Goodbyes

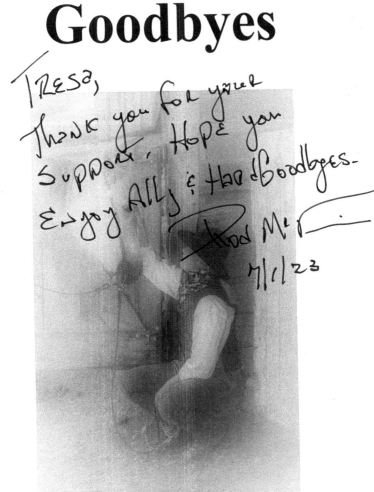

Tresa,
Thank you for your
Support, Hope you
Enjoy All; & Hard Goodbyes.
Rod McFain
7/1/23

Rod McFain

2021 White Bird Publications, LLC

Copyright © 2021 by Rod McFain

Published in the United States
by White Bird Publications, LLC, Austin, Texas
www.whitebirdpublications.com

Paperback ISBN 978-1-63363-507-4
eBook ISBN 978-1-63363-508-1
Library of Congress Control Number: 2021936790

PRINTED IN THE UNITED STATES OF AMERICA

Dedication

To Linda
Who has made my life wonderful

Hard
Goodbyes

**White Bird
Publications**

Chapter One

Southeast Wyoming Near Fort Laramie 1860

Either a nasty spring cold or some allergy kept Ally Hart miserable for the better part of two weeks. She rubbed her nose raw with the constant blowing, and between the sore red nose and bloodshot eyes, she looked as bad as she felt. She spent an entire day in bed, hiding from Elijah's relentless mothering.

The seventy-year-old man had appointed himself her personal knight in shining armor after her husband Sam died several months ago. However, when he demanded she spend a second day flat on her back, she put her foot down.

Another argument took place when she insisted Elijah go to town for supplies. Her gentle friend thought it out of the question to leave her while so weak with the fever. He forced her to promise both a morning and afternoon nap before he hitched the team to the old wagon and squeaked off for food and a needed jar of salve to heal cracked lips and chapped skin.

Ally's loneliness, after only one night alone, took her by surprise. By mid-morning, as she tinkered around the kitchen wishing for late afternoon or evening when Elijah would return, sadness overtook her, robbing her of her little energy. She poured herself the last cup of morning tea, which she preferred to coffee, and sat down at the table she and Sam purchased in Hays City.

When Sam died, and she buried him under the larger of the two oak trees growing on their place, she resolved to put flowers on his grave at least once a week. However, the sadness became too much for her. Now, she seldom went to the grave, let alone with a flower arrangement. In truth, she resented Sam for dying and leaving her here, without the means to move. The ranch had been his dream, not hers. Now she found herself angry he didn't make better provision for her. Of course, he might have if he expected to die, instead of being gored.

That was another disagreement between Ally and Elijah. Her bull, the one that did the goring, was running around somewhere out on the range. Elijah said she needed a bull to have any hope of making a living off the cattle. Since she lacked the cash to buy another one, bringing this one back was necessary. Ally argued she did not want ever to lay eyes on the vulgar beast again. So that's how things stood. The bull running loose, Elijah concerned, and Ally not caring.

Ally decided she sat in her self-pity long enough. She picked up the old wooden bucket she carried water in and went out the kitchen door and across what made do for a yard toward the well.

About halfway to the well, too far from the house to go back, Ally saw an Indian sitting on a pinto horse only a few yards away. She froze. However, the Indian made no move toward her. For what seemed like minutes, but really only the briefest of time, they stared at each other. Ally let her eyes dart around, both looking for any way of escape and searching for other Indians. Seeing neither, she turned to face him.

After a moment, the man squeezed his bare legs against his horse, moving slowly toward Ally. She held the bucket in front of her chest. Either for protection—or to throw up. He rode a small circle around her, stopping in front of her. He sat on his horse, looking her over as if trying to decide what he wanted to do with her. The blade at the end of that lance was going to hurt. Will it cut smooth and clean? Or, will it rip through her soft skin, tearing her wide open? How will death come? Quick? Or in suffering?

She tried to remember what Sam and Elijah told her to do if caught out when Indians showed up. Don't show fear. Not showing fear is critical. But how, this frightened, could she not show it? "What do you want?" she said, her boldness surprising her. It occurred to her the Indian might not, in fact, probably didn't speak English. "What do you want?" she asked again, this time afraid about fear showing in her voice.

"Water for my horse."

Relieved by hearing him speak English, she regained some composure. "Yes. Yes, of course." Ally pointed to the well. You're welcome to my water."

"Sometimes we may cross here," he said.

He looked at her with what Ally thought was sympathy, not anger. Yet, why would an Indian extend sympathy to a white woman?

"Do not be afraid of us. Cheyenne do not make war on women whose men are dead and who now live with old men. Roman Nose," he said, tapping on his chest.

Ally assumed he was introducing himself.

"Do not fear the Cheyenne."

As he moved his horse away, Ally managed to stammer, her name. "I won't be afraid. Thank you." The stammering embarrassed her. After all, this was Roman Nose, a Cheyenne Chief, speaking clearly and calmly in English. What kind of impression was she making, stammering in her language?

Chapter Two

"Good heavens, Mrs. Hart. Roman Nose hisself?"

"Yes," Ally said as she placed the bowl of stew in front of Elijah.

"Roman Nose hisself. Good heavens." Elijah picked up his spoon but hesitated before dipping into the stew. "And he said, don't be afraid if you see Cheyenne?"

"Not to be afraid," Ally said, enjoying the amazement of her friend. "He said Cheyenne don't make war on widows." Ally did not tell Elijah the part about Cheyenne not making war on women who live with old men. Elijah did not believe himself old.

"Well, Mrs. Hart, this is positive news indeed."

"Why yes, I suppose so," Ally said, smiling.

After eating dinner, Elijah started to rock in a straight-backed rocker he brought from his place in town. As Ally opened a book, Elijah began gabbing about the work he should accomplish the first thing in the morning.

"I think I'll ride a little further out and scare up some of those strays. It's a lost burden, not have to be worried about gettin' a Cheyenne arrow in me."

Ally chuckled at how relieved Elijah was over the Cheyenne declaration of peace.

"What are you finding so funny, Mrs. Hart?"

"Nothing, Elijah, nothing. I'm enjoying your company." Ally did enjoy his company. He was never cross with her, never tried to change her. Her welfare became his primary concern. When he knew she was wrong, like when regarding the bull, he let her have her way. He would try to persuade but never got mad.

The two sat for a while, with only the squeaking of Elijah's rocking chair breaking the silence. Finally, Elijah stopped rocking, giving Ally an enjoyable quiet time.

"You say Roman Nose wanted to water his horse?"

"So he said."

"I swear," Elijah said, still trying to understand Roman Nose's visit.

Chapter Three

Joshua McCormick reined his horse to a stop beside the young corporal, dismounted, and stretched his aching back.

"The Hart place is about six or eight miles," the young corporal said, pointing out into the plains. "She's got an old man helping her out, but I doubt if he amounts to much. Saving her scrub ranch from ruin will take a bit of doing; I'll let you in on that."

"Six to eight miles?" Joshua's voice sounded dismal as he gazed off at the treeless landscape.

"About six or eight. Not much else out on those plains, except prairie dogs, some buffalo, and of course, Indians."

Joshua shuddered at the warning about Indians. "Are you having Indian trouble around here?"

"Not particularly," the corporal said, "but you always want to keep your guard up. They can be unpredictable. One time they don't pay any attention to you. Other times, if they figure the odds are right, they'll attack without any blamed cause."

"How well do you know this Hart woman?"

"Not at all," the corporal said. "I used to see her once in a while, back before her husband died. Don't think I've seen her since. Not a bad-lookin' woman. In her later thirties, I suppose."

Joshua had not asked the old Judge who sent him on this fool's mission about the woman's features. Joshua took for granted she'd have gray hair and would look older than she was, weathered, and worn out. Joshua assumed that living in a rough, unsettled country like this would do that to a woman. The thought was decent news, although he did not know why. Beautiful women could be as ugly of temperament as unattractive ones. Besides, what a corporal out in this desolate place thought of as attractive might not be his idea.

"Where's the road to her place?"

"Road?" The corporal laughed. "Not too many roads out here."

"How do I find a place six miles or more away, with no road?"

The corporal laughed again. "I can't help you. I never been to her place myself. I understand it's not a grand place. I think the house is on the Platte, right on the other side, I believe. I guess if you can find the North Platte, you'll be able to find her little ranch."

"Well, how am I supposed to find the river?" Frustrated over the soldier having a bit of fun at his expense, Joshua clenched and unclenched his fists. He took a step toward the man.

The unconcerned soldier laughed again. "Well, hell, man, what do you think is right over there?" He pointed out in the distance.

"Why didn't you say follow the river?"

The young soldier shook his head. "Boy, are you green. If you follow the river from here, you'll add three, four miles, or more to the distance. You need to go straight north and hit the river up there. You'll save way over an hour. I'll try to find someone who's been to her place, and they can give you better directions."

It took some time to locate a soldier who had been to the Hart Ranch, and while waiting, the sergeant who brought Joshua and a small group of soldiers from St. Louis walked up and offered his hand. "Accountant, I misjudged you. You did well on our little trip."

The sergeant's friendliness befuddled Joshua. He stumbled a little, trying to return a compliment, wondering if he sounded anywhere near earnest.

"I want to ask you something," the non-commissioned officer said, sitting on the ground and motioning for Joshua to do the same. The sergeant wondered what Joshua, a city man with access to news, thought about the possibility of a conflict coming with the Southern States. He said most military men had concerns about a fight and didn't believe the Army was always honest with them.

Joshua was thoughtful in his answer, not wanting to set the sergeant off if he took the wrong side. "I wouldn't bet either way. The South is starting to talk more defiant." Joshua thought a little more before continuing. "Only my opinion, Sarge. I'm sure no political expert, but my thought is if Lincoln, from over in Illinois, happens to get elected president, the likelihood of war will increase."

The sergeant thought over McCormick's statement before asking him if he thought Lincoln wanted a war. Joshua had no proof Lincoln wanted war, but he believed Southerners would consider Lincoln a real threat to slavery and, therefore, to their economic well-being. The sergeant told Joshua he thought most soldiers were hoping to avoid a war. He asked Joshua if he had any personal feelings on the subject.

Joshua was hesitant to respond. Revealing himself as a southern sympathizer might not be wise.

The sergeant got tired of waiting for an answer and expressed his own opinion. "If a war starts, the South will start it. They would be betraying their own nation, taking up arms against their countrymen. I'd side with the North." The sergeant again said he would hate war, but he'd fight to preserve the nation.

Both men stood. The sergeant extended his hand. "Luck to you, accountant. I hope we don't meet up again shooting at each other in a war."

"I hope not too," Joshua said. "Luck to you, Sarge. I appreciate you getting me out here." The sergeant slapped Joshua on the shoulder. The accountant, well, former accountant since the fiasco in St. Louis, watched the soldier walk away, noticing for the first time that he walked with a slight limp. "I guess I should be a little less judgmental of people," he muttered to himself, wondering for the first time if he, himself, might be worth a second chance.

When the corporal returned with a captain who had been to the Hart Ranch, he assured Joshua he would have no problem finding the place. "Go straight north until you hit the river. You can tell north, can't you?"

The look on Josh's face must have made the captain have doubts, and he added some detail. "About a quarter-mile that way, you'll come to a deep gully heading north, runs better than two miles. Follow it to the end. You'll come to a little rise. Go up to the top, and you'll be able to see a stand of trees off in the distance. They'll be the only thing. They're growing around a little pond due north of the gulley. Keep going, right past them. A couple of miles, and you'll hit the Platte. Turn left; that'll be west. Follow the river west; it'll lead you right on to the Hart place."

"The corporal said she's on the other side of the river," Joshua said.

"No, it's on this side." The captain walked Joshua to his horse and made a few admiring comments about the stout animal. "Listen," he said, as Joshua stepped up into the saddle, "Mrs. Hart has had a rough time. You'll be a help to her. She's a decent woman who deserves better than she's been dealt. I hope you'll treat her well."

Joshua was a little surprised by the captain's admonition

to him. Turning his horse north, he believed for the first time in a long time; he was doing a generous thing, a fine thing for someone other than himself—his first step to redemption. Something he desperately needed.

Chapter Four

The fort was barely out of sight when Joshua came upon buffalo, likely 400 of them. He'd seen stuffed ones. But alive, they were much bigger. A couple of young bulls jousted with each other. Then a bull tried to mount one of the cows. Otherwise, there was little movement in the herd. Joshua watched them for several minutes, not because he was spellbound, but he didn't know how to go around them. He hoped his horse could outrun a buffalo.

He sure didn't want to find out. He moved off to the left, giving them plenty of room as he passed. The giant animals, thank the Lord, paid no attention as he circled them.

He was still shaken by the buffalo encounter when he got his first view of the Hart place. The corporal had been right about its appearance, not grand. The weather-beaten house, the corrals, and the barn needed repairing. Joshua saw no sign of cattle, only a few horses as he rode through the gate and toward the house.

Before he stepped from his horse, the front door opened

and a woman came out on the porch. "Mrs. Hart?" As the young soldier hinted, the woman was attractive. But she did not answer him. Joshua clumsily extended his hand. "I'm Joshua McCormick."

"The outlaw Judge Dan sent me," Ally said, bringing a chill to the air. She ignored his stretched-out hand. "I've no use for convicts. Or for drunkards either."

This was not the reception Joshua expected. As a result, he took a moment to react. "I uh...don't plan to be either one again," Their initial meeting was going damn poorly.

Why was the woman so angry? Attractive or not, her antagonism would scare little children.

"Judge Dan sent you without my permission. I sent a letter back telling him not to."

She paused, scrutinizing him, which he didn't like. He was ordinary. A little on the short side, and he should have removed his hat, but he wasn't unpleasant looking.

"Regrettably, you must have been on your way when he got my letter."

Ally started to go back inside the house but turned back toward him.

"Just so you understand, absolutely understand," she said. "I have no intention of trying to rehabilitate a drunkard."

Joshua took a step back off the porch toward his horse before turning back to his antagonist. "Lady, I don't plan on being a problem for you. I intend to do as the Judge promised and be of some help to you. But, if you expect me to be afraid of you or be some kind of bootlicker, you've made a major error in judgment, and perhaps I should go back to St. Louis and serve out the remainder of my time."

Ally made no effort to hide her contempt. "Don't provoke me. And call me Mrs. Hart, not lady. You'll find Elijah down at the barn. He'll show you where to put your things." She turned and went back into the house, slamming the door behind her.

"Well," he muttered to himself as he turned to lead his

roan horse toward the barn, "the trip was rather long, but without any real problems. Thanks for asking, Mrs. Hart."

The reception from Elijah Yancey was different from the one he received at the house. Elijah showed him an area he cleared away below the hayloft for his living space. He assured Joshua he could bunk in the new room Ally insisted he build for himself on the side of the barn.

"I built on the east side. The sun helps me wake up in the morning and won't keep me awake at night when I need to fall asleep early."

Elijah brimmed with delight regarding all the work they needed to accomplish for "Mrs. Hart." Their conversation was amusing to Joshua after the unfriendly welcome at the house.

Once his new working partner took time for a breath, Joshua told him his greeting from Mrs. Hart had not been warm. Elijah was surprised and a bit confused. He stared for a moment at the house and shifted from foot to foot.

He spat a stream of tobacco. "She weren't friendly?" Elijah's eyes widened.

"That would be a fair assessment."

Elijah's mood darkened. He shook his head. "That's not like Mrs. Hart."

"Well, maybe she takes a little while to warm up to someone." Wanting to change the topic, Joshua asked, "How many head of cattle do you run?" An accountant should have known the question was inappropriate, like asking how much money Mrs. Hart had.

Elijah swept an arm at the plains as he answered, "Only about twenty or thirty, I reckon. We've lost a few over the past couple of months. Five or six near as I can tell could be as many as ten." Elijah took off his hat, an old floppy gray one, and wiped the sweatband with his handkerchief. "We need to double the size of the herd for Mrs. Hart to make any money off this place," he said with the authority of a real ranch foreman. "Won't be hard to do, though," he continued as he put his hat back on, covering the bald spot on the back of his head. "Plenty of strays wanderin' around these parts. All we got to do is round 'em up. Why, shoot, with a week's work from both of us, we can increase the herd up to thirty-five, fifty, if we're lucky."

"Don't those strays belong on some other ranch?"

"Naw, most of 'em calved out right on the range from cattle strayed off from somewhere. Ain't none of 'em wearin' no brand. If they were, the other close-by ranches, and there were only two of them to start with, ain't here anymore. The dry weather did one in, and the Cheyenne burned the other one."

"Cheyenne? Are Indians around?" On the trip from St. Louis, the sergeant instilled considerable fear of Indians in Joshua, and Elijah's remark rekindled his fright.

Elijah spat a stream of tobacco and gave his loins a vigorous scratching. "Who did you think you'd find around here? A bunch of Quakers? Of course, there's Cheyenne. Cheyenne, and Sioux, and Arapaho, and Crow. More Indians roamin' about than you can shake a stick at, but you better have more'n a stick. I'll point them out to you every time I notice 'em." Elijah, a practicing scalawag, waited before offering a bit of a reprieve. "Course we don't need to worry about Cheyennes. Roman Nose hisself told Mrs. Hart, sittin' on his horse right over there, they weren't gonna bother her on account of her husband dying. He said they don't make war on women."

Joshua should have been relieved, at least a little, and he was, briefly. Then he began to wonder if his presence would cancel Roman Nose's promise. Elijah might find Indians humorous; find it funny to make a city man uncomfortable. Joshua did not. While he came here to escape prison, he also wanted to help the woman. His intentions were decent. He resented how the woman treated him. He was confused about why the old man, initially friendly, decided to treat him like a buffoon. It might be a long three months. Joshua started to store some of his gear and spread his blanket out.

"We'll build you a cot to sleep on," Elijah said, friendly,

again. "I'd have done it already, but I didn't know what size a man to build for. Glad I waited. I expected a taller fella."

"I can make do here on the ground for a few nights," Joshua said, hanging his saddlebags over one of the stalls, not yet ready to trust Elijah's benevolence.

"The first thing we need to do is bring the bull back." Elijah sat on a crate and took off his boot to scratch his foot. "But, Mrs. Hart, she doesn't want Satan back," Elijah grumbled as he pulled the boot back on. "Satan, she's called the bull Satan since the beast gored Mr. Hart," he said. "I hate to, but I'm afraid we're going to have to buck her on this one," Elijah said, discomfort clear in his voice. "You can't run a cattle operation without a bull."

"No, I wouldn't think so."

"I didn't tell you before, but there is one more ranch, a little more than a day's ride away, on out past Emigrant's Wash Tub," Elijah said as if Joshua would know what or where that was. "This other one is sizeable, belongs to a man named Kane. He's not a nice fella. I think Mrs. Hart might be a little afraid of him." Elijah spat a long stream of tobacco. "Don't want to mention him when Mrs. Hart is around."

Hostile Indians, hostile neighbors, a hostile boss, what had Joshua done to himself?

Chapter Five

The evening was unsettling, full of the spookiness that comes with absolute stillness in the air, casting a peculiar and unnatural mood out on the plains, often meaning an approaching storm, a nasty one. Joshua could sense the approaching storm as he strode toward the house for supper.

"The horses are restless, Mrs. Hart," Elijah said as he and Joshua came in the front door. "They don't like the silence," he said, directing his comment at Joshua.

"Elijah has great concern regarding storms." Ally set a ham in the middle of the table. "Why don't you sit here, Mr. McCormick?" she said as she pulled a chair back. "Elijah and I are used to our regular places." After Elijah's somewhat lengthy saying of grace, Ally cut a slice of meat for Joshua. "I hope you like ham. We'll have more tomorrow evening."

"I'm fond of ham, of all pork," Joshua said, doubting the woman cared. He took a bowl of mashed turnips from Elijah. Reaching for a knife, Joshua asked Ally if she would like him to cut the bread. Should he have asked before picking up the knife? He didn't want to be presumptuous.

Out of practice eating with a woman, everything he did was wrong or clumsy. He didn't know how many slices he should cut or how thick to slice them. Since he thought this loaf might be the only bread in the house, he cut only three slices and sliced them thin.

Josh sensed Ally was also uneasy about his presence at dinner. He wondered if she was embarrassed about her earlier rudeness or that there might not be enough food to satisfy two men. "I might put the ham in a pot of beans for tomorrow night. They can cook all day, and I can help Elijah show you around."

"Ham and beans will be fine, Mrs. Hart, but you don't need to worry yourself about showing him the place. I can show McCormick around."

"Is this your first time away from St. Louis," she asked.

"No, but my first time west." The start between them had been so poor, Joshua wondered if Ally was implying he was too inept to survive outside a city.

After a long silence, Elijah, fond of conversation, even ones that made no sense, could no longer tolerate the quiet. "Well, Mrs. Hart, what would you like us to do tomorrow?"

"Mr. McCormick's un-calloused hands don't look ready for much physical work." Joshua scrutinized her, although he tried to be more discrete. She didn't smile much. He had not seen her smile once. Her eyes also caught his attention. They were always gazing far away, wavering between sadness and boredom.

To be friendly, Joshua picked up the coffee pot and asked Ally if she would like more.

"I'm drinking tea, not coffee."

It was going to be a long three months.

Chapter Six

The first two weeks of Joshua's time in Wyoming passed. Somewhere within that time, Ally decided not to run him off. He and Elijah fixed the corral and barn roof. They put a single coat of whitewash on the house, although it needed a second. Joshua also put some callouses on his hands.

So far, there had been no attempt to return Satan to the ranch. However, most of the work around the barn and corral was getting finished. Elijah started working on Joshua to bring the topic up with Mrs. Hart. Giving in, Joshua agreed to undertake the task at supper. Something he dreaded.

For the third night in the last five, the men sat down to a plate of stew for supper. With each serving, the stew got thinner and contained less meat. Even Elijah sensed Ally's embarrassment over the meal.

"We need to butcher a steer. We're nearly out of meat," Ally said as she dabbed her bread into the weak stew. "Elijah doesn't want me to kill one until some of the cows are bred, but I'm not going to have men working for me without being properly fed." A mischievous smirk crossed her lips. "Besides, Mr. Yancey, a steer can't breed a cow."

Joshua glanced at Elijah before looking over at Ally. "Mrs. Hart, we've wanted to talk about something for several days now, and I guess now is as good a time as any."

Ally, her brown eyes full of fire, interrupted before Joshua breached the topic. "That bull is not coming back on my ranch," she said.

"I think I can understand," Joshua said, looking down instead of at his hostess. "But Elijah is right. You must have a bull."

"No." Ally gave Joshua a dirty glare before fixing her eyes on Elijah. "And if you bring him back here, I'll put a rifle ball in his head, and one in your hind-end."

"Oh, now, Mrs. Hart, you don't want to shoot the bull," Elijah said as he put both hands palm down on the table. "Besides, if you did shoot him with that old muzzleloader you've got hanging over the fireplace, all you'd do is make him good and mad."

"I might not kill the beast, but I'd give him a pounding headache," she replied before her chin quivered as she broke into a laugh at herself over the foolishness of her remark.

Elijah got caught up in her laughing before agreeing she would give the "old boy a whopper of a headache."

That thwarted Joshua from again approaching the necessity of the bull's return. Ally poured each of the men a fresh cup of coffee.

"There is something else we need to discuss," she said, pushing her plate back and her hair out of her face. "Elijah knows about this," she said, with considerable affection for the aging man showing. Both men were looking at her, Joshua, more intently. A somber tone invaded her voice as she started to speak. "About a week after Sam died, Dierden Kane visited me. Not a friendly visit, I'm afraid. He told me a woman has no business trying to run cattle out here, and if I make any effort to do so, he will make me sorry."

Elijah reached over and patted her hand. Ally gave some

explanation as to who he was. "He's a cattleman."

Elijah interrupted, "He's a damn crook and a killer. ."

"Well, he may be a killer, but he's still running one of the biggest herds in southeast Wyoming," Ally replied without looking up. "It's better if we just raise our food and don't buck him."

Joshua watched Ally for a brief time, wondering if it was out of line for him to speak. He decided to take a chance. "Mrs. Hart, you're far too intelligent to think that can be any solution. If you raise your food, you'll still need to sell cattle to have money. It doesn't take an accountant to figure that out," he said as a smile slipped over his mouth.

Ally didn't return the smile. She was condescending, "You don't know Dierden Kane," Ally said, her smug words keeping Joshua in his place. "He's the kind of a man who's willing to hurt others for what he wants, and he wants everything out here."

Joshua tried to hold his ground. "I've handled enough money for other people to know what greed is. I don't doubt what you say at all."

A truce in the relationship might be developing as a half-smile flitted across Ally's face.

"Mr. Hart would never let Kane push him around," Elijah said with a lot of boldness in his voice. "He wouldn't have caved in."

"No. Sam wouldn't have," Ally conceded. "But, if Sam were here and that damn bull you seem so fond of was back," she said, glancing at Elijah, "we still couldn't stand up to a man like Kane. I think he has at least twenty men working for him."

Elijah tried to defend himself regarding any fondness for old Satan. "Well now, Mrs. Hart, it ain't I'm fond of that ol' bull. I ain't fond of him at all. It's just; well, it's just you have to have a bull."

Ally wanted to be warm, soft, feminine, but she struggled with those characteristics. She had never lived a comfortable life. Her dreams always fell short, and disappointments outnumbered gratifications. Nevertheless, she stayed resilient. She smiled at her old friend before giving a quick wink at Joshua, which surprised him.

"Kane may have twenty men," Joshua said, "but it doesn't mean they'd fight in some kind of range war. At least I wouldn't think an honest man would," he said, looking first at Ally, then at Elijah.

"An honest cowhand wouldn't," Elijah agreed. "But the men working for Kane ain't honest." Elijah shook his head. "Men like them; if they figure it might help feather their bed, they'll do anything."

"Well, it doesn't matter," Ally said. "We couldn't make a worthy fight. He hasn't done anything yet. I hope he won't."

"Hasn't done anything? Why you know as well as I do, he rustled those cows we're missing. The ol' boy is jist bidden his time, waiting to see if you leave on your own. When you don't, he'll come. He wants everything, thinks he's one of them, what do you call 'em? Cattle barons. Ain't no reasoning with him." Elijah broke off a chunk of tobacco and stuck it in his jaw before taking his chaw right back out when Ally asked him where he planned to spit the stuff. "Kane is plain damn mean," Elijah said. "He plain likes hurting people. He don't need no reason. He likes it."

Joshua stared at her. "I'm no gunman, Mrs. Hart, but I don't think we can allow a man to destroy your life because he's greedy."

Ally smiled at him, looking as if she was going to answer him, but she changed the subject. "I believe I need to apologize, Mr. McCormick, for being rude to you." Apologies were hard for Ally, she assumed they were for everyone, but she was tired of being mad at McCormick. She was tired of being mad, period.

Joshua stared at his plate before responding. "Ma'am, I lost my family, a wife, and a child, and I lost my way. However, my intention is not to be an affliction to you. I intend to be the assistance to you Judge Starrett promised. I'll not be a burden. I want to relieve you of some of your current burdens."

Ally nodded at him. "From now on, your help will be met with gratitude. Elijah and I have both had our loads lightened since your arrival." Ally paused. "You may as well call me Ally; everyone else does…except for Elijah." She laughed, "I wore out trying to persuade him to use my first name."

"All right, if you'll call me Joshua."

Ally studied him. "I think I'll call you Josh. I believe Josh suits you better."

Chapter Seven

Elijah created quite a problem for Josh. Josh had seen few sunrises before taking up residence in Ally Hart's barn. Over the past two weeks, they became a daily occurrence. Josh preferred a soft pillow and a warm bed over watching the sunrise. Elijah found too much pleasure in life and in sunrises to let them slip by without partaking. Making it worse, once awake, he tended to whistle or hum, and not quietly either. He also bumped into things in the still dark morning, which puzzled Josh since the room included only two chairs.

By the time Josh gave up on getting more sleep, Elijah was out tending the morning chores. He watered the five horses and threw them several forks of hay. He scattered some feed for the chickens and got pecked by a hateful old hen while gathering the fresh eggs, which he would sit next to Ally's front door. Elijah always helped himself to a dipper or two of well water. He particularly enjoyed the water's coolness at the start of the day.

Pulling on his boots, Josh wished he was asleep instead

of listening to Elijah greet Ally, who always came out on the porch about sunup. Josh memorized Elijah's greeting, "Morin', Mrs. Hart. Sure, a beautiful sunrise today. Did you sleep soundly last night?"

Whether Ally did or not, she always told her friend she slept well. Otherwise, he would be coddling her, fussing every time she sighed. Lord forbid, she would yawn.

"How would you like your eggs this morning?" Ally asked Elijah every morning, although he never surprised her; he wanted them fried hard. He never wanted them scrambled, or poached, or sunny-side up. Easy to please, regarding eggs, Elijah never required or desired any variety in his diet. "Breakfast will be on in about thirty minutes. Make sure Josh is awake. Tell him I'll scramble his."

Josh limped out of the barn on an ankle he sprained two days ago when he stepped awkwardly off Ally's porch while trying to avoid her old hound.

"Morning, McCormick. Did you catch what Mrs. Hart said about your eggs?"

"Scrambled is fine," Josh said, not much caring whether they came scrambled, fried, or hardboiled.

"The bay gelding needs to be shod. I'll shoe him before I head off for supplies. You might want to ride him when you go off looking for some of Mrs. Hart's cows," Elijah said, walking back toward the barn.

"You don't need to shoe him," Josh said, having no idea why Elijah would think such a thing. "I can ride my horse or any of the others. Don't bother shoeing one for me."

"Well, he's real cowy. I expect you best take him. I'll shoe him right after breakfast."

In Josh's short time on the Hart place, he discovered Elijah's mind could not be changed once an idea took root.

By the time the two men went into the house, Ally finished putting the breakfast on the table. Meals were much different from when Josh first arrived. Those early mealtimes had been tense, unfriendly, sometimes almost hostile. Breaking bread with Ally and Elijah became a time of sharing, affable conversation, a part of the day Josh enjoyed. "The eggs are small this morning, so I fried you three instead of two," Ally said as Elijah sat down.

"Fine, Mrs. Hart. I'm plenty hungry. Won't be any problem with eating them." Elijah tucked his napkin into the collar of his gray flannel shirt, which despite the morning being hot, he buttoned to the top. "What do you plan to do today while I'm gone for supplies, and McCormick is out lookin' fer cows?"

"I think I might ride along with Josh to help find the cattle." For some reason, this surprised Josh. He did not expect a woman would involve herself in men's chores. In St. Louis, such a thing would never be done. Not even on one of the farms or ranches. The men would do the outdoor work while the women busied themselves with house cleaning and cooking substantial meals for all the hands to sit and eat. A city woman would never do any kind of outside physical labor.

"Surprised, Josh? Don't you think I can chase after a cow?"

"No, I guess I didn't." Josh was trying to imagine Ally straddling a horse and yelling giddyap.

"Well, you'll be glad I'm along if you find more than a couple to push back home. Cattle wandering the range for a while can be difficult to drive. You'll appreciate the help."

"I'm sure I will."

"Mrs. Hart's a capable rider," Elijah said. "A woman on a ranch out here can't afford the luxury of not participating in the work. Mrs. Hart can toss a rope a bit," he said.

"A bit?" Ally asked. "I throw a rope as well as you do. Better!"

Josh enjoyed Ally razzing Elijah. When playful, she changed. Childlike joy rebloomed. She laughed out loud. Occasionally she would give Elijah a little jab. Elijah, himself, smiled over a pat on the arm. Once, she gave him a small pinch in the ribs, which he grinned about all day.

Josh finished his breakfast, contemplating the difference

in life out on the prairie and back in St. Louis, differences continually surprising him. Ally, unlike women back in St. Louis, did not behave according to the whims of men. Not Ally Hart. She lived unfettered by gender rules, indeed by any rules. Josh liked her more every day.

Chapter Eight

By the time Elijah shoed the bay and Josh harnessed the team, Ally prepared a list of supplies. "Don't let that shopkeeper pass off any second-rate cornmeal on you," she warned Elijah. "He'll sell you some that's beetle-infested if you don't keep a sharp eye on him."

"I'll pay particular attention," Elijah promised. "I'll check real thorough."

Ally wished him a safe trip.

"If it gets too late in the day, you stay in town and come back in the morning."

The town wasn't much from what Josh remembered, only a few stores, an eatery, and a saloon sitting right next to the fort.

"No sense in your traveling after dark."

"Yes, ma'am. But I should be back before night lays in."

Josh followed his new friend over to the wagon and gave him a bit of a boost as he climbed up to the old wooden seat. "Elijah," he said, glancing toward Ally to make sure she wouldn't overhear. "Do a little inquiring about Dierden Kane."

"What do you want me to find out? He ain't worth a pinch of manure. I don't need to inquire about that."

Josh put his hand on Elijah's knee and dropped his voice a little more. "Listen for any talk about him doing something to Ally. Or selling any cattle he might not own."

"You mean Mrs. Hart's?" Elijah asked, wide-eyed.

"You said some are missing," Josh said matter-of-factly.

"Good heavens," Elijah's voice wavered. "I never thought about Kane rustling from us."

"Be careful about what you say to somebody or ask. Don't be too direct." The confused expression on Elijah's face made Josh regret bringing up the matter. He now doubted Elijah being subtle enough to investigate anything without everyone in town knowing. Asking straight out if Kane was selling stolen cattle was more Elijah's style.

He was about to tell Elijah not to worry about checking when Ally came out and ran over to them, telling Elijah she also wanted him to bring back a sack of flour, something she neglected to mention earlier.

"Now remember what I said about spending the night. I do not want you coming home after dark."

"I still expect I can make it, but if not, I'll stay the night," he said as he slapped the reins to the two-horse team and departed.

"I always worry when Elijah goes off alone."

Josh started to reassure her, but for some reason, he changed his mind and instead said he would go and saddle a couple of horses.

By mid-morning, the front of Josh's hat dripped with sweat. Ally said it was showing all the signs of being a hot summer.

"If we turn dry, it'll be the third draught in the last five years," she said.

"Does your river ever run dry? The only worry with the Mississippi is flooding in the spring."

"Never," Ally responded. "At least not since I've been here. Last summer and most of the winter was wet. Lord, I got tired of wading through snow. Ally grew weary of discussing the weather. Sunshine, rain, snow, and wind were things she didn't control. She found no point in idle chatter about the weather.

Josh was beginning to understand Ally's lack of interest in talking about trifling topics. Anything out of her control, she considered trifling. Most of his wife's friends talked for hours about the silliest of subjects. They would clamor on and on about the proper stitching with which to hem a dress, but not Ally. She lived a more difficult life, not in a place allowing a woman many pleasures. Wyoming's ruggedness, the hard work, and the long days left little time for idle chat. The closest Ally ever came to a casual conversation with Josh came one night when she asked him a little about Sarah, specifically if they caught the man who shot her. When he told her no, she didn't ask anything else about his wife.

"Any idea where we might find some of the cows?" Josh asked, not knowing if the question made much sense.

"About two miles over." Ally was pointing off to the southwest, "we'll find a ravine full of brush and thicket. For some reason beyond me, they like to hide down in that tangled mess. Probably because they're so damn hard to chase out," she said, surprising Josh by the use of a swear word.

When they reached the ravine, the chasm filled with brush and hedge trees was much more extensive than Josh anticipated. Ally rode up one side and Josh the other. Josh turned the bay horse down a trail leading into the gully's deepest part. At the bottom, he started to weave through the bushes, keeping an eye out for any cattle lying down in the thicket, attempting to find shade from the hot sun.

"One is about fifty yards out in front of you," Ally

called from the top of the bank. "She's off to your left under the tall hedge tree."

Josh strained to find the beast, but the animal was hidden deep in the thick, thorny brush. "Is she down or up?"

"She's lying down. Holler and make some noise. She'll jump and run."

"Cow! Cow!" Josh hollered out, waving his rope around like a clod, or a drunk. The "cow" turned out to be an underweight steer. He got up and ambled up the ravine. Josh finally found the animal, a black beast with long horns. "Git! Git up outta here." He nudged his horse forward, spooking the steer into a quicker escape. "Go on, git up out of here."

For some reason, Josh thought about an enormous oil painting hanging in one of the banks back in St. Louis. Painted in oranges, reds, and yellows, it depicted a group of cowboys moving a cattle herd across some plains full of scruffy sagebrush. Josh chuckled over all the times he admired the painting, never once expecting he would be a cowboy chasing cattle. Of course, he was not much of a cowboy, and one shabby steer did not make for much of a herd.

"Two more on your right," Ally yelled. "I think you may be able to sneak down below them and chase them out. I'm going to ride on along the top. I don't want to miss any. After I do, I'll come down and try to help you push them up and out."

Josh spotted these two quicker than the steer. Slipping past them, he chased the two, a cow and her calf, up the bank. The skittish cow lunged out with the calf bawling after her.

While watching the cow and calf go over the lip of the ravine, Josh lost track of the black steer when the beast cut back into the arroyo and thicket. Thorny, high-hanging branches provided Josh with a couple of deep scratches. One at the top of his left eyebrow started a trickle of blood running down his cheek, drawing a swarm of mosquitoes. Twice Josh backed his horse out when the brush got too thick to negotiate. He now understood why Ally cussed the blame ditch.

"Where the hell did you go?" he whispered to himself, irritated about letting the animal disappear. He spent another five or ten minutes working his way through the thorny underbrush before hearing Ally's voice.

"I rode up to the end, but I didn't find any more. The gully flattens out about half a mile or so from here. No place for them to hide."

"Can you see the black one? I lost him getting those other two out," Josh said, irritated by his lack of competence.

"He's likely buried himself back in some thick brush," she said, pointing back up the ravine. "I'll ride down from this side, and hopefully, between us, we can flush him." Ally found the steer first and pushed her horse down close to him; he lowered his horns and threw his head up in a mock charge. "Move! Move!" Ally slapped her rope several times across some of the brush. She urged her horse in close as the steer turned away. She bumped her horse's chest up against the stubborn animal and slapped his rump with her rope. The beast charged out and whirled to his left, back toward Josh. "Don't let him past you. Cut him off."

Cut him off? Incompetence, mixed with fear, took over. They were his downfall. The bay horse he was riding, at Elijah's insistence, was a natural-born cow cutter. Josh was not. The horse took charge, cutting over in front of the running steer. The bay's front end bounced immediately back and forth, left and right, staying in front of the steer, instantly going from full speed to a complete stop and back to full speed. Josh was all over the saddle, on the horn, way to the left, so far back, his head bounced off the horse's hindquarters.

The steer, much faster than Josh expected, turned away from the horse and toward the top of the ditch. Josh's horse planted his back end, at the same time, swinging his front end ninety degrees to the right in pursuit of the fleeing steer. Desperately, Josh grabbed at the saddle horn, but to no avail. He hit the ground hard enough to knock the wind out of him. The steer and the horse, that damn horse Elijah put him on, went up and over the bank, leaving him lying in the dirt.

"Are you all right?" Ally jumped from her horse and took Josh's arm to help him up.

"I think so," Josh said sheepishly. "I think my pride's the only thing injured."

Ally laughed at Josh. "I almost warned you about riding Peppy. He's real cowy."

"Yes, so Elijah said." Josh stretched out his arms and neck, both to work out a couple of kinks and to check if everything still worked.

Ally regained her composure, not completely, but mostly.

"What are you smiling at?" Josh asked, noticing the broad smile still on Ally's lips.

"You didn't know what 'cowy' meant, did you?" she said with a warmth in her voice.

Josh laughed a bit at himself. "No idea," he said. "Next time, I'll ask. You can bet on that."

Chapter Nine

By mid-afternoon, Elijah basically asked almost everyone in town if Dierden Kane was selling stolen cattle. A friendly bartender pulled Elijah aside and told him he should be careful talking about Dierden Kane, especially accusing him of stealing cows.

"Kane may be the troublemaker you think he is," the bartender said. "But he has friends around here."

Elijah condescendingly grunted.

"Grunt, if you want, doesn't change the fact he has friends." The bartender leaned over closer to Elijah so he wouldn't talk so loudly. "He deals fair with the Army, gives them a fair price on his cows. He gives the storekeepers a lot of business. Pays his bills, never asks for credit."

"He's a damn rustler, thief, and murderer. That's what the hell he is."

The bartender sighed and shook his head. "You may be right, likely are, but nobody's proved anything. Kane might be a snake, but he's a smart one, recognizes who to strike and who to slither away from." You best not be asking any more questions about Kane, least not if you want to stay healthy."

Elijah wandered on down the street until he ran into an old buffalo hunter, for whom Elijah spent a couple of winters skinning, sitting down at the end of the street watching one of Dierden Kane's wranglers shoe a horse.

"That man is a worthless piece of crap," he whispered as Elijah sat next to him. "Poor animal's taken a beating." The horse jerked a foot away from Kane's wrangler.

"You jarhead," Kane's man screamed as he jabbed the rasp into his horse's stomach. "Gimme your damn foot," he said, grabbing at the animal.

The gelding jerked away, pulling back on the lead rope tied to a post. For a minute, Elijah thought the horse would break free, but the man gave him another slap with the rasp before jerking hard on the lead rope. "Come 'ere, damn ya." The cowboy got the horse's foot back up, and after so much swearing, he caught the attention of two men across the street.

In his late twenties, one of the men didn't care for the cowboy's despicable behavior. The horse kicked away again, drawing three sharp beatings with the rasp. The blows cut the horse open above the hock, inflicting enough pain to cause the animal to shift his weight off the leg. Tossing the rasp on the ground behind him, the man grabbed a horseshoe and hammer.

Elijah started to rise out of his chair, but the buffalo hunter put his arm out to stop him, shaking his head as a warning to his friend.

"Don't get in the middle."

Elijah sat back down, ashamed of himself for not doing something. The man from the other side of the street charged toward Kane's cowhand. In a dead run, he reached down, grabbing the rasp.

"Hey!"

While a rasp is an excellent tool for filing the hoof of a horse, it plays hell with a man's face. Kane's cowhand's cadence was off. He glanced up just in time to see the backhanded swing delivering the rasp, not in time to duck. The sound was something similar to, but not quite like, the noise a watermelon makes when dropped on hard ground. Blood splattered all over, mostly on the paint horse.

"How do you like it?" A second blow, more of a jab, cut a nasty gash over the victim's eye. The next was another backhand. "I'm gonna knock the hell out of you. How do you like it?" The man went almost crazy with anger. He pulled up Kane's man by his hair and ears, only to knock him down again. Dropping the rasp, he jerked the man out of the dirt and rammed his head three times into the hitching post. Elijah and the hunter both got out of their chairs, attempting to stay out of harm's way. The man slammed his fist into the cowboy's stomach—twice before grabbing a handful of his hair in both hands and slamming his head into the post one more time.

Blood sprayed. Teeth flew. He struck the man, square in the face sending him sprawling backward over the hitching rail. Finally, the man's companion tried to separate them.

"You're gonna kill him, Gray. Before he pulled his friend, the man landed one last swift kick to the bent-over horse beater's chest.

"Somebody oughta kill him," the one called Gray spat out, red-hot anger flashing in his voice and eyes.

"Yeah, but not today," the younger man said, trying to stay in between his friend and the near unconscious victim.

The man doing the beating reached into his shirt pocket and pulled out some money. He walked over to where the thrashed man lay and bent down over him. "Hey. Hey, can you hear me?" The barely conscious man moaned and tried to put his arm up over his face to protect himself. "Here's ten dollars. This horse belongs to me now. Do you understand me? I said, do you understand me?" Kane's cowhand, whose face looking like someone had taken a plow to it, groaned and may or may not have nodded his head.

"You're a witness," the horse savior said, looking up at Elijah. "He sold me this horse."

Elijah stepped down off the sidewalk and leaned over the beaten man. "He don't look too good."

"You wouldn't either if somebody beat the hell out of you," the young man half-laughed.

"No, I suppose I wouldn't."

The man called Gray examined the horse's hock. "Easy, easy, I'm not going to hurt you," he said in a soft, calm voice when the horse wanted to pull away. "Stand still now, stand easy." The man gently rubbed his skinned-up hand over the horse's leg and wiped the blood on his pants. "Come on, let's go find something to doctor you with."

"You might want to find some of his friends if he's got any," the horse savior's partner said, glancing at Elijah. "I suppose somebody ought to drag him off the street."

"He can lay there 'til he dies and rots," the old buffalo hunter said, spitting a wad of tobacco at the moaning cowboy.

"Suit yourselves. He's no friend of mine."

"I'm Elijah Yancey," Elijah said, sticking his hand out to the young stranger.

"J. B. Hickok."

"I don't believe we've met," Elijah said while staring again at the near unconscious wrangler. "His lip is tore near clear off."

Hickok glanced at the man but didn't care about his lip. "My partner and I brought some cattle down from the north for the Army. We're going to do a little scouting for Fort Laramie."

"Fort Laramie? I spend a lot of time at the fort," the buffalo hunter said, stepping down off the sidewalk. "Harry Calhoun's my name."

"I guess I better go and catch up to my partner," Hickok said after shaking Harry's hand.

"I guess you best," Elijah laughed. "'Fore he kills somebody for kickin' a dog."

"Oh, he doesn't like dogs much." Hickok cackled as he turned to leave. "He's a horseman."

"I see he is," Elijah said.

Hickok jogged a little to catch up to his friend, who did not acknowledge his return. "You're probably gonna have to kill him when he gets well enough to come after you."

"I'd have killed him now if you hadn't interfered."

Chapter Ten

Between snooping for information about Kane and watching the man be half-beat to death, Elijah neglected to pick up the supplies before the general store closed and had to hang around town until the store opened at nine. By the time Elijah loaded the wagon and made his way back home, it was after one in the afternoon.

Ally stood on the porch when Elijah pulled to a stop at the front of the house. "I was getting worried about you."

Josh strolled across the yard from the corral, wiping his hands on his bandana.

"No need, Mrs. Hart. I got sort of a late start this morning."

"Well, I'm glad you're home safe," Ally said as she started to unload.

Once Ally went to the house, Josh asked if Elijah found out anything about Dierden Kane. "Nothin' much. Some of his cowhands were in town, but not Kane. Nobody would say much about how many cows he's been selling."

Josh glanced at the front door before replying. "I guess I let my imagination run away with me. I imagine those cows wandered off on their own."

"One of Kane's men ran into a little trouble," Elijah said, clearly delighted. "He gave a horse a beatin' with a rasp, and some fella, a stranger to me, objected. He liked to beat Kane's man to death. I never saw a man so upset over a horse. Especially one that weren't his.

Chapter Eleven

Cow Camp North of Fort Laramie

An eye-catching blue-eyed blond woman wandered over to the man who slapped around Kane's cowhand. "Jimmy says you ran into a little trouble."

"Not much," Gray Wehr said, sounding annoyed.

"Jimmy says you nearly killed a man."

"Not hardly," Gray responded before taking a drink of the coffee, shifting his eyes away from the woman.

Gray Wehr was not exactly uncommunicative, but his disposition did turn toward the quiet side. Not yet thirty years old, he had a reputation as a man not to trifle with. His unruly blond hair gave him a roguish quality, and his probing green eyes cut right through you. Women found him a dashing figure.

The blond woman started to speak again but changed her mind and, without saying anything else, went back toward the cook fire built in the center of a medium-sized camp. She talked to a dark-haired woman before they both picked up water buckets and headed off to the stream a few hundred yards away. "He didn't say much." the dark-haired woman said.

"Not much. You didn't expect him to, did you, Annie?"

With a little black puppy bouncing along behind him, Hickok walked over to where Gray stood leaning against an old oak tree.

"What'd you tell my sister?" Gray asked in an unpleasant voice.

"I'm not sure I mentioned anything," Hickok said, picking up the pup.

"You're the only one in this camp she calls 'Jimmy,'" Gray said, not expecting much of an answer.

"Oh, I guess I may have pointed out your particular affection for horses." Hickok laughed. "And...it doesn't serve a man to slap one around in front of you."

Gray grunted, disinterested in pursuing the matter.

"I'm going to give this pup to her," Hickok said, expecting his friend to be impressed.

"Jeannie doesn't need a dog."

"I ain't givin' him to her because she needs him; I figure she'll enjoy him. What do you think we ought to name him?" He held the dog up for Gray's inspection.

"How about Nuisance," Gray snickered.

Chapter Twelve

Elijah stopped digging out the stump to study the lone rider coming along the river. "I swear, that's Burton Brown." He shook out a red bandanna before wiping the sweat from his face. "He's a cattle buyer. Mr. Hart used to sell to him every spring."

"You suppose he's looking to pick some up from Ally?"

"Naw," Elijah said, waving his bandana at the rider. "He's aware Mr. Hart died, and Mrs. Hart is struggling."

"Mighty hot afternoon to be digging at an old stump," Brown said as he stepped down off his horse and extended his hand. "How you been, Elijah?"

"We're getting by." Elijah pointed an old, boney, bent finger toward Josh. "This is Josh McCormick. He's helping Mrs. Hart out for the next couple of months. He used to be an accountant in St. Louis." Elijah paused and chuckled. "Now, he's learnin' to be a cowhand."

Josh believed he dodged a bullet when Elijah did not tell

the man anything about his past beyond being an accountant. "Elijah says you're a cattle buyer. I wish we had some business for you," he said as he shook the man's hand.

Brown spat out a stream of tobacco, which splattered against a flat rock. Josh was still having trouble getting accustomed to every male in Wyoming over nine years old, ceaselessly spitting tobacco juice.

"Cattle are why I stopped by."

Baffled, Elijah barked, "Hell, Mrs. Hart's in no position to sell cattle."

"Of course not. You dammed old fool." Brown spat another stream of juice and wiped his sleeve across his mouth, mostly hidden by a huge salt n pepper mustache. "I believe I can help her procure some cattle," Brown spoke with an air of self-satisfaction in his voice.

Elijah winked at Josh. "He means he may have a way up his sleeve for Mrs. Hart to get some cattle," Elijah said. "Burton likes to use fancy words he don't think I'll understand. But I ain't such a damn fool as he wants to think I am." Elijah laughed, giving Josh a wink. "Why don't you drag your skinny butt up to the house with us? We may be able to procure a cup of coffee out of Mrs. Hart."

About halfway across what, after much work out of Ally and Josh, resembled a front yard, Elijah hollered out at the house. "Mrs. Hart, we've got company. If you can call this cousin of a skunk company."

Ally, smiling brightly, gave Burton a quick hug. "I didn't expect you this spring."

"I suppose our luck can't last forever," Elijah half-growled.

"Don't pay any attention to these two sniping at each other," Ally said. "They're dear old friends."

"We ain't neither. I wouldn't spit on him if he was on fire."

"If you were on fire, I wouldn't..." Brown cut himself off as he glanced over at Ally. "I wouldn't...throw dirt on you."

"I have coffee inside, and supper is less than an hour away." She took Brown's arm in hers and walked him toward the house.

"You can go back to diggin' on your stump while Alice and I drink our coffee," Brown said, looking back over his shoulder at Elijah.

"I will," Elijah shot back. "The stump is sure better company than you. Come on, McCormick, we can dig the tree out while this old loafer sits on his backside, watching Mrs. Hart cook his dinner."

Josh and Elijah headed back to the stump. "Do many people call her Alice?"

"Naw," Elijah said, his voice grumpy. "He's jist putting on airs. Thinks he impresses Mrs. Hart. She realizes he's full of crap."

"I'm happy to see you, Burton," Ally said, sitting a cup of coffee in front of her guest. "Visitors are scarce these last months."

The house smelled of the sausage Ally cooked for breakfast. The drawn curtains and closed windows blocked the light, and fresh air, making the atmosphere stifling and depressing. A painting, one painted in understated tones, Burton remembered hanging on the wall at the darker end of the room was missing. He took a long drink of the coffee and contemplated Ally.

"How you been, Ally? Have you been able to make ends meet out here?"

Ally sat across the heavy oak dining table from her old friend and started to talk with him, talk more honestly than she talked with anyone since Sam's death. "Life's been challenging, Burton, more difficult than I expected." Brown reached over the table and patted her hand before giving it an affectionate squeeze and holding on to it. Ally made eye contact before again starting to speak. "If not for Elijah, I don't know if I could survive. Certainly not out here," she said. "And I don't know where else I could go."

"He's an able man. And he thinks the world of you." Burton went into the kitchen, where he opened the dark green curtains and window. Maybe light and fresh air would lift Ally's melancholy.

"This McCormick fellow," Brown said as he sat back down. "Elijah called him an accountant. How'd he end up out here at your place?"

Ally smiled—slightly. "He's a gift from Judge Starrett." She half-laughed. "The judge freed him from jail on the condition he spends three months working for me."

Concern grew evident in Brown's face as he listened to Ally. "What did this fella do? Are you safe having him around here?"

"Judge Dan jailed him for being a drunkard," Ally said. "His daughter died." Ally continued with empathy in her voice. "About five months later, a burglar killed his wife. He started trying to drown his sorrows in whiskey."

"Some men do," Brown said, not in a sympathetic tone.

Ally knew Burton Brown was not a drinker, but his father had been a terrible one, and a mean drunk. He had told Ally and Sam long ago about his father. As a boy, he was helpless when the brute broke his mother's nose, an arm, and numerous ribs. The beatings and abuse to his mother long ago hardened him regarding the shortcomings of a drunk.

Ally was somewhat puzzled at finding herself defending Josh. "He's been a help to Elijah and me. Judge Dan wrote to me about him being a respectable man before the tragedies. If he's not a decent man again, he's on his way. At least I think he is." Ally did think so. She was thinking a lot about Josh, including about her feelings for him. She was starting to like him but wasn't sure if that was good or bad.

"Well, I hope you're right, Burton said, drawing Ally back into the present moment. "I don't mean to be cruel in saying this, but you've had enough heartache and hardship without a swill belly bringing you more."

A rather uncomfortable silence filled the room for two or three full minutes while Ally unsuccessfully tried to think of how to answer Brown.

Brown got up and poured himself more coffee. "I suppose if he ain't caused you no problem so far, he may turn out to be all right. I hope so, for your sake." Brown sat back down across from Ally. He reached across the table and again patted Ally's hand. "Anyway," he said in a much cheerier voice, "I believe I have some good news for you."

"It would be well received." Ally smiled. "We haven't had a whole lot of happy news around here lately."

"How would you like about twenty-five or thirty head of new stock?" Brown asked. "And not some scrub, half-starved cattle you might round up out in the sagebrush. I'm talkin' about twenty-five or thirty quality cows, most of them bred, and a young bull to boot."

Ally half-laughed, not a pleasant laugh, but a lost-sounding laugh. The way people losing hope sometimes laugh. "I should buy a hundred head or two hundred." She chuckled again, this time more lightheartedly. "I have about as much chance coming up with the money for a hundred as I would for twenty-five."

"I didn't say you need any money," Brown said.

"Oh, you know someone who's giving cattle away, do you?"

"Well, now, I didn't say they were giving them away. I said you might not need any money, not immediately." Brown took on a more earnest demeanor. "Are you familiar with the Wehr/Joseph Ranch?"

"From up north?"

"Up in the Bighorns," Brown said.

"I think everyone has." Despite being in a more remote place than Ally herself, the Wehr/Joseph Ranch was the most successful cattle operation in Wyoming, as esteemed as any in Kansas or anywhere on the plains. Only in Texas would a bigger one be found. A Texas ranch would only be more significant in size, not in success.

"They've got more'n two hundred head north of here. Less than a two-hour ride from here."

Ally finished her coffee before standing up to start supper. "Burton, you must think I'm better off than I am." She turned back toward the cattle buyer. "I couldn't buy one cow. The truth is," she said, surprised she was not embarrassed, "we're going to need to sell a cow or two for enough money to buy some supplies." She turned away and started to peel the five potatoes sitting next to the pump.

Brown sat quietly, looking at her.

Ally was a bit embarrassed about him staring. She had lost so much weight she feared she looked a little sickly. The cream-colored blouse she wore drooped off her shoulders. She brushed her brown hair back away from her face, revealing a bit of perspiration on her brow.

"Alice . . ."

Hearing him call her Alice, caused her to stop and turn toward him. "I hope I've not overstepped myself, but I talked to those folks about you and your situation."

Ally scowled at him and leaned forward.

Brown hastened his words. "They're exceptional people, Ally; both the Wehrs and the Josephs. They want to help you."

Ally reacted negatively. "You told them about me? You asked them to give me charity?" For some reason, Burton, a tall but skinny man, stood before speaking. Perhaps towering above the woman added to his confidence.

"I did no such thing," he growled. "I told them about your difficulties. They want to help you. There is no charity involved. You can pay them after your first crop of calves sell. You'll want to work out a fair rate of interest."

Ally leaned back against her countertop, not much more than a rough old plank Sam carved out of an old log and sanded smooth before heavily varnishing.

"They're business people; they'll want a fair profit."

Ally, angry at Burton, embarrassed he asked, asked

without her consent or knowledge, for someone to help her, turned away from Burton Brown and stared out at the oak tree towering over Sam's grave. She bit her lip, trying to hold back tears of embarrassment. She spoke without turning around. "You had no right to ask them to help me." The tears now started to roll down her cheeks. "I won't take charity."

Burton walked behind her. He put his hands on her shoulders, firmly turning her to face him and looking directly into her eyes. She turned her face away.

"Look at me, Ally."

She did not.

He tightened his grip on her shoulders. "Look at me, Alice." When she did not, he took her chin and raised it. "Look at me. There is no charity involved. And it isn't about my rights. This is about doing what's right."

The tears flowed harder. "Let me go." She trembled as she spoke. "Let go."

Brown let her go. She did not turn away or move away.

He answered in a much softer voice. "Ally, answer me this. If the situation was the other way around, if someone needed help you could provide, what would you do?"

Ally bowed her head. She didn't speak, only stood still.

"Well?" he asked.

After a moment or two, she leaned against Burton's chest. "I'd help them," she whispered after taking a deep breath.

"You're a fine person, in these circumstances, not by your fault."

Burton bordered on lecturing when he told her not to let foolish pride prevent her from accepting help, especially help willingly given. Knowing she was a Christian woman, he used scripture, reminding her pride comes before a fall. At last, she agreed while making no commitments. She would at least seek input from Elijah and Josh.

When, over supper, Burton told Elijah and Josh about his proposal, both men unreservedly expressed Ally should make the two-hour trip to talk with them. Elijah did not hide his excitement when Ally insisted her two hands make the journey with her.

Brown started to explain the details of how the meeting with the people from High Meadows, a little town in the Bighorns, should go. "Now, the patriarchs are not along," Brown said. "They're getting older and seldom leave the valley anymore. Three Josephs are in camp," Brown said, looking at Ally. "Alan, he's the oldest, about thirty-two, I suppose, as well as James and Zach. You'll want to deal with Alan, as far as the Josephs go. James is a quiet man; he'll let Alan negotiate. Zach, he's...." Brown paused. "Ah, hell, Zach's a borderline fool. And he frequently crosses the border."

"You mean he's dim?" Elijah asked.

Burton rubbed his face, a bit exasperated at Elijah's question. "Naw, he ain't dim, you old clod." Burton's eyes were twinkling. He glanced at Ally. "Now, pardon what I'm about to say, Alice. But Zach is full of shit."

Ally took no offense. She laughed heartily.

"A lot of people suffer that affliction," Josh said. "I might put that damned old judge in that category," he said, raising another laugh out of Ally. Josh smiled at her. "I enjoy you laughing, Ally. Laughing suits you."

"Sure does, Mrs. Hart. Sure does," Elijah said, reaching over and patting her shoulder.

Much to Ally's relief, Burton Brown again picked up the conversation, saving her any embarrassment her emotions might cause.

"Two of the Wehr kids, Gray and his sister Jean, are with the herd. They're in their mid to late twenties, so they're not kids. Jean is likely the one you'll end up dealing with, though she's younger than her brother. It will depend on Gray's mood. He can be moody."

Elijah said, "I swear, I never put that together."

"What?" Ally asked, glancing at her friend.

"Gray Wehr being one of those Wehrs," he said. "I swear."

"Gray earned himself a bit of a reputation," Burton said. "He's got a little wild in him."

"You're talking about whom Ally should deal. I thought these people already agreed," Josh said.

"They have," Burton said. "But they'll still want to agree on a price and when Ally will pay."

Josh did not say anything.

"Jean can be a firebrand too," Burton said. "She's got a lot of her brother in her. Nevertheless, she's a girl who will go a long way to help someone she thinks deserves a hand. One other person is with them, who you'll want to pay some mind." Her name is Annie Laurie. She's not a Wehr or Joseph, but she keeps a tight rein on Gray. He's likely to ask her opinion," Burton said.

He described Annie as a gentle woman with a soft heart. Burton said her folks owned the general store up in High Meadows. "She's raising some beautiful horses," he said. "She's going to be successful on her own and has about a dozen with her to sell. If you need a fine horse or two, you should talk to her."

"Good Lord," Elijah said, cutting Burton off, "Is there anybody in Wyoming not in that cow camp?"

Burton laughed at Elijah's insight. "Oh, shut up, you old fool."

"Well, I hate to sound like the pessimist here," Josh said. "But can we drive these cattle home by ourselves?"

Chapter Thirteen

When Burton Brown rolled out of his bedroll two hours before daylight, he was noisier than Elijah. "What time does Ally feed folks? I need some strong coffee."

Josh sleepily said breakfast occurred right after daybreak. "I cannot grasp the need for everyone out in this God-forsaken country to get up in the middle of the damn night. It's too dark to work, and I don't understand why you can't spend another hour or two in bed like any civilized people."

"Because any rancher laying around in his bed will soon be broke," Brown said sarcastically.

Josh decided any further conversation on the topic would be meaningless. He pulled his boots on and headed out the door to gather up the horses he, Ally, and Elijah would ride. Josh selected the cowy bay for Elijah and got his horse for himself. Cowy or not, his roan horse came across Missouri, Kansas, Colorado, and up into Wyoming without throwing him one time, and he was not going to have Elijah pick him out one to break his neck the first time they encountered a cow.

Ally sat reading her Bible when the three men stepped up on her porch. "Some time in the good book?" Burton Brown asked as they walked in the front door.

"Helps me find peace in the world." Ally laid the tattered book on a table next to the window.

"What particular book are you studying?" Burton asked as he hung his hat on a rough old coat tree and ran his fingers through his graying hair.

"Proverbs," Ally said while putting plates on the table for breakfast.

"Trust in the Lord with all thine heart and lean not to thine own understanding. In all thy ways acknowledge him, and he shall direct thy paths."

"Why, Burton, I didn't expect you were a Biblical scholar," Ally said.

"Not a scholar, Ally, not a scholar," Brown said, sitting down to the breakfast of scrambled eggs, biscuits, and gravy. "Quite a spread here this morning; smells delicious. Well, what are you looking at?" he snapped, seeing Elijah staring at him. "Don't you think I behave like a theologian?"

Chapter Fourteen

Cow camps are seldom neat and clean, and they don't smell like roses. This one was no exception, full of cowhands and horseflies and smelling like cow shit and burned beans. The only difference between this camp and any other cow camp was the two beautiful women in this one. Jean Wehr, seeing riders coming up from the south, glanced at her dark-haired friend. "Must be Burton Brown and the woman he told us about."

As the four riders came splashing out of the river at the Wehr/Joseph encampment, Brown waved his broad-brimmed hat. "Hello, ladies." Two women walked down toward the sloping riverbank to meet them. "Jean, Annie, this is Alice Hart," Burton said as he and the others stepped down off their horses. "The woman I told you about."

"Mrs. Hart, I'm Jean Wehr. This is my friend Annie Laurie."

"It's Ally. Everyone calls me Ally," she said, taking Jean's hand. "These are my friends Elijah Yancey and Josh

McCormick. Josh recently came from St. Louis."

How was your ride up here?" Annie asked, extending her hand to Ally.

"Fine," Ally smiled. "Took us a little less than three hours."

"We left right after breakfast, soon as Mrs. Hart finished her Bible study," Elijah added after giving Annie's hand a vigorous shake.

"Lunch is only a little more than an hour away," Jean said. "We'll eat first and go pick you out some cattle."

Ally glanced at Burton, a bit surprised at Jean's directness. Despite Burton's having told her she would acquire the cattle, she expected some type of negotiations or discussion about her situation first.

"I sent someone after Gray and Alan when we saw you coming," Jean said.

Jean led everyone over to the fire.

"This country must be quite a change from St. Louis," Annie said to Josh as she and Jean poured each of the four a cup of coffee.

"I'm afraid this is strong," Jean told them. "The pot's been sitting on the flames since early this morning."

"It is different," Josh answered. "I'm getting used to the differences. I find some kind of harsh attraction."

Ally was disheartened by Josh's reaction to their country, saying the place had a harsh attraction. *Harsh? Yes, probably.* She still did not like an outsider judging. *Perhaps you're a little too soft for this country.*

"I suppose some think our land is harsh...I don't," Jean said, sitting down on one of three campstools, which the cook pulled out of the chuckwagon, an act of chivalry toward the females.

"You fellers can git along sittin' on the ground," the cook told them through a mouth missing all its front upper teeth. "Lost them to a nasty-spirited mule," he said with a laugh when he caught Ally staring at his toothless smile. "Damned animal was trying to take my head off, but I were too quick for him. All he got for his effort was some teeth."

"Your valley is much prettier than Ally's ranch," Burton Brown said. "I told Ally on the way up here this morning she should give up this fool notion of raising cattle and move to Kansas or someplace where life would be a bit easier for her. Your little valley would be a better spot yet. Ally would be safe and would soon make several friends. Ally's a smart woman, capable of taking over the school teaching when your mother retires," he said to Jean. "If the land and the work where she is don't kill her," he said, talking as if Ally were not present, "some Indian will take her scalp some morning after he's done some other things."

"Why, you old fool, I told you last night Roman Nose hisself told Mrs. Hart she'd be safe," Elijah said.

"Yeah? Well, I guess he doesn't speak for all the Cheyenne, and he sure doesn't speak for the Sioux." Brown stood and pointed at the coffeepot to ensure the cook's permission before he poured himself another cup.

"Here come Gray and Alan," Annie said, putting her hand on Ally's forearm.

"I swear!" Elijah blurted out as Gray Wehr stepped from behind his blue roan horse. "He's the fella what beat the hell out of Kane's man." He gave Josh's shoulder a push. "What do you think of that?"

Seeing Gray, Ally blushed. After Elijah described the man beating the hell out of Kane's cowhand, she expected him to be brutal looking, at least rough and mean. This man was handsome.

"I guess Elijah has seen you before," Jean said to Gray before adding, "the other day when you were, how did you put it, Elijah, beating hell out of some fella?"

Ally caught Annie smiling and shaking her head as Jean continued.

"Oh, don't worry, though, Elijah, he doesn't beat the hell out of people when Annie's around. So, you should be safe enough. As long as you don't speak ill of a horse."

"My sister's kind of mouthy. It's best to ignore her."

When Jean picked up the coffee pot, offering some to Alan Joseph and her brother, Gray sat down on her stool. "Burton says you have a ranch you need back on its feet," Gray said, nodding at both Josh and Elijah.

"If you don't want a lap full of hot coffee, you better get off my stool," Jean snarled at her brother after pouring Alan's coffee.

"I see Stu has lunch ready to serve," Alan Joseph, a dark-haired man with a large, droopy mustache, said, speaking for the first time. "Why don't we fill our plates and talk while we eat?"

During the lunch of cornbread and fish, Ally explained in-depth about losing her husband, with Elijah adding she now called the bull Satan.

"Well, we've talked a bit, Mrs. Hart," Alan Joseph said. "We're comfortable to give you thirty bred cows, ten unbred heifers, and a young bull. You can pay us when you sell the first crop of calves." Alan refilled his coffee cup and offered more to the others. "We'd also like fifteen percent of the profit from the following year's calf crop in return for delaying the initial payment. We feel we're fair to both parties." Alan poured honey onto a new piece of cornbread and continued without waiting for any response from Ally. "Gray will help you drive the cattle home. We can sort them out for you this afternoon, and you can be on your way at your convenience tomorrow." Jean added they'd be more than welcome to rest for a second day before they started for home.

So, there it was. Ally Hart acquired forty head of cows and a fine young bull without speaking a word.

The acquisition took Ally from an almost hopeless future to a position of security. At least as secure as one could be as a widow.

"You can take some horses out of our remuda if you want to

give your animals a rest," Jean said as they prepared to sort out Ally's cattle. "Yours might like a rest."

"Thanks, but I'll stick with my horse." Josh laughed. "I had one experience with a horse cowier than I am." Josh spent the afternoon practicing caution as the cows moved.

"They'll quiet down here in a little while," Alan Joseph said, speaking to Josh in somewhat hushed tones.

"This is my first real experience at cattle work," Josh said. "Back in St. Louis, you see all those paintings of cattle drives where the cowboys are riding at a dead run, dust blowing, makes it look exciting. I'm learning it's not much like that."

Alan chuckled at Josh's observation. "No, not too often. Slow and easy is the best way to work a bunch of cows. There's not much need to hurry them. Hurrying them creates a lot of extra work."

Josh stared for a moment at the man sitting next to him. He did look like the dime novels portrayed a cowboy— rugged, tan, lean, and reliable. Josh thought the large mustache drooping from his upper lip befit the man.

"So, what do you think of our country and our way of life out here?" Alan asked.

Josh thought about the man's question. At first, he wondered why Alan asked. Idle conversation, he hoped. "You know," Josh said, pausing to look over the cows and out across the horizon. "I like it. I can see the appeal of it. Maybe more so for a man than a woman, but I can see its appeal. I'm starting to understand the attraction to this life, the feeling you're making something, something worthwhile. When I go to bed, I feel I accomplished something with lasting value to it."

"Well, hell, talking like that, you may turn into a cowman if you don't watch yourself," Alan said.

Josh thought Alan might be mocking him.

"I have a lot to learn and a lot of skills to improve on before I dare call myself cowman," Josh said in a relaxed manner. "Hell, Ally is a better hand on a horse than I am.

But," he continued after a slight pause, "it's a life I believe I could come to enjoy."

Alan looked at Josh as if trying to determine his sincerity before responding. "I believe a man, if it's possible at all, should do what he enjoys. As far as the woman being a better hand than you, there ain't nothing says a woman can't handle a horse. Jean Wehr and Annie Laurie can both sit one as well as any man I know. But, don't you ever let either of them know I said that," he added with a wink and a smile as he spat a stream of tobacco. "Course they also clean up a lot prettier than the rest of us do." He laughed.

"I understand Gray and Jean have a brother."

Alan raised his rope at a white-faced cow, starting to wander away from the others. "Get back over there." The cow turned and moved back. "His name's Paxton. We left him back home. Jean tends to boss him a bit. Not her other brother, though. Not Gray. Ain't nobody gonna boss him." Alan motioned toward Gray, sitting his horse on the opposite end of the cowboys. "Gray, he's the finest horseman I've ever seen, nobody else even close. But the damn wild streak in him is gonna cause him problems someday if he ain't careful."

Burton Brown rode casually over to Alan and Josh. "They're settling down. Don't look like they'll be any trouble."

Alan looked over at the two men and let his eyes drift back and forth between them. Burton Brown's face was weather-beaten and wrinkled. McCormick's face also looked beaten, though not by the weather.

"This Hart woman, does she have the sand to make a go of her ranch?"

Josh, not sure who the question was for, presumed it was for Brown. A muscle in his jaw twitched over Brown's answer.

"I don't know, don't know."

Alan Joseph didn't respond. Josh clamped his jaws together, determined to help Ally make her ranch pay.

Chapter Fifteen

"It's a little more than six miles to Fort Laramie," Ally said, responding to a question from Annie. "I guess the nearest neighbor is ten or twelve miles away. So, no, there's not much opportunity for visiting. It's pretty much Elijah, Josh, and me."

"As remote as we are up in our valley," Annie said, "all our homes are close to town, so it makes for a close-knit little community."

"I admit I long for friends," Ally said, perhaps a touch of sadness showing in her voice. "The winters are the hardest. The days are so short, and this last winter weeks at a time would pass without the sun shining, dreary gray day after dreary gray day."

Ally could sense Annie felt sorry for her. Why wouldn't she? She led a lonely existence made more so by the loss of a husband. Ally was trapped by circumstances, not always able to act on others' sound advice.

"Do you have any brothers or sisters?" Annie asked.

"A sister, but she lives down in Texas. Lord, it's more desolate than my little ranch. I count my blessings when I think of where she is."

"I had a brother and a sister. They were killed about a year ago," Annie said, looking off into the evening dusk. "A man named Harvey Kehn murdered them. He's a lowlife who's been hurting people out here for a long time."

"He wasn't caught?" Ally asked.

"No. But, maybe someday," Annie said, almost matter-of-factly. "Maybe someday, I hope so, at least. I don't think he's a candidate for redemption. I believe he's a man who will keep hurting until he's stopped."

Ally thought the comment about redemption peculiar. It sounded as if the man's redemption would have been preferable to Annie. She could not help thinking if someone, a person instead of a beast, killed Sam, she would have hoped more for punishment than for redemption. "They didn't catch the man who killed Josh's wife either," she said after a brief pause. "We don't talk about it much, but from what Josh tells me, there's not much chance he ever will be."

"Do they know who killed her?" Annie asked.

"No. A man who escaped from a nearby jail fit the description. They showed Josh a drawing of his face. However, Josh could not be sure. He never got a good look at him."

"Such a shame." Annie sighed. "I imagine it's a heavy burden for him to carry."

Ally didn't respond. Her feelings about Josh remained mixed.

Chapter Sixteen

The air remained still and hot as Ally walked through the small stand of trees down toward the river, where she hoped she might find some breeze and a bit of relief from the heat. Clouds moving over the dappled half-moon made the night dark, and her walk through the small woods careful going. A large rock protruded from the river's edge, and Ally sat on it, lifting her chocolate brown skirt to her knees and removing her boots and socks to put her feet into the water and allow its coolness to bring some relaxation to her tense body.

"Can't sleep?"

The sound of the man's voice startled her, and she jumped.

"I'm sorry. I didn't mean to scare you."

"You didn't really scare me," Ally said, embarrassed about jumping. "You surprised me a little."

"Well, I didn't mean to startle you either," Gray said, moving out of the shadows and toward Ally.

He wore a dark-colored shirt with a faded red bandana

hanging loosely around his neck. Gray was a tall man. Ally thought about six feet. Lean and graceful in his movements, there was just enough light for Ally to see him smiling at her. A soft smile making her feel comfortable in his presence.

"To answer your question, I couldn't sleep. But not sleeping is nothing unusual," Ally said, sliding across the rock to allow room for her new companion to sit. "Here, there's plenty of room," she smiled, patting the rock with her hand. "Are you the camp guard tonight?"

"No." Gray laughed. "We don't post a guard. We've got a couple of nighthawks with the herd, but there's no reason to post a guard over the camp. I'm a troubled sleeper too."

"How late is it?" Ally asked as Gray slipped down next to her.

He pulled out his pocket watch. "Two forty-five," he said after struggling to see the watch's face in the dark. He dropped the watch back into his shirt pocket.

"You can scoot on around if you want to put your feet in the water."

Ally's bare legs and feet moved up and down in the cold river.

"I'm fine right here," he said, sounding out of place.

"Well, if you change your mind, there's room."

Gray let the offer pass.

After a brief silence, Ally touched Gray's knee and began to speak in a soft but steady voice. "I want you to know how much I appreciate what you and your family are doing for me. It's kind, and I know you are taking a bit of a risk on me."

Gray shrugged. "I don't suppose it's too much of a risk," he replied. "You should do well with this bunch of cows."

"Would you like to take a walk along the river?" Ally asked, sensing the togetherness on the rock might be a bit much for her companion. She believed men were either too bold or too shy in relationships with women, and this one was of the shy variety.

"Sure," Gray said. Ally sensed he was relieved to get off

the rock.

"I don't think many people would help someone who is in the same business they are," Ally said as she pulled on her boots and dropped her skirt down. Gray's relief about the skirt was so obvious she almost chuckled out loud.

"I don't know why not," Gray said as they started to walk along the riverbank. "Helping one cattleman helps the whole business. Besides, there may come a time when we'll need your help."

Ally laughed. "I can't imagine the Wehr/Joseph Ranch needing my help. But, if you ever do," she said, "you can count on it. Still, I know not everyone feels the way you do. Some want no competition, and especially not from a woman."

"Is someone giving you trouble?"

"Not yet. They've just promised to."

Gray stopped, looking down at the thin, tired woman. "You've been threatened? By who?"

Ally hesitated, not sure she should make any accusations. It also crossed her mind the Wehrs and Josephs might be friendly with Kane. Kane did know who to push and who to accommodate.

"Mrs. Hart?"

Ally stopped walking and looked first at the ground, then at Gray. "Dierden Kane."

"Humph." Gray glanced away before responding. "Doesn't surprise me."

Chapter Seventeen

Josh rolled out of his bedroll a little before sunup thinking he would get a head start on the others in preparing for the day's drive. Worry about how he would perform moving cattle in the company of real cowhands disturbed his sleep, making him glad to rise early. When he fell off his horse trying to get one rogue steer out of a gully, Ally laughed at him. But it was warm and friendly laughing, not judgmental. She had not been critical of his shoddy work but made him feel, perhaps for the first time, she thought well of him, valued his desire to help her, and was starting to appreciate him as a friend.

However, Burton Brown and this Gray Wehr, they were not women or kindhearted like Elijah but real cowmen, hardened and toughened by both years and miles of trail experience. They would not put up with mediocre work, certainly not shoddy work.

Ally's new cattle grazed along the river about a half-mile from the camp. The cattle being right on the river troubled Josh most. With no time to get accustomed to working with the herd, he would help get them across a river. Even with no experience at all, he knew river crossing could be a dangerous task. He heard many stories of terrible disasters when drives crossed rivers. Cattle sometimes managed to drown themselves and sometimes a cowboy in the process.

If they didn't drown him, one of them might hook him. Range cows could be aggressive, flat-out mean. He did not care if Burton Brown called them *high-quality* cattle or not. A *high-quality* cow could hook you the same as a low-quality cow, in his opinion. A serious hooking was more worrisome to Josh than drowning. After Sarah's murder, when Josh spent every hour finding the bottom of whiskey bottles, he thought about drowning himself in the Mississippi on more than one occasion. Once you drown, the worries and hurts of this life disappeared. But a hooking, even a bad hooking, could leave you crippled instead of dead, a fate worse than death.

The talk during breakfast did nothing to ease Josh's concerns about the day. When Alan Joseph mentioned some of the cowboys would help get the cattle across the river, his anxiety didn't wane. The opposite, it confirmed to him the danger of river crossings. Why else would they provide extra help?

Gray, not coming to breakfast, also disturbed him. Instead of being with the others, where Josh might be able to get a reading of the man's attitude about driving cows with a greenhorn, Wehr spent the morning over by the remuda.

Gray's sister and Annie Laurie, whom Josh judged to be romantically interested in Wehr, took him a plate of biscuits and gravy.

"How long do you think you'll be gone?" Annie asked, handing the plate to Gray.

"Oh, I don't know. I guess I hadn't thought much about it," Gray said, rubbing the face of a sorrel gelding nudging his back. "She's been threatened by Dierden Kane. Did you know?" Gray asked, not directing the question at either woman.

After a brief but a bit awkward silence, Jean replied to her brother. "None of our business."

"I think I'll take Doc," Gray said, looking over at the blue roan stallion. "It'll be a good experience for a young horse like him."

"Did you hear what I said?" Jean half-snapped at her brother.

"No, I suppose it's not our business," he said, giving his sister only the briefest glance.

"I guess I'll go ask the Hart woman how soon she wants to leave," Annie said before turning back for the breakfast area.

As soon as Annie was out of earshot, Jean turned on her brother. "Have you lost your mind?"

"What?"

"Have you lost your mind? Don't give me that look. You know what I mean. You've got it in your head to get into a scrap with Dierden Kane."

"I've no such thing," Gray said, vexed by his sister's manner.

"Not much, you don't. You don't like Kane, and you figure this will give you an excuse to get into it with him."

"I don't like the kind of man he is. People thinking they have a right to push others around doesn't sit well with me."

"They're going to leave as soon as they get saddled," Jean told Annie when she returned from the tiff with her brother.

"I wouldn't be surprised if he doesn't show up again for a month," Jean growled while shooting a nasty look at Gray.

Chapter Eighteen

"I notice you'd have missed your breakfast if not for Annie," Burton Brown said to Gray as he rode over to the river where they planned to cross the cattle.

"Our camp cook makes breakfast too greasy to suit me," Gray said. "We should've given him the boot years ago. But he's been with the ranch almost since the beginning. The folks would never stand for getting rid of him."

"Loyalty can be an admirable quality," Burton said.

"I suppose so," Gray said.

"Look at Elijah, loyal as a dog to Ally. He's been a help to her."

"What about McCormick? He much help to her?" Gray asked.

"Well, I suspect he wants to be," Burton said. "But he's got so damn much to learn it's hard to say at this point."

Alan Joseph rode up, interrupting any further discussion of Josh McCormick and his value to Ally. "You ready to start these cattle?"

"We are," Gray said before questioning with a bit of a laugh whether the Hart woman and her two hands were.

"Now, you're underestimating Alice," Brown said. "She may not be operating a spread the size of yours, but she'll not shirk a day's work. And she'll cook you a tasty supper when we get to her place tonight."

Joseph waved his rope over his head to tell his men to start the cattle moving. "Let those cattle spread out a little bit crossing the river," he yelled. "We'll group 'em up on the other side."

"I'll go push the little bull out in the water," Gray said as he started his horse toward the herd. "Once he gets going, the others will follow right along."

Jean Wehr and Annie Laurie walked down to the riverbank as the cattle started to cross. They watched silently as the herd crossed the river without trouble. With the cattle on the other bank, Gray realized neither his sister nor Annie helped get them across, meaning he was in trouble with them. Both suggested Zach and Jimmy Hickok take the cattle to the Hart place, and Gray stay with them. He thought for a moment about riding back and saying goodbye, getting a kiss from Annie.

He decided against it because Jean would let fly a cross word or two for him. Instead, he raised his arm and waved goodbye, a gesture only halfheartedly returned by Annie, not at all by Jean.

"Well, good luck to you, Mrs. Hart," Alan Joseph said as he turned his dun gelding back toward the river. "Try not to let Gray shoot that damn Dierden Kane," he said to Burton as he shook the man's hand.

Chapter Nineteen

With the river crossing behind them, Josh's mood improved. He mentioned his unneeded concern over the river crossing to Burton Brown. Josh now felt comfortable about the trip, which would take most of the day back to Ally's ranch. He allowed himself to imagine what the Wehr/Joseph ranch might look like, picturing it in a beautiful valley of dark green pastures and meadows with thousands of cattle settled peacefully under big shade trees. In his mind, the ranch hands sat quietly on their cow horses, having to do no more than observe the serene surroundings.

"McCormick—Josh!"

Burton's yell brought him back to the much different reality of dust and sage-filled high desert.

"These cows may try to drift apart at first. Don't let them get behind you and push 'em back to the group if they start to move away. Once we're down the trail, they'll settle in together."

"Where should I ride?" Josh asked.

"Trail along behind them, over to the left like you are. You and Elijah and I will push them. Ally and Wehr can ride flank."

Josh noticed the first embarrassing difference in how he worked cows and how Gray Wehr did. Wehr's horse quickly went from a slow, lazy pace to a dead run. It amazed him how fast Wehr's horse could slam his hindquarters underneath himself, pivot, and change directions. Josh's horse was taller and much stockier, but much slower, especially about changing his course. For Josh, slow was a good thing. If his horse performed like Wehr's stud, he'd be on the ground the way he was when Ally's cowy horse whirled out from under him.

Josh judged Wehr to be around ten, maybe a dozen years younger. Thinking about it made him a bit envious. More troubling, though, he noticed Ally's gaze drift toward the man several times throughout the morning. It made him a bit jealous, which worried him since it meant he might be having some feelings for the woman. He wasn't sure he was ready himself or if she would welcome them from him.

Josh snapped out of his daydreaming when Ally called out across the herd to ask if anyone wanted to stop and eat the sandwiches she'd packed into her saddlebags.

"Is it time?" Elijah asked. "It don't seem like we've been riding long."

It did to Josh. All morning a moderate breeze blew the dust the cattle stirred up right back into his face.

"It's half-past one," Ally said, replying to Elijah.

Wehr, the one whom Josh thought might want to keep pushing the cattle, said he seldom turned down a chance to eat before he eased his horse out in front of the herd, stopping their slow walk through the thickening brush.

Once the cattle settled, which took only a short time, Ally and the four men sat in a circle to have their lunch. Surprising Ally, Gray brought up Dierden Kane, a man he admitted strongly disliking.

"I know you whipped the hell out of his man in town,"

Elijah said when Gray asked him and Josh what they knew about Kane and his threats toward Ally. "And I know he ain't worth a pinch of manure," Elijah said.

Gray called Kane worthless, contemptible, and cruel, an unflattering combination. Gray eyed Ally, "I told you last night, Kane won't hesitate to hurt you. He's not bluffing. He'll take something he wants and do it by whatever means he thinks necessary."

Gray's reference to last night disturbed Josh. He was unaware Ally spent time with Wehr, and he thought Gray's comment a little too bold because it made it sound as if the two spent time alone. *How much?* And worse, *what were they doing?* Josh watched Ally, maybe a little too intently. She glanced at him and flashed a quick smile. Why? Was she telling him he had nothing to worry about; she was his? Or was it some sly, shameful confirmation of a good time with Wehr?

Thinking about a woman other than Sarah troubled Josh, made him feel guilty. He resented Ally Hart attracting him. Still, she did charm.

When they finished lunch, Elijah started talking about all the mean and ornery men he encountered during his life. Buffalo hunters, he said, tended to be the orneriest. He amended his conclusion to say, "skinners were most ornery." He speculated it was because they had the dirtiest and stinkiest part of the work. As Elijah gave more and more discourse on his theories about the causes of meanness in men, he concluded greed was another cause, and he figured greed was the particular cause in the case of Dierden Kane.

"Greed will make some men ruthless," Josh said, trying to put his thoughts of Ally and Gray being alone the night before out of his head.

"Well, whatever it is," Gray said, "causing a man like Kane to be the way he is. It's been my experience; you can't ignore them. At some point, you're going to have to stand up to him. And I believe the sooner you do it, the better off you'll be."

Until this point, Ally listened quietly. Nevertheless, what Gray said bothered her. Partly because she suspected it was the truth and partly because she was, in reality, afraid of a confrontation with Kane. Ally could see no way she would be able to win such a conflict if it arose. She thought that what would happen was Kane would end up with all the new cattle, killing someone if not all of them in the process. "You men keep saying I'll have to stand up to him, but how? And if I try, are cattle worth getting killed for?"

Gray's response was callous. "They would be for me."

Chapter Twenty

Gray's comment weighed on Ally the rest of the afternoon. She suspected Burton, and maybe Elijah agreed with what he'd said. She remembered Sam once or twice mentioned he might have to face up to some bullying someday. Now, Ally wondered if he had been talking about Dierden Kane. If so, she wished he had told her so. It might have readied her for the threats coming after his death. At least she wouldn't have been so unprepared when Kane rode onto her place, all full of himself, telling her to move to town. Of course, she hadn't given Sam's words much thought back when he said it. They had three men working for them, not counting Elijah, who was around only part-time when extra work justified a little added expense.

The presence of Sam and three other strong men always made her feel reasonably safe. One of the men, a big and burly Swede, had been thrown from his horse and broken his neck while coming back from town. Sam had not told Ally the man had gotten good and drunk before starting home.

Another married a woman he met when a wagon train passed heading west. Without notice, he joined the train and went with her. That was when Elijah came to the ranch more or less full-time.

The other hand left when, while sleepwalking, he knocked over a lantern in the middle of the night and burned down the little frame cabin he and Elijah used. Ally had heard of people sleepwalking but had never seen anyone do it until he hired on. He would go for weeks with no episodes before everyone on the place would be awakened in the middle of the night when he crashed into something while wandering around in the dark.

The cabin he burned down hadn't amounted to much, an empty room with six cots and a potbellied stove. Still, he felt so bad about it he left the ranch without collecting his last two weeks' pay. His departure made Ally feel downright gloomy for a couple of weeks. Sam tried to talk her out of her melancholy, telling her it was late fall, and they wouldn't need much help for a while. Sam's assessment did not make sense to her, except it would save the expense of paying a hired man.

Two cows wandered off from the group. When Josh moved over to push them back, they bolted. Running up a brushy little knob, they disappeared over its crown down into a thicket of scrub brush, thorns, and sage. Josh's big roan gave him a rough ride down the backside of the hill, jarring Josh, who cussed both him and the cattle as Gray arrived. "They got down in there before I could get 'em turned." His face burned. "How are we gonna get 'em out?"

The patch of brush and scrubby trees ran three, four hundred yards down through a dry creek bed. In most places, it was fifty to seventy-five yards wide. "Can we get them out of there?" It wasn't a question. It was bellyaching.

Gray studied the thicket. "Where'd they go in, do you

know?"

Josh slung his rope at the lower side of the creek bed. He jerked a glove off. "Down along there someplace," he said. "I took my eyes off of them for a minute, trying to get down the damn hill. Why the hell do they always get in somewhere like that with all this open ground? They too shittin' dumb to run for open ground?"

Gray snorted. "A cow doesn't run any farther than she has, too," he said. "If they figure they can hide, they'll do that instead." He moved his horse down along the edges of the brush. Moving slowly, he slipped on a pair of old leather gloves and untied his rope. "Get on down to the other end of this mess and work back toward me. Wait a minute, wait a minute," he called out before Josh got on his way. "I've got 'em." Before moving toward the two cows standing down in a massive part of the brush forty or fifty feet away, he took a minute to decide where they might head in an escape effort. "Well, you blame fools; you've got yourself in a mess down in there." The two cows were in a tangle of sage and thorny hedge so thick the only way they'd be able to go would be out to the open ground or straight at Gray.

Gray half-glared at Josh and motioned with his rope. "Go on down about where that old hedge tree is standing. Soon as you get down there, I'll move in and bust 'em out. As soon as they come out, holler and charge at them. Make sure they head back toward the herd and not in the other direction. Now charge at them pretty hard; otherwise, they may take off past you."

For the first time all day, Josh had a specific task required of him. Until now, he'd been riding along behind the herd, doing nothing except following. Now he was going to have to turn a cow, not a task he was unconcerned about accomplishing. "Charge right at them?" he asked.

"Come fast and come hollerin'," Gray said without as much as casting a glance in Josh's direction.

Once Josh was in position, Gray started down at the cows. "Shhhhh, calf, git up out of there. Shhhhh. Shhhhh."

Gray raised his rope and slapped it down on his chaps. "Git, now, git." The larger of the two animals backed away and turned toward the mess of brush and thicket. She lunged at the tangled mess of sage and scrub, but it was too dense for her to get through. "Get out of there, get out of there!" Gray gave the horse a kick and his reins a quick jerk to the left. "C'mon, Doc, get in there." The stud sprung at the two cows, coming close enough for Wehr to slap one across the hind end with his coiled rope. "Yaw, yaw, get out of there!" Both cows broke for the open ground. As soon as they busted through the brush, Josh charged his big roan at them. It was a somewhat awkward charge, but he did it, hollering and waving his rope.

The two wide-eyed beasts turned, slinging spit and snot, in a dead run back toward the hill and the rest of the herd. "Shall I chase 'em?" Josh yelled out to Gray, who was somewhat gingerly picking his way back out the thicket.

"Naw, Burton'll get 'em as soon as they go over the knob. They'll head back into the rest of the herd anyway."

Josh, calmer, had a strong desire to ask if he had performed his task well enough but decided that would be like an apprentice accountant asking if he had correctly added up four and four. Instead, he mentioned they were within two or three miles of Ally's ranch.

Chapter Twenty-One

"Mrs. Hart, the barn's gone!"

Elijah pulled the cowy bay horse, the one who threw Josh, around and spurred him toward the right side of the herd and Ally. Ally did not respond to her aging friend. She sat her horse staring blankly at the area where the barn stood. When he got no response, Elijah repeated the obvious.

"Yes, Elijah, I can see that," she said, but not unkindly.

"Good heavens," Elijah said, spurring his horse and heading for the barn at full gallop.

The prospect of getting to the barn before anyone but Elijah and having to listen to never-ending exclamations of "good heavens" was more than she could bear. Instead of heading toward the fallen barn, she turned her horse and started toward the back of the herd. Josh was coming toward her, his big roan in a rough trot, making him bounce in the saddle.

"This is distressing," she said when Josh pulled his horse up alongside her. Immediately, she wished she had not said it. It sounded not only cold but also foolish. "I'm sorry, Josh, I know all of your things were in the barn. I'm sorry."

"Ally," Josh said, "I can replace shirts and pants. But your barn is gone." Both sat for a minute, staring at the barn, and Elijah, picking through ashes like a bummer picking through a garbage pile. "Do you suspect Indians?" Josh asked.

Ally did not answer, not knowing what to say.

Burton and Gray rode up together. "We'll let the cattle stay here, Mrs. Hart," Wehr said. "They won't go anywhere except over to the creek."

Ally nodded, and the four of them rode over to the burned-down barn where the air still had an acrid smell.

"Do you think Indians did this?" Josh asked again, this time of Gray.

"No. Indians wouldn't have burned only the barn. And they wouldn't have left the stock." Ally noticed Gray did not as much as give Josh a stern look. Still, she could see Josh now felt foolish for asking the question.

"I suppose it was lightning," Ally said as she stepped down off her horse.

"It's common this time of year," Gray said, dropping his reins on the ground and kicking at some of the charred lumber.

Ally walked over to where Elijah was trying to open a burned old metal chest holding some of his belongings. As Ally left, Gray glanced at Burton Brown and shook his head, which Burton also did in response. The brief exchange between the two alarmed Josh, who was still a bright man, despite being green to cowhanding and the West. "It wasn't lightning?" he asked in a low voice after walking over to the other two men.

"No. We'll talk about it a little later," Gray said as the last of the day started to die away.

Josh nodded before going over to Ally and Elijah to help sift through anything that might have survived the fire. Ally was sympathetic to the two men but showed no sense of personal loss regarding the barn. She talked only of getting their clothes and belongings replaced, never mentioning a new barn or anything she might have lost in the fire.

"What was in her barn?" Gray asked as he and Brown watched the other three. "Anything of particular value?"

"Not much," Burton said when Josh was out of earshot. "Maybe Sam's saddle and bridle, a little latigo. Not much, I don't suppose, a few tools, shovels, and the like. As far as what the two men had in there, I wouldn't know. I wouldn't think McCormick would have had too much. He came out here on horseback. I doubt Elijah was storing sacks of money." Brown paused. "I suppose here's where we'll start to find out how much sand there is in Alice."

Chapter Twenty-Two

Sorrow, for Ally, was an emotion to be held inside. It was not for others to see. In truth, she hated it more than any other feeling. Grieving, she believed, was for women who were vulnerable and fragile. Sam's death had not brought any tears. She had been sad, of course, but not the way other women were when their husbands died, not uncontrollably so. She felt a degree of emptiness, hollowness. In truth, her sorrow was somewhat shallow, like the marriage had been.

Ally had tried to sow the seeds of a good marriage. She believed Sam had also tried. Yet, the roots never grew deep. It had produced no children, though they both wanted them. Whether children would have improved the marriage, Ally didn't know. She did not dwell on those kinds of questions. She did not let them discourage her.

When Sam died, she heard other women, in whispers not intended for her ears, say she put up a good front. In reality, though, it was not a good front. It was Ally's true character. She was strong, not only strong-willed, as Sam had often accused her of being but strong in her nature. She instinctively knew how to control good and bad circumstances—and people.

Ally had always been strong. At first, as a young woman, she thought she was fooling herself into believing she was strong. It was an act. Ally soon learned it was no act. For her, strength was a replacement for feelings. If there were no feelings, there could be no pain.

It was not until she closed her bedroom door and sat on her bed; the heartache started to swell up inside her. She hurt not only for herself; she hurt for Elijah and Josh. Before, but especially since Sam's passing Elijah had been kind to Ally. Most days, he picked flowers for her. When he went to town, he brought back gifts for her. He always complimented her looks, even when she knew she was a mess.

Secretly she had felt excellent about the way she had treated Elijah. She always thanked him for the friendship and help he had been to her. Her appreciation was sincere. She knew it would have been hard without him. Elijah had been sort of a lost soul most of his life. He had no family. Ally felt she had, in some ways, rescued him from loneliness. Strangely, they made a good pairing.

She also felt Josh needed her as much as she needed him, which kept her from feeling beholden to him. Now, because of helping her, they had lost, at least in Elijah's case, everything.

She undressed and, in the cool dreariness of the night, washed the dirt and smell of the burnt barn away before slipping into her nightgown and bed. Her bedroom was a lonely place. She felt she might vanish if she lay quiet enough. Vanishing might be a good thing. But she didn't disappear. Instead, she started to cry. It was her first crying spell in years, and it angered her. She tried to use her anger to control the weeping, but she could not. She rolled over on her side, trying to muffle the sound in her pillow. The sobbing continued until her chest ached.

When sleep came, Ally dreamed about Josh. He was

smiling and talking about her hands. He said they were pretty and reached out to touch them. His touch was soft and made her feel safe.

It remained a rough night. Sleep was sporadic. During the times when she was awake, Elijah, Josh, and Gray all disturbed her thoughts. She worried over Elijah, agonized over him losing his belongings. She felt both sympathy and grief for him. Josh perplexed her. She couldn't sort out her feelings about him, but she worried he was getting interested in her romantically. She could not resolve how she felt about him. There was no lack of clarity about Gray. She liked him, found him tempting, physically and emotionally. About him, she felt unnerved.

Chapter Twenty-Three

When Ally again awoke, the sun was already shining through her bedroom window, and she could hear men's voices. They were a little way off, perhaps out by where the barn had been, but they were getting closer and more distinct.

"If lightning had hit an empty barn, it would have left a definite mark, if not a hole in the ground," Gray said. "It wasn't lightning."

Josh's was the next voice she heard.

"So, you both think this Kane burned it down?"

"Thinking it is one thing, proving it's another," Burton Brown said.

"I wonder why he didn't do more than just burn the barn," Josh asked.

"I don't know. That does seem odd," Gray said. "Maybe he thought that would be enough to scare her off. On the other hand, maybe we're wrong about it."

"I doubt the hell out of that," Burton said. "But I have to admit it's peculiar."

Ally got out of bed and reached for the brown riding skirt she had been wearing yesterday but picked up her dressing gown instead. She was not feeling particularly shy, and these men had probably all seen a woman in sleepwear anyway. She rapidly wrapped the green robe tightly around her waist as she headed barefoot for her bedroom door.

"Mornin', Mrs. Hart. Did you sleep well?" Elijah, who was sitting in the parlor rocker having a cup of coffee, asked as she shot across the room toward the front door.

All three men looked surprised when Ally came through the front door like fired from a cannon. She flew across the porch and down the two steps.

"You believe somebody burned my barn down?" Her face was red hot.

The firey intensity in her eyes caused hesitation in the men. Finally, Gray gathered his wits about him enough to speak. "We didn't mean for you to hear us."

"Answer my question!"

The men glanced back and forth at each other, shifting around a bit. Had Ally not been so heated, it would have almost been comical.

"Ally," Gray began, using her first name for only the second or third time since they had met, "it wasn't lightning that set that barn on fire. And barns don't just burn themselves down."

"You're sure it wasn't lightning?"

"It wasn't lightning," Gray repeated sympathetically.

"Have I missed something this morning?" Elijah asked, coming out and joining the others.

"Dierden Kane burned my barn!"

"Now, Alice, we can't prove that," Burton said. "I don't know how we'd prove it."

There was little talk over breakfast. Ally told the men they were sleeping in the house from now on, not out on the hard ground. The stern tone of her voice eliminated any argument, even from Elijah. Finally, Burton Brown did bring up the barn.

"Ally, Kane burned that barn. You can bet your life on that. You're going to have to deal with that man." As Burton spoke, Ally poured each of the men another cup of coffee and started to clear the table. "Now, you need to sit here a minute and let us talk to you. Elijah and McCormick tell me that you're dead-set to avoid a confrontation."

Ally looked sadly at Burton but then sat back down.

"Avoiding trouble is an admirable quality," he said. "Unfortunately, it can't always be done."

"I didn't expect him to do something like that," Ally said, her temper having cooled. "I thought he would threaten and bully, maybe try to scare cattle buyers away from me, but I didn't expect this."

Wehr spoke in a soft, tranquil voice that seemed to contradict his words. It did make Ally believe what he said.

"I've known Kane since I was just a kid, and I've known men like him. I'm surprised he didn't hurt you more, steal or kill those horses in the corral or burn your house. The next time he will."

"What do I do? There's no honest law around here. The town sheriff isn't going to help me. At least I doubt it."

"Let's think about what options you may have," Gray said, leaning forward just a little. "As I see it, and I may not know everything, but as I see it, you can stay put, which means a fight. Or, you could sell out. I don't know whether you could find a buyer or not. Or, you could just walk away and start someplace else. I don't know how much that would appeal to you. But those are the only three options I can see."

"I mentioned this to you when we were in the cow camp," Burton said. "I think you should consider High Meadows, where Gray lives."

Ally had thought about that after her conversation with Annie Laurie. The woman had made the place sound so wonderful. It sounded beautiful, and it sounded friendly.

But, what about Elijah and Josh? What would they do? Although she wasn't responsible for them, she felt she was. If she went and if they wanted to go along, she would have to see to it that there was a place for them. She wondered to herself how she had become a caretaker of a half-addled old man and a tenderfoot entirely out of his element.

"I'll need to think," she finally said to Gray. "I guess I'll have to think about what I should do."

"Don't think too long," Burton said. "Kane's not likely to give you that privilege."

Ally's problem was that in all the time she had lived in this country, she still didn't know what men meant when they said they were going to have to fight. Did they mean that they planned to persevere even through hardship—not to be run off? Or did it mean they were going to pick up a gun? Looking at Gray Wehr, she believed she knew the answer.

"Well, we'd better start getting those cows where you want them," Gray said, "otherwise they may be sitting up in that rocking chair on your porch."

Chapter Twenty-Four

Ally's twelve or so head, along with maybe ten or fifteen of the strays Elijah rounded up, had moved into the cattle they brought from the Wehr/Joseph herd. The strays now with the herd included Satan, giving Josh his first look at the bull Ally so despised.

He was a long-horned, skinny, brown and white beast with reddish eyes snorting and pawing at everything in sight. He charged the first horse that got anywhere near him. Luckily, Ally thought, it was Burton Brown's horse and not Josh's. Burton spurred the sorrel, a good animal that avoided the charge and kept his head about him.

"I'd stay away from him," Gray hollered. "I don't believe he likes you."

"Aw, that ornery sonuvabitch, I'll throw a rope around his neck and hang him from that tall tree behind the house," Burton laughed once he was out of harm's way. "He ain't no match for me. I'm too witty for him."

"I hate that animal," Ally said as she pulled her horse up next to Gray.

"Butcher him and eat him through the winter," Gray said drolly.

"That's what I should do now that I've got a new bull," Ally said.

Without saying a word, Gray pulled his rifle out of its scabbard and shot the beast right behind the left ear. Ally was looking out across her new cattle herd. She shrieked when the rifle cracked and shot Gray a look of pure amazement. Gray had a crooked little smile. He looked so pleased with himself. Ally didn't know why she was laughing, but all of a sudden, she couldn't stop. Tears danced in the corners of her eyes, before spilling over. Her breath came in quick gasps between unrelenting giggles. The laughing caused her stomach to jump up and down. It was delicious laughing, her best laughing in a long time, coming from deep within her.

Elijah and Josh were both sitting about seventy-five yards away and looking dumbfounded. "What on earth?" Elijah asked. Josh just sat gawking at Ally and Gray.

"Thank you," Ally said when she finally caught enough of her breath. "Thank you very much."

"Think nothing of it," Gray smiled.

"I guess he don't have so much affection for a bull as he does a horse," Elijah said as he turned his horse and rode off toward the dead animal.

As Elijah and Josh headed toward them in a stiff trot, Ally turned toward Gray. "Good heavens, Mrs. Hart, good heavens," she laughed, gently mocking what she knew would be the first words out of Elijah's mouth.

She reached over and patted Gray's hand when the two men arrived. "Good heavens, Mrs. Hart, good heavens."

"I told you I wasn't having that beast on my ranch," she said with an air of satisfaction clearly in her voice.

"Yes, ma'am, that's what you did say," Elijah said, casting another wide-eyed look, first at Gray and then the now deceased bull. "That is what you said."

"He'll keep you folks in meat for a while," Gray said, matter-of-factly.

"Yes, I suppose he will," Elijah said, cracking a bit of a smile himself. "Good heavens, I suppose he will."

Chapter Twenty-Five

Josh and Elijah spent the rest of the morning and a good part of the afternoon in the bloody business of skinning and cutting up Satan, a duty that confirmed what Josh already suspected—he was low man on the ranch, even beneath Elijah. It should not have upset him. After all, he had no experience in any of the work, and it was justifiably the proper role for him to fill.

Still, the assignment of the most menial tasks, like helping Elijah cut up the animal, was insulting. He had even hoped that Ally might have interceded for him when Burton said that she, Gray, and he would move the cattle to a proper place for grazing while Elijah cut up the bull.

His exact words had been, "McCormick, you stay and help Elijah. Pulling a hide can be a two-man job." Nevertheless, Ally said nothing; she just rode off with the other two men, leaving him alone as a helper to Elijah.

The job was hot and messy and seemed to draw every single fly in Wyoming. Besides that annoyance, ever so often, Elijah would have another laughing fit about what Wehr had done, making Josh even more ready for the others' company.

"I won't miss this job," he said as he and Elijah saddled their horses to join the others.

"Oh, it's no worse than other jobs," Elijah said with a bit of amusement. "A lot of ranch work can be nasty. And you ain't a top hand jist yet, so you'll have yer share of that work," he added with a bit of a twinkle in his eye. "When we go to make those spring bulls steers, you'll find that ain't the sweetest work."

The afternoon grew hot and muggy. All of the romance Josh felt about cowboying back when he sat talking with Alan Joseph was starting to lose its allure. He could see now that there was much more to ranch work than just sitting a good horse and moving cattle from one place to another. He could see that working the livestock was going to require much more skill than painting the house and corral or even making repairs to the barn.

By the time they rode the nearly three miles to where Ally, Gray, and Burton were bedding down the cattle, in a little clearing just off a medium-sized pond, the cattle, still weary from the drive the day before, had grown lethargic and were offering no opposition to staying put.

"We'll get Ally's brand on 'em tomorrow," Burton Brown said to Elijah as he and Josh joined the others.

"How long will that take?" Josh asked.

"We'll finish in a day," Burton replied. "Then I suppose I better head on over toward Cheyenne. A couple of small ranchers will be wondering what's happened to me."

Josh sensed Brown was fighting some reluctance about leaving. Josh knew the man was fond of Ally and enjoyed being around her. When the others drifted away, Josh asked Brown if he thought there was any chance Gray would stay around a while.

Brown shrugged. "He's unpredictable. The man is wild as hell, but there is a little do-gooder in him. There is some old bad blood between him and Kane. I suppose I could ask him."

Across a brushy gully, Elijah moved his horse over next to Ally's. "Would you like me to spend the night out here with the herd?"

"No. We can't keep someone out with the herd every night. They'll be fine."

"Well, I just thought maybe for a night or two," Elijah said. "We don't want them to wander off before they're used to the place."

Without really meaning to, Ally glanced at Gray, who must have caught the flicker of worry in her eyes.

"They'll be fine," Gray said. "They've got grass and water; they won't wander very far."

Josh and Burton returned in time to hear Elijah say he was more concerned about Dierden Kane than the cattle straying. A concern shared by Ally. It worried Elijah what Kane might do next, and that there was no real law available to help Ally. Here in the rough country of Wyoming, if Ally herself was not strong enough to stop this man, he could do whatever he pleased. When no one else brought up rustling, Josh did.

Wehr straightforwardly responded to him. "It's one thing to burn her barn. That's hard to prove unless he gets caught red-handed. And frankly, who knows what happens to him, but you steal cows, you hang. He won't take that chance."

"But they don't have Ally's brand on them yet," Josh said.

Burton Brown laughed at him. "No, but they sure got a W/J on their rumps. You try to sell a cow with that mark west of the Mississippi; you better have a bill of sale. Otherwise, if there's no rope right handy, you'll be shot. Kane ain't nervy enough, or dumb enough for that matter, to steal these cows."

Elijah appeared satisfied with the explanation of why the cows would be safe from rustling. His thoughts turned to his stomach. "Does anybody have a watch with 'em? I'm starting to feel hungry."

Josh shook his head and hoped Gray was correct in his pronouncement about Kane.

Chapter Twenty-Six

After supper, Josh and Ally sat on the front porch while the other men went off to look over the little remuda Ally had.

"We'll have a blue moon tonight," Ally said.

Josh sat quietly. "Sarah," he finally said, sounding almost like he was speaking to himself instead of to Ally, "she always liked a blue moon. She said it was romantic," he added before laughing just a little. "I guess she was more romantic than I was. I'd have never even known it was a blue moon if she'd not mentioned it."

"Sam was like that," Ally said. "I guess you men just don't have that kind of romance in you."

"I guess not," Josh said, his thoughts running back to Sarah. It was odd the way he missed her. Sometimes, Josh could put her out of his mind entirely. Let her go, he supposed, which was what some back in St. Louis had told him he must try to do. Other times, like now, she came back to him as real as if she were sitting right next to him. He could smell her freshly washed hair and hear her whisper his name. He remembered how she moved, the feel of her touch, funny little expressions she would get on her face. He remembered how she would smile at him. Perhaps that's what he remembered most of all. It was her smile that first attracted him to her. She smiled as much with her eyes as with her lips. He had always found warmth in her smiles. When Hanna, their daughter, died, it seemed that something in Sarah's smile also died. Often Josh wanted to tell her how he missed her smile, but the words never came.

"Ally, do you ever wish you had said things to Sam that you never did?"

The question shocked Ally. Josh had never talked about his wife to her and never asked her about Sam.

Ally was not sure she wanted to answer him. In fact, she knew she did not. Answering him might open up feelings that she did not want to face. Feelings that she should have been more tender toward Sam, the way some women were to their husbands, even though their husbands did not treat them nearly as tenderly as Sam treated her. But Ally was not like most women. Showing deep affection came hard for her. It was something that, for some reason, made her afraid.

Why—She didn't know. Perhaps, down deep, she was scared the object of her feelings might not return them. Perhaps it was her life, which forced her to be strong. Maybe it also robbed her of tenderness. Whatever it was, she always felt that it was a failure in her. There had been times that she wanted to go to Sam, to tell him how deeply she loved him, but it was so hard for her. All of her life, she wanted to be in control. Now that Sam was gone, she tried to convince herself that he did know the actual depth of her feelings, not just that she loved him, but how deeply she loved him. Still, the impression that he may not have known would not pass. It wore on her emotionally and even physically, making her feel tired. Sometimes, she knew her face looked drawn, hollow. Perhaps others didn't see it, but she did.

"The past is gone, Josh. There is nothing that will give us a second chance. I have to live the life I have today. I don't want to feel guilty about some pain that may never have even been there." That was easy to say, harder to do.

Her answer surprised Josh. He hadn't even been thinking about guilt or pain. He simply wished he'd been more loving. The last thing Sarah ever said to him was, "be careful." The last thing he said to her was "lock the door." Why hadn't he said *I love you*?

"I suppose you're right," he said to Ally. "We live the best we can and have to accept that's what we've done."

They sat quietly for the next hour, watching the dusk darken and the moon climb up over the stand of trees out beyond the corrals.

"I think I'll take a walk down the river," Ally said, standing and pushing her chair back against the house. "Why don't you come along?"

As Josh stood and started toward the creek with Ally, he felt the sadness that had come over him begin to fade. As they walked, a refreshing and welcome breeze drifted through. He heard the cattle lowing. Even though they were well down the river, the night air was carrying the sound down the little hollow and out into the meadows on the other side of Ally's house.

"I've felt like a bit of a fool the last few days," he said as Ally picked up a stick and tossed it into the stream. "I didn't realize I'd be so inept with the cattle." Ally looked at him and smiled but did not say anything. However, she surprised him by putting her arm in his as they started down the little clearing. It not only surprised Josh, it unnerved him a bit. "I like it here, though. I feel—comfortable, I guess," he said after hesitating briefly. Ally squeezed his arm and laid her head momentarily on his shoulder. Josh thought she was going to say something but then didn't. He stole a glance at her, but it was just a glance since he certainly did not want to be caught. She was walking with her eyes almost shut and a peaceful look on her face.

His spirits picked up even more as he realized that he was enjoying himself in the woman's company. He thought for a moment about slipping his arm around her waist and giving her a slight hug, but the thought went away very quickly. He needed time to think about the propriety of that, rehearse it in his mind before attempting such a thing.

Soon, the sound of the other men's voices interrupted Josh's romanticizing. They weren't close enough to understand their words, but he could tell that they were sitting alongside the house laughing about something.

"I suppose we should head back home," Ally said. "Otherwise, Elijah will start to go crazy with worry. He'll convince himself that we've fallen in the river and drowned, or that you've carried me off to ravage me," she added with a chuckle.

As they returned to the house, they found the other men sitting on the north end, where the breeze was a little stronger. Ally's old hound was lying sound asleep with his head in Elijah's lap. Elijah was also sleeping.

Burton Brown looked up and gave a bit of a wink at Ally. "Well, we were beginning to worry that you two had wandered off and gotten scalped."

"Do you have many Indians up around your valley?" Josh asked, looking over at Gray.

"A band of Lakota at the far end of our valley," Gray said. "We've always been good neighbors to each other. We haven't had a real Indian threat since I was little, seven or eight, I guess. The only time we've had any real concern was when the Army killed Conquering Bear over that Mormon's cow."

"That even made the St. Louis papers," Josh said. "Mostly about the Indians massacring the soldiers. The papers said that Conquering Bear was the big Sioux chief. The story said he was killed when he attacked some soldiers for no reason."

"That's not true," Gray replied.

"No, it's not," Burton snorted.

"Some lieutenant that didn't know anything about Indians opened fire on them with no reason, killing Conquering Bear. The damn fool only had thirty-one men with him. There may have been 1,200 Sioux there. They made quick work of the cavalry. Then when the cavalry retaliated, things were pretty edgy out here for a while." Gray paused and glanced around the area.

"We went to Fort Laramie for almost a month when that happened. It was the only time Sam ever left the ranch worried over an Indian threat," Ally said. She tapped on Elijah's shoulder. "Do you remember the time that you, Sam, and I were out looking for strays and rode over a ridge right into a Sioux camp?"

"Lordy, that was a surprise," Elijah said as he sat up.

"Daylight stays late out here in the summer." Ally said, directing her comment to Josh. "We'd searched all day for those cows. It was right at dusk, and the shadows were long when we topped a ridge. A Sioux camp was right there in the valley. Elijah said there was no doubt they'd seen us, so it was better if we rode on down and tried to talk to them. It was the first time I had ever seen, let alone been in an Indian village. The camp had an almost mystical presence as Indians danced and skipped around small fires to the sound of drums and chanting. Some of them were painted and feathered, giving them an almost grotesque appearance against the flickering of fire in the fading light. I thought I was going to pee myself."

Gray laughed.

Josh, although embarrassed over Ally's remark, did manage to ask if the Indians were threatening.

"No. It was a little tense at first, but Elijah could speak enough Lakota to tell them why we were there. They offered us food and even allowed us to sleep in their camp. If it hadn't been for Elijah, I don't know how it would have gone."

No one said any more about the Indians, and finally, Josh commented on it being a clear night, just to break the silence.

"We need a good rain," Ally said. "But I doubt that we'll get any this time of year. It may not rain for the rest of the summer."

That was something else that Josh was having trouble getting used to about Wyoming. In St. Louis, it would usually rain at least every week or so. It wasn't like that out here where it hadn't rained since he had been here. The night air here wasn't like it was in St. Louis, either. There, if it were hot during the day, it would probably stay hot and muggy through the night. Here it could bake you in the daytime but still turn almost chilly at night, something that did make sleeping more comfortable.

No one else said anything about the weather as the quietness of the evening just seemed to take over. Josh gazed out across the horizon, taking in the moon and stars, which dimly lit the rugged landscape outline.

For some odd reason, it caused Josh to recall the old tintypes that Sarah's parents had hanging in the sitting room of their home back in St. Louis, the ones taken when Sarah's family had first come west. The men all had big mustaches that would have fit right in with these Wyoming cowboys. The women in the pictures, Sarah's mother and aunts mostly, had drained, worn-looking faces. Josh had always looked up to them for having the courage to face and defeat the frontier hardships that were prevalent, even in St. Louis, when they first come west. He wondered why they had not demanded that their men take them back east, back to where life would have been at least a little bit easier.

He believed that Ally's situation was similar, perhaps a bit unkinder. She was more isolated and faced more dangers. She had not only remoteness to battle; there were also Indians and outlaws with little law for protection. Also, there was the loneliness, which Josh thought must be the most constant of her sorrows. Still, at least in his view, Ally did not have the haggard or beaten look of those women in the photographs. Her eyes were bright, and her outlook, at least in front of others, was mostly cheery.

Elijah looked around when the dog started moving from place to place. His joints popped and cracked, drawing a laugh from Ally when he tried to stand and stretch.

"You sound like you need oiling," she said. "I've got some in the barn." She chuckled. "Well, there was, anyway," she said.

"That's all right, Mrs. Hart, we'll get you another barn put up. And we'll see to it that no one burns the next one," he said soberly.

Chapter Twenty-Seven

When Burton Brown came back from seeing a man about a horse—his morning trip to the outhouse, Ally had breakfast on the table. "How long will it take to brand Ally's new stock?" Josh asked as Brown sat across from him.

"It's hard to determine," Burton said, piling scrambled eggs on his plate. "You know, them ain't calves we're gonna be throwin', and..." he muttered after passing the eggs to Elijah and taking the bacon from Wehr, "we're working with a stiff old man and a greenhorn."

"That's true enough." Elijah snorted. "I guess Wehr and I will have to work extra hard to compensate for your worthlessness. Not that you were worth much more before you got old and stiff."

Ally laughed and patted Gray's forearm. "Would you pass me the coffee? I wouldn't want either of these stiff older men to strain themselves. Or have their minds distracted from their wit."

Ally poured her coffee and put three slices of bacon on

her plate. "Are you growing a mustache, Josh?" she asked quite offhandedly.

Everyone at the table glanced at his upper lip, and for some reason, Josh felt hotly embarrassed. Involuntarily, he put his hand to his mouth and ran his thumb and forefinger over his lip. "Well," he said, still running his fingers over the stubble, "it seemed like everyone out here wears one. I thought maybe I could at least start to look the part of a ranch hand," he said, trying to laugh just a bit.

Ally gave him a warm smile. "I like it when you laugh at yourself. And, I'm sure it will be quite becoming on you," she said.

Elijah finished his last forkful of eggs and said, "Well, I guess I'd better go out and try to dig your branding irons out of those barn ashes."

"Do you want some help?" Josh asked.

"Naw, I know right where they'll be. The irons will be one of the few things not burned up," Elijah said on his way to the door.

"Why don't you and I go saddle some horses?" Gray said, looking over at Josh. "You can see how they like that new mustache."

When they arrived at the corral, Elijah had leaned two branding irons up against his saddle and was opening the gate. "You want your blue roan?" he asked without looking up at Wehr. "Or do you want to ride one of these others?"

"Doc will do," Wehr said, picking up his bridle and following the old man into the corral.

"I suppose you want that roan of yours," Elijah said to Josh, in a tone of voice indicating he felt Josh should make another selection.

"Elijah doesn't think my horse is cowy enough," Josh told Gray as he followed him through the gate.

"Why don't you try one of the others, then," Gray said. "That sorrel over there is well-built."

"Oh, he doesn't want him." Elijah snickered. "He's rank." Elijah gave the sorrel a hard look. "Meaner'n hell, that one."

Gray Wehr looked over the sorrel and took a few slow steps toward him.

"I wouldn't do that." There was a good deal of concern in Elijah's voice as he stopped walking the brown gelding he had selected for himself toward the corral gate. "I'm not a kiddin' ya; he's rank."

Gray stopped and continued to look the horse over. "That's a nice-looking horse, not to be earning his keep," Gray said. He took a few more steps at the sorrel before the animal seemed to pay him much attention. When the horse did fix his gaze on the man, the animal looked defiant. He tossed his head up and down and gave a couple of unfriendly sounding grunts. "Oh, don't get your back up," Gray said quietly, stopping several feet from the horse. "Nobody's gonna hurt you."

The animal backed up a step before throwing his nose out and stomping a foot in a more threatening manner. The horse was a muscular animal, probably just over fifteen hands high. He had no white on him anywhere, save a small white ring around his left rear foot. His mane tangled from wind, and lack of brushing added to his beastly appearance. His brown eyes were full of fire, and he kept a keen look on Wehr as he stood several feet away.

"So, you're rank, are you?" Gray said, speaking again in a quiet, relaxed voice. "You really rank, or have you just got everybody around here, buffaloed?" Wehr turned somewhat sideways to the horse and moved a step or two closer, a maneuver that drew some snorting in response. Gray backed away a few steps and turned more squarely toward the horse. "I haven't got the time now, but maybe before I leave, we can get to know each other a little bit. What would you think of that? Maybe a little later." Wehr turned and put the bridle he had in his hand on his own horse. "Come on, Doc, he doesn't want to be friendly today."

Although Wehr had done nothing more than walk over toward the horse, Josh felt that something extraordinary had taken place. While he certainly couldn't identify what it was, it caused him to admire Gray. He led his roan over next to Wehr. "Can anything be done with a horse like that?"

Gray looked at him and then over toward the sorrel. "Most of the time. Not every time, but most of the time."

"How do you get him to come around?"

Gray looked at Josh as if trying to decide why the man wanted to know. "You go slow, gentle him down. Gain his trust."

Wehr continued to look at Josh in a way that made Josh just a bit uncomfortable.

"You treat him decent and do it for a long time."

Chapter Twenty-Eight

"You and Ally can do the branding," Burton said as he scooted one of the irons around in the red coals of the fire. "When we throw them, shove the iron down on their rump. Roll it just a little bit and lift it off," he said, demonstrating what he meant on a stump of wood.

"I want the iron completely red when I brand?" Josh asked.

"That's best," Elijah said before throwing a few more pieces of wood on their fire. "By the time Ally and Gray get out here, the coals should be ready."

The others had gone off ahead of Gray and Ally when Gray found that his horse had a loose shoe and the bread Ally was baking for lunch wasn't quite done. It had taken only a few minutes to nail the shoe back on, and Gray was now sitting in the kitchen having another cup of coffee while Ally's bread, which Gray thought smelled wonderful, finished.

"Hello, in the house. Hart woman, come out here!"

At the sound of the man's voice, Ally startled. She peaked through the window. "It's Kane and two other men," she said, fear if not near panic, causing her voice to quiver.

Ally looked at Gray, who nodded for her to go out on the porch. "Go ahead. I'll stay here and listen for a little while. Don't let him know you're not alone." He could see by the look on her face that Ally was not happy with what he had said. "Go ahead. I won't let you get hurt."

Ally stepped out onto the porch, leaving the door slightly ajar behind her. "What do you want?"

Gray positioned himself to see Kane but in the shadows to not be seen.

Dierden Kane, a big, ugly, unshaven man with pasty-looking skin, stepped down off his horse and up onto the porch, intimidating Ally enough that she stepped off to the side, leaving Kane standing right in front of the solid oak door. "Not going to ask me in out of the heat?" The man's audacity was so offensive that it had the opposite of its intended effect on Ally. Rather than causing her to shrink away from him, the absurdness of his behavior emboldened her. Her chin raised, and her back stiffened.

"I said, what do you want?"

"Well now, missy, that's not a very friendly way to receive a guest. It might make a man feel completely unwelcome."

"You are unwelcome."

The nastiness of Ally's remark drew a laugh from one of the two men with Kane.

"Shut the hell up." Kane snarled.

Kane's face flushed red when he turned back at Ally. He advanced on her enough that she could smell his awful breath, a vulgar mix of whiskey, tobacco, and unbrushed teeth. "By hell, woman, I told you not to try and run cows out here. I told you to get off this damn land. I guess you ain't smart enough to listen to good neighborly advice."

Kane raised his hand, at first causing Gray to think he was going to strike Ally. Instead, he jabbed his long fat finger toward her.

Wehr had hoped for the man to make some kind of statement about the barn fire, but when he jabbed at the woman, Wehr's contempt for Kane came flooding back over him. As clear as if it were yesterday, he recalled how, at thirteen, he and fourteen-year-old Zach Joseph had the job of watching over a corral full of beef while their fathers had gone into the office of a cavalry major to be paid for the animals.

Kane came over with an oak cane in his hand and climbed in with the Wehr/Joseph herd. He walked through them, giving a steer a hard slap across the rump with his cane before giving another one a hard slap on the side. Gray took extreme exception to the abuse. He jumped down into the corral, yelling for Kane to stop. Kane laughed at the boy. Instead of stopping, he gave another steer two hard whacks with the cane. Gray pushed through the cattle and tried to grab Kane by the arm. For his trouble, he took a fist in the mouth.

The blow sent him sprawling on the ground, but he did not stay there. He scrambled to his feet and charged the full-grown man. This time he got a harsh blow across the chest with the cane, one that doubled him up in great pain. Kane hit him again, this time across the back, once again sending the boy down into the dirt. Laying on the ground, he took a swift kick to the face and then one to the ribs. The second kick lifted him into the air and rolling into one of the cows, who stepped on him in an attempt at fleeing. It took two weeks before Gray could move around without hurting and another six weeks before the two broken ribs had healed.

Gray had never been a man of great patience. He was not about to allow this brute to beat a woman. Kane was slow to notice the door opening, and when he did turn toward it, it was just in time to see a clenched fist hard on its way toward his face. The punch hit him just under his eye. Gray heard his cheekbone crack. The force of the blow knocked him clear off the porch. Wehr jumped down and kicked him square in the face when he started to rise. The kick sent him sprawling onto his back, only half-conscious. Gray then grabbed the shirt of the man who had laughed, jerking him hard off his horse and onto the ground, landing on his head and collarbone. Gray gave Kane one more kick before pulling his pistol and pointing it at the only man still mounted. "Throw that pistol away," he snapped. "Do it now!" The man unlashed his revolver and tossed it toward the porch. "The rifle too."

When the third cowboy had disposed of his rifle, Gray leaned over the man he had jerked off the horse. "Where's your pistol? Where is it?" The man rolled off his side, and Gray took an old cap and ball away from him. "Hold this on them," he said to Ally, in none too gentle a tone. "If they move, shoot 'em." Ally took the pistol from Gray, cocked it, and pointed it at Dierden Kane.

Gray went over to the horse belonging to the man who was now laying on the ground moaning. He took the knife sheathed on the back of his gun belt and cut the cinch strap before pulling the saddle off on the ground. Gray then took off the horse's bridle and waved his arms to scare the animal away. He leaned down over Kane's cowboy and grabbed him by the neck, causing Ally to gasp. "Every time I see you around a horse—I'm gonna beat hell out of you."

Turning back to Kane, he reached down and pulled the still-dazed man up by his coat collar. "Get on your horse and get out of here." Kane's hat was still lying in the dust when Gray grabbed a fistful of the man's hair. He got very close to Kane's bloody face before he spoke.

"Now, Dierden, I want you to listen real close to me. If I see you on her ranch again, Dierden, you have no idea how much you'll regret it. If I see one of your men on her ranch, Dierden, you have no idea how much you'll both regret it. Now get your ass on that horse and get out of here." Gray shoved him toward his horse, kicking him in the hind-end, sending him once again face down in the dirt.

Grabbing his stirrup, Kane managed to pull himself up

on his horse and was backing away when Gray grabbed hold of the reins. "One more thing, Dierden, the next time you beat the hell out of a thirteen-year-old kid, you might remember that kid is gonna grow up someday." Wehr turned the horse's head away and slapped his rump, almost causing Kane to lose his seat when the horse bolted.

"Now you two git," Gray said.

"How am I supposed to go?" the man asked, cradling his arm against his belly, still carrying the rasp marks from his last encounter with Wehr, and now standing wobbly on his feet.

"Climb up behind me," the third cowboy said, moving his horse toward his shaken partner.

"You move one step toward that horse, and I told you what'll happen!"

The man looked over at Gray, and believing what he said; he started walking with a considerable limp toward Ally's ranch's front gate. Once they were a couple of hundred yards past the gate, the third man stopped his horse, and his horseless friend climbed up behind him. Gray grabbed the rifle he had made the man throw down and took a shot out toward the two out-of-range cowboys who quickly galloped away. Wehr was still glaring at them when Ally asked if he was really trying to shoot them. He smiled at her. "If I were, they'd be shot."

Chapter Twenty-Nine

"The fella with Kane was the man Gray whipped in town?" Elijah asked.

"That's what he said later," Ally said.

"And he said he was gonna 'kick his ass' anytime he saw him around a horse?"

"That's what he said."

Elijah again started to rock back and forth in the straight-backed rocker. "Good heavens. That feller better learn to like walking."

Ally laughed. "Or stay away from our young friend."

"And he told Kane he'd shoot him if he came back on your place?"

"He told him that he'd 'regret it,'" Ally said more somberly.

"And he kept calling him by his first name?"

"Dierden. Dierden. Dierden," Ally said, again laughing, although she felt a little bit bad about it.

"Good heavens. Good heavens."

Chapter Thirty

"You know you should have shot him," Burton muttered the words out the side of his mouth without looking over at Wehr. "Knocking him around may have amused you, but it won't help Alice any. Not in the long run." Brown brushed a little more dust from his horse's back before smoothing out the saddle blanket and throwing on the saddle. "You should have shot him," he repeated more sternly.

Wehr gave his cinch a final tug and looked disgustedly across his saddle at the older man. "You can't go around shooting people just because it suits you," he said.

Brown shot a quick look off at the house. "I can see I should never have left you alone with her," he said, drawing a quizzical look from Gray, who was now leading his horse away.

"What does that mean?" Wehr asked, turning back toward Brown.

"Means I should have stayed here with you."

Wehr's face was as gray as the dawn, his voice flat and

impersonal. "Stay wherever you want."

Brown silently watched as Wehr led his horse away. "Impetuous SOB," he muttered to himself. "You always have been self-centered," he said, intending that Gray would hear him. Wehr, however, ignored him. He stepped gracefully upon his horse and muttered something to Elijah before riding off toward where the cattle were. Burton left his sorrel tied to the corral and strode briskly toward Elijah. "What did he say to you?"

"Said he was going out to count how many head still need to be branded," Elijah said. "Seemed a bit aggravated 'bout something." The two men stood watching as Wehr rode slowly away. "Hope it's not something I done. I'd hate to have that man aggravated at me," Elijah said, drawing an annoyed grunt from Burton Brown.

"Now, what would you have done to make him mad?"

"I don't know. Nothin', I hope."

"He's mad at me," Brown said. "I told him he should have shot Kane, and he doesn't like people telling him what he should have done. Or what he ought to do, for that matter. He's always been like that." Brown continued to stare at Wehr's back, thinking he would wave him back if Gray turned around in the saddle. But, Wehr did not turn. He just rode slowly toward the bawling of the cattle. "Stubborn jackass." Bown thought for a moment of firing off his pistol so that he could call the man back but decided against it. *Let him go. Let him miss his breakfast.*

When Burton went back into the house, Ally had a brief flash of anger toward Burton for making Gray mad but decided not to say much about it. If she'd known he told Wehr that he should have shot Kane, she would have said plenty. Ally decided to pack a biscuit and some bacon and take it out to Wehr. If the opportunity came, she would tell him that Burton had no right to make any comments.

As she poured the coffee, Ally glanced over at Elijah. "Elijah," she said with firmness in her voice, "Burton and Gray and I can handle the rest of the branding. I want you and Josh to go into town today and replace some of the things you lost in the fire. Put it on my bill at the general store."

Elijah started to protest, but Ally, even more firmly, put a quick stop to it.

The uncomfortable tension hanging over the morning increased as Ally's anger over Gray started to churn up again, and this time she did not remain silent. "Why did you let him ride off with no breakfast?" The men stared awkwardly at each other without responding. When Burton reached for another slice of bacon, Ally jabbed a fork at his hand, barely missing his knuckles. "That's for Gray. I'm not letting him go without any breakfast." She scooted her chair back.

"I don't see why you're upset, Mrs. Hart. Wehr rode off on his own; no one told him to skip breakfast. As far as I'm concerned, he's a grown man. He can skip any meal he wants to."

Josh and Burton braced for the explosion. Ally almost did, but settled for shaking her head.

"I'm going to change before we go out to brand. You two get started on your way to town so that you don't end up having to spend the night there."

Ally's bedroom was on the northeast corner of the house. There was nothing romantic about the room. It was a fairly large room, at least in proportion to the rest of the house. Its sparse furnishings made it feel even larger—and emptier without a husband to share the room and the bed. The double bed centered between the room's only two windows had a brass frame that Ally regularly polished. There was a dark blue quilt on it that Ally made the first year she and Sam lived in the house. There was a small wooden table on each side of the bed and two straight-backed wooden chairs across the room. An oval-shaped Oriental rug that Sam purchased in Denver as an anniversary present lay in front of the bed. Other than the area covered by the rug, which Ally said Sam spent too much money on, the floor was bare wood.

Ally opened the second drawer of the chest of drawers and took out a pair of tan trousers. Some folks frowned on women wearing pants. She'd heard there was an actual law against females wearing pants, but she'd never heard of a woman arrested for it, and in her world, they were a practical necessity. Stepping out of her dress, she sat on the bed and looked out the window, toward the little valley and her cattle. She pictured Gray Wehr gracefully working through the cows, inspecting the branding and counting the number of head still unbranded. Then, for just the briefest time, she thought of herself with him. Listening to his soothing voice, thinking about what his touch might feel like, even of making love with him. "Enough," she said half-aloud. She would allow herself no delusions, no fanciful feelings.

Their ride through the valley was leisurely and unhurried. Burton had attempted to apologize to Ally for causing Wehr to ride off in a sulk. The flash shooting from her eyes and the tension that pursed her lips warned him that he might have used a poor choice of words.

"I wish that rogue would stay here with you a while. You could use his help, and maybe his protection," he said after spitting a stream of tobacco juice. "But he's tough to constrain, always has been."

"We'll be fine," Ally said, but without the usual confidence that most people sensed about her, even when she was unsure of herself.

"You may be, but you may not be," Burton said, an abruptness in his voice that caused Ally to glance over at him.

He was sitting very erect in the saddle. His slouch hat pushed high on his forehead. "Don't be lookin' at me as if I don't know what I'm talkin' about. I do, better than you may imagine. You told me it stunned you. I believe that's the word you used, how hard Gray went after those men. You need to understand." It was now Burton's eyes that were piercing hard. "This ain't gonna be no schoolyard tussle 'tween boys. Kane's a hellhound, Alice. He'll hurt you."

Ally didn't answer. She just stared straight ahead, avoiding Burton's look.

"This water may be too deep for you. You got nothing but an old man and a greenhorn beginner that doesn't know his butt from cow crap for help. And hell, there ain't no guarantee that next week you might not have the Cheyenne or Sioux down on you."

Ally still didn't reply.

"Well, that's fine. I'll just shut up."

Suddenly, and unexpectedly, Ally jerked her horse to a stop. "Just what am I supposed to do?" Her words were cutting and shrill.

Burton's face flushed. "Go to a town, Ally, someplace you'll be safe. Go to High Meadows, where Wehr lives. I think you'd like it there."

Rod McFain

Chapter Thirty-One

Elijah Yancey had been around too many curs in his life, dogs, and men, not to know the difference between one that bites and one that just barks. The barkers were all bluff, big on bluster and intimidation, but slow to back their bluff. They preferred to sneak up from behind and fight only when they had a definite advantage. They were, in reality, cowards who lacked the spine to back up their bluffs when challenged. Then there were the real curs, the mean ones, the ones who were willing to be torn up themselves to hurt somebody else. They'd fight dirty, but they would attack, and they would fight. Elijah wasn't sure that Josh McCormick completely understood that Dierden Kane was one of the real curs.

The storekeeper handed the gun to Josh. "This is an 1858 Army Remington. It's the newest model we have. Quite a gun."

"You buyin' yourself a pistol?" Elijah asked as he looked at the weapon Josh was now holding out at arm's length as if aiming at a target.

"I thought I should," Josh said, sounding as if he might not want Elijah's input.

"Why?"

"Why what?"

"Why do you figure you need a pistol?" Elijah shifted a toothpick to the other side of his mouth and studied Josh's expression.

Josh turned more squarely to the older man. "Everyone at the ranch feels there is going to be trouble. I need to be able to help stop it. I need to be prepared," he said after a brief hesitation to examine Elijah's face.

Elijah, who thought the comment sounded like an accountant talking, leaned back against the counter, removed his hat, and wiped the sweatband with an old bandana. "Well, that weapon will stop it, man or beast." He motioned at a tin of snuff, which the shopkeeper handed him. He packed his lower lip and used his tongue to position the tobacco into just the right spot. "'Course, a feller has to be able to hit what he's aimin' at. Can you do that, McCormick?" He replaced his hat and dropped the snuff tin into his shirt pocket. "Cause if you can't, you ought to get yourself a shotgun. It'd give you a little margin for error."

Josh's jaw muscles clenched. "I'll take it," he said, handing the pistol back to the store clerk. "And a holster."

"Cross-draw, or hip," the skinny clerk asked without looking back at Josh.

"Cross-draw," Elijah said, removing his toothpick. Josh shot him an irritated look, which Elijah responded to by shrugging his shoulders. "Only gunnies use hip rigs."

Josh's mouth opened then closed with a snap, trapping his words inside.

"You'll probably walk a little lopsided 'til you get used to all that extra weight," Elijah said as the two men left the store.

Chapter Thirty-Two

Josh's new pistol raised Ally's ire a bit, which disappointed him, especially since she showed no displeasure about Gray Wehr carrying a gun. Rightly, or wrongly, he resented another indication she thought him incompetent, or at least severely limited in his abilities.

"Well, one thing about this pistol," Gray pointed out, "if you miss him, the thing is heavy enough to hit him with and knock his head clear off."

"Is this a hunk of old Satan we're having tonight?" Elijah asked, laughing at his humor.

Ally smacked her lips, chuckling as a glimmer of happiness twinkled in her eyes. "He's delicious, isn't he."

After eating, Ally washed and put away the dishes. She asked Gray to speak with him for a few minutes. "She's going to ask him to stay around for a while," Burton Brown said when he caught Josh glaring at the two going out on the porch. "A fight's coming, and she's going to need some help."

"I suspect she's going to need more'n one man," Elijah said. "But he'll be a good start."

"Let's walk along the river," Ally said, stepping off the porch and heading around the house. She and Gray walked a couple of hundred yards up the creek in silence while Ally worked up her courage. "I need to ask you something, Gray, and this doesn't come easy for me." She stopped and looked directly at the man. She had a hard time putting the words together. Her head dropped, and she started to tremble. Without looking up, she spoke in low tones. "I'm aware that you plan to leave tomorrow or at least by the next day. Burton has convinced me to do something that I've never done in my life." Ally stopped speaking. She took hold of Gray's arm for support. "I need to ask for help."

She continued to stare at the ground. She had no idea how the man would respond, although she had hoped he would immediately say yes. He did not. Instead, he just watched her.

Ally had no delusions as the man stood looking at her. He was going to say no. She turned away and started down closer to the water.

Several minutes passed before Gray walked down behind her. "What do you want me to help you do, Ally? Two men are enough to run your place." Gray waited for an answer, but none came.

What Ally needed was clear to her. But she tried to push that reality away, to convince herself there wouldn't be a fight. Ally wanted to make herself believe Wehr's presence would be enough. She tried to make herself assume when Dierden Kane found out Wehr was helping her, he would back down, back down, and leave her alone. He'd let her go about her business of running her little ranch in peace. That wasn't true. She was asking a man, and worse, a man she barely knew, to fight her fight. A fight with guns. A fight in which people would die.

Finally, Wehr gave up on getting an answer, and despite not being told exactly what she wanted, he replied to her.

"I'm not in the habit of hiring out for that kind of work." He paused, threw a stone in the river. "Besides, you need more than one man for a fight like that. Take Burton's other advice. Pack up and go someplace else."

"Is that what you'd do? Leave everything?" Wehr might be right, but she didn't like anyone telling her what to do. All her life, people dictated what she should do: let Judge Starrett care for you and your sister, marry Sam, go to Wyoming, a fine place to make a start.

Elijah and Josh behaved the same way when they insisted on her bringing Satan back—damned bull. They didn't consult her, ask for her opinion, or consider her feelings. They declared, like some kind of gods, the bull had to come back. She decided this time she was at least going to have an answer. She raised her eyes, then her head.

"Well," she asked again, "would you leave everything?"

"I'm not a woman all alone."

Ally's ears burned. "The ranch is mine. Why should I lose my home because I'm female?"

"Because you can't hold it," Gray said flatly.

"I'm sorry. I had no right to ask," Ally said as she stomped off toward her home.

Chapter Thirty-Three

In the three weeks since Gray's departure, they had no trouble. No cattle were stolen or slaughtered, nothing set on fire. This night, Elijah Yancey was sick with a fever. Sensing something wrong around midnight, Josh went out to the corral to find out what was spooking the horses. On his way back, he found an Indian lance in the front yard, standing straight up its red and yellow shaft looking like some kind of maypole for children. Josh froze. The lance was not stuck in the path when he went to the corral. Fear cut through him. He dashed across the yard and porch. Flinging the door open, he startled Ally. Startled her enough, she dropped the plate she was washing. "Are you all right?" he asked.

"What? Why?"

"Are you all right?" Josh shouted.

"Yes, I'm all right," she said. "Why? What's wrong with you?"

Josh's eyes darted back and forth across the dimly lit room before he turned and slammed the door closed behind him. "An Indian lance is sticking in the front yard," he said. Anxiously he jerked back the curtain from a window to peer into the darkness. "They stuck that lance in while I was at the corral. I'm lucky they didn't kill me." Nervously, he switched windows again, tearing at the curtain to gape into the shadowy night. "I can't see anything."

Ally first glanced at and then rushed into the bedroom where Elijah was sleeping restlessly. The dark room might be hiding an intruder. She stood stiffly, listening, hearing Elijah's labored breathing, nothing else. Moments later, she went to the window and pulled the forest green curtain back far enough to peek out across the almost otherworldly landscape toward the creek—nothing.

Josh kept rattling around in his belongings, looking for his new pistol. Blindly rummaging through drawers, Josh found his Colt—not loaded—hell. "I don't understand," he half-mumbled.

Ally came back into the room and peeked out another window. "Understand what?" she half-whispered.

"Why they would stick one lance in the yard and ride off. Do you think they left?"

Ally tried to make out something, or someone, in the darkness. Josh thought back to the night Sarah died, the night he failed to protect her. "Get down!" he snapped when Ally headed toward the kitchen to look out another window toward the river. "Please stay down," he repeated, this time with tenderness in his voice. "Please, I don't want you hurt."

Chapter Thirty-Four

Rain was falling when morning came. "They stuck that in the yard and rode off?" Elijah said, mostly to himself, as he stared at the Cheyenne lance.

"You should be in bed," Ally said.

"My fever's broke. Ain't no reason for me to lay in a bed. We've got work to do." Elijah opened the front door and went out on the porch. "Kind of a fancy thing," he said as he went down the steps and out toward the red and yellow lance decorated with feathers and colored strips of cloth.

Josh half-expected to take an arrow in his chest as he followed Elijah out into the yard. "What do we do with this thing?"

"I'll swear, I never thought about what to do," Elijah said. "I wonder if we should leave the thing alone, in case it's a sign?"

"What kind of a sign?" Josh asked skeptically.

"Well, how should I know what kind of sign? I'm no Cheyenne."

"You've lived out here your whole life. Surely you've learned something about Indians."

"Of course, I have. Just not what this blame lance means."

"Maybe it's a warning?" Josh said.

"What kind of warning?" Elijah asked.

Josh grew frustrated with the old man. "Maybe they're telling us to leave."

"Are you daft, McCormick? I told you Roman Nose hisself told us we're safe here. He told Mrs. Hart, sitting on his paint horse right over by that oak, the Cheyenne wouldn't bother us."

"What if the lance is Sioux, not Cheyenne?" Josh asked.

Elijah did not reply. Ally came out, holding a brown shawl over her head to protect her from the rain. "Breakfast is almost ready." She pointed at the lance. "What does a red and yellow lance mean?" she asked Elijah.

"He thinks it's some kind of sign," Josh answered sarcastically.

"I said it might be a sign. I didn't say it was a sign," the older man snapped back.

"We can ride over to the fort later on and ask why they would stick a lance in the yard," Ally said. "Breakfast is ready."

Josh spent most of the meal wondering how the other two stayed so calm and wishing Elijah would think of some job to do and give him a few minutes alone with Ally. During the night, she fell asleep leaning against the wall next to the front door. For some reason, Josh used his finger to draw across her forehead and down her nose before lightly touching her lips, something he often did to Sarah when he wanted to wake her in the night. "I'm sorry, Ally," he mumbled when she woke the second time. He touched her face to push her hair back. She smiled slightly and pretended to fall back to sleep, although Josh wasn't fooled. For the rest of the night, he sat embarrassed across the room, wishing for daylight.

Elijah headed off to check on the cattle and look for the tracks of Indian ponies. Ally busied herself with straightening the kitchen. "Ally, about last night," Josh began.

Ally turned toward him. "Josh, don't say anything. I'm not upset with you."

He turned his face away from her, with no idea what to say.

"I understand loneliness," she said quietly.

"Ally, I would never…"

She again interrupted, this time by stepping close to him and putting two fingers to his lips. She shook her head before catching his eyes. "Shhh," she breathed. "You should try to find Elijah and give him a hand."

As Josh saddled his horse, he understood the touch had been given to ease his mind and nothing more, but he was unsure why he touched her face.

After watching Josh ride off, Ally thought about touching his lips. If asked, well, if asked by the right person, Ally would admit to being lonely, something she did not like. Did she touch his lips because of loneliness? Did she miss the affection of a man more than she realized? What would she have done last night if Josh had behaved differently when she woke up? What if he hadn't apologized, but instead tried to take her into his arms and kiss her? Honestly, Ally did wonder. For now, she would put touching out of her mind, let their touching go. But what if they touched again? That thought was harder to put out of her mind.

Chapter Thirty-Five

Pushing her blond hair away from her suntanned face, Jean Wehr walked with her brother toward the corral, where a group of weanlings whinnied for their just-separated mothers. Over dinner, Gray and their father decided Gray should make a trip down to check on the Hart woman and the cattle. Along with their mother, Jean opposed the decision.

"Tell me something," she said, leaning against the corral. Do you think that woman and those cows need checking on, or do you want a clash with Kane?"

Gray half glared at his sister. "Both," he said. Jean shook her head slightly as she turned away. Some people would have been surprised by Gray's bluntness. Not Jean; they were always honest with each other.

"Why do you care," Gray said. "No one is asking you to go."

She turned and glared at him. "You could be killed."

Gray did not expect that response.

"I'm not going to get myself killed."

His sister turned and walked away from him, stopping only when one of the weanlings came up along the fence to her. "You're a friendly little thing," she said as she put her hand out under his chin. The young horse, a dapple-gray stud colt with big black eyes, raised his head as she rubbed his jaw. "You like your jaw scratched, don't you?" Jean slid through the fence to pet the little colt. "This one is a sweetheart," she said when Gray walked up to her and the colt.

"Maybe you should keep him for yourself."

"I think I might," she said, scratching the horse behind his ears. "He'll let me touch his ears. I think I'll name him Jack."

"He's good-looking," Gray said, watching his sister handle the colt for a few more minutes before speaking. This was not a chance or casual encounter. Jean rarely had chance encounters.

"Do you want to talk?" he asked.

Jean turned toward her brother; surprisingly, her blue eyes were a little misty. Her chest raised and lowered when she took and released a deep breath. "Yes, I do. But let's go for a ride while we talk."

Gray nodded and went to saddle her catty sorrel, and Doc, his blue roan.

They rode aimlessly, no one saying anything, for a couple of miles before Gray asked what she wanted. "Jeannie?" he said when she didn't answer.

He knew she wanted to talk; she just struggled to put her heart into words. Despite all the brashness Jean displayed, like her brother, Jean suffered through times of insidious melancholy: "the blues," their mother called those periods. When they hit, they brought terrible sadness and discouragement. Jean would withdraw deep within herself, locking out everyone, everyone except Gray. Annie Laurie would try to draw her out and sometimes would succeed. But only Gray could bring her back when she spiraled into the deepest depths of sadness. He alone understood, as she alone understood when Gray went to that same dark, terrible place.

Jean took her brother's arm. "Let's go sit under one of those trees."

They sat down in deep meadow grass, and Jean scooted around to be in front of her brother. She looked tired and worn.

"Sometimes, I think I can see your very soul in your eyes."

Gray laughed. "Some would argue I don't have a soul."

"Don't say that. You have a kind soul." She turned away. "We needle each other, all the time, and we yell back and forth...a lot," she said with a mischievous laugh. She raised her knees and dropped her head between them. Straightening up, she brushed her hair back from her face. "You would tear to pieces anyone who hurt or tried to hurt me."

"Where did you come up with an idea like that?" Gray asked with a snicker. "You're tougher than I am."

She punched his shoulder. "You love me." She laughed.

He gave his sister a nudge. "Have you been into the cooking sherry?"

Jean took a deep breath. "I love you." She took his hand. "No one in this world has a more wonderful brother. Gray, I don't want you to go down to her ranch. I'm afraid."

Jean had a habit of disarming her brother. He didn't expect such an emotional outpouring and was at a loss for how to respond. Was he supposed to say, "Jeanie, I love you too?" This wasn't Annie. This was his sister. He did love her. But who goes around telling their sister you love her?

Finally, he gazed off in the opposite direction. Emotions, either hers or his, were embarrassing him. "As sisters go, you're as good as any...I guess."

Jean's face lit up. Slapping her brother on the knee, she laughed at his tenderheartedness. "Come on now," she teased, tugging his shirt a couple of times. She leaned over close, her face touching his. "I won't tell anybody. Come on now, you can say it."

Laughing at himself, Gray quickly kissed the side of her face, a peck. A silly one. "Oh, hell, Jeannie, I love you too." He hesitated. "Happy now?"

"Overjoyed," she laughed. She took her brother by the arm. "I know you do. You're also my protector. Sometimes I want to protect you. I don't want you to go."

His mood became more serious. "Let's walk a little," Gray said, reaching down to pull his sister up. "We can't live our lives afraid of things," he said as they walked through the tall grass. "The woman needs help. She asked me for help before I left. The truth is," Gray said, "I feel guilty about leaving." Gray, sensing he was losing, changed his argument. His demeanor became very business-like. "Don't forget, we also have an investment to protect."

Jean laughed right out loud. "Oh my, you know damn well I'm not going to swallow that. You already admitted you want another chance to beat the hell out of Dierden Kane. That's why you want to go."

"That might be one reason, I'll admit, I enjoy thinking about, but it's not the only one."

"My ass," Jean said.

That made Gray laugh out loud. "Did our mother ever wash your mouth out with soap?"

"I'm far too smart to cuss in front of her," she said. Let's ride into town; Nellie's baking pies this morning."

A slow rain started to fall as Jean and Gray rode into the small village of High Meadows. Nellie's Restaurant was at the north end of the north/south running Main Street. Laurie Mercantile, owned by Annie's parents, sat halfway down the street. Gray told his sister he'd stop and grab Annie. They'd meet her at Nellie's.

Annie was in the back of the store straightening shelves when Gray came in, announced by the little bell over the front door. She was, in his opinion, in fact everyone's view, a beautiful woman. Annie was tall and thin. Her dark brown hair reflected a hint of auburn when the sun hit her just right. "You're a pretty sight," Gray said. "I should write poetry about your exquisiteness."

"Your brother was in a little while ago," she said. "Don't you Wehrs have any work to do out at that cattle company?"

Gray's romantic thoughts deflated. "Naw, those cows tend themselves. No need for us to worry about them."

"Well, good because Paxton said you're heading back down to Alice Hart's place." Annie could complicate things. Arguments suitable for others often sounded utterly foolish on her. Gray wanted to ignore Annie's comment, but she wouldn't allow that. He wished his younger brother kept his mouth shut because now he needed some way to justify the trip. Gray began to consider his options.

"Going to ignore me?" Annie asked, sounding casual.

Gray figured this was going to be her strategy to draw him into an argument he would not win. If he won an opening round, she would bring Jean in on her side. Even if his argument were better and more logical, which in this case, wasn't true, he would lose. Unless he steadfastly maintained Dierden Kane would take the cattle and maybe kill the Hart woman and her two men. That argument would still meet resistance from Jean and probably the Josephs. They would argue if the Hart woman can't hold what she has on her own, giving her help would only postpone the inevitable.

"Dad and I both think I should go," Gray said.

"Then you're both foolish," Annie said.

"Well, I didn't come in here to discuss the depth of my foolishness," Gray said. "I came in to ask you if you wanted a piece of pie over at Nellie's with me."

Nellie Bascomb, a feisty gal who loved harassing Gray Wehr, was serving pie to Jean when Gray and Annie came into the restaurant. "I swear, your sister doesn't look like she's slept in about a week," Nellie said, looking at Gray. "You take poor care of her."

"Well, thank you. You look great yourself," Jean said.

"Jeannie looks fine to me. Besides, a grown woman ought to be able to take care of herself," Gray snorted. He picked up his sister's fork and took a bite of her apple pie.

"Bring me peach pie."

"Where do you think I'd find peaches this time of year?" Nellie asked.

"He doesn't even like peach pie," Annie said.

"I've got apple for you, Annie. But all I've got left for you, Mr. Wehr, is custard," Nellie said, heading off to the kitchen.

"Rather eat cow slobber," Gray said, starting to take another bite of his sister's pie before getting his hand slapped away. Gray was pouring himself a second cup of coffee when Millie, Nellie's adopted daughter, came racing through the front door. She ran to Gray, throwing her arms around him.

"Hello, Little Bit," Gray said, picking the girl up and kissing her on the cheek. "I swear you grow bigger every day," he said as he put her down. Two months short of her ninth birthday, Gray told the brown-haired girl she was as beautiful as a valley sunrise. And she was. While most girls her age had little pug noses, and cute little smiles, Millie had classic beauty: long eyelashes, large eyes, high cheekbones, a heart-shaped symmetrical face. She had been with Nellie since word came to High Meadows about a band of Sioux along Crazy Woman Creek with a white infant child in their camp. Nellie insisted Gray take her to find the Indians and persuaded A Man Afraid of His Horse to let her take the girl child. The girl adopted Gray as her daddy by the time she learned to walk.

"I thought you were playing with Carrie Swain," Nellie said to the girl, who was climbing back up into Gray's lap and picking up his coffee cup.

"You're not drinking my coffee," Gray said while taking the cup away from her.

"Doc's tied out front, so I came home," Millie said. "Just give me one swallow. I'm old enough, and I like coffee."

"Do you give this child coffee?" Annie asked, giving Nellie a *how could you* stare.

"Of course not. I give her whiskey and cigars." Nellie

got up to fetch a slice of pie for the girl. As soon as she went into the kitchen, Gray gave the girl a couple of swallows of his coffee.

"Nellie's going to shoot you if she catches you offering her coffee," Jean said good-naturedly.

"Nellie never carries a gun," Gray said.

"She doesn't." Millie chuckled. "But she's got a big one hid in the bread box."

"How much coffee did you give her?" Nellie asked when she returned with the pie.

"Three swallows," Millie said.

"If she's up all night, I'm bringing her to your house," Nellie said, pointing at Gray.

Gray almost grew comfortable about no one mentioning his going to the Hart ranch. He should have known better.

"Did my brother tell you he's going down to the Hart place?" Jean asked Annie.

"Your other brother told me," Annie said nonchalantly.

"More or less, he wants to shoot Dierden Kane," Jean said.

A frown went over Gray's face as he glared a bit at his sister and nodded slightly toward the girl on his knee. Jean gave an, I'm sorry, glance at both Gray and Nellie. She interrupted her brother's teasing of Millie about cow slobber custard pie. Jean asked Nellie to let them take Millie home for the night since her brother planned to leave the valley for a while. Nellie consented, asking Millie if she'd like her own cup of coffee.

Chapter Thirty-Six

A cinnamon sky like the one now hanging over the plains often indicated a brewing storm. Ally wished earlier this morning that a storm would churn itself up. They badly needed rain, and a shower would be a welcome change in the monotony of the dry summer.

An hour later, Ally got her wish, and the rain drove Josh and Elijah off the half-finished roof over her new barn. Neighbors provided as much help as possible, but with few neighbors, all with their own work to do, the barn raising proceeded slowly.

"I enjoy a slow rainstorm," Elijah said as he, Ally, and Josh sat on the front porch.

"According to Wehr, your sorrel can be a fine horse," Josh said. "Gray said he'd be a fine cow horse with some time and patience."

"You better leave him alone," Elijah said. "He's rank as hell. He's a devil. He'll break your neck. My advice is to leave him be."

"He ought to be earning his keep instead of lazin' around and get'n fat," Josh said.

"You try to climb on him, and he'll fix you to where you can't earn your keep," Elijah said as he filled his old corncob pipe and struck a match. "The horse is rank. The best thing we can do with him is to sell him if anybody's fool enough to buy him."

"Maybe Gray'll buy him," Ally laughed. "He's the one saying he'll be a fine animal."

"We probably won't see that rogue again 'til we sell cattle," Elijah said. "I think we're foolish letting a worthless horse stand around. Ought to take him into town and sell him. Or to the cavalry, they always need horses."

The Army often restocked on horses in St. Louis before heading out on the plains, so Josh suspected the cavalry would purchase the animal at a reasonable price. Still, breaking the sorrel held a strong appeal to him. Breaking the horse would prove him capable, something that ate away at him every time Elijah laughed at one of his blunders.

Chapter Thirty-Seven

Much to his wife's disapproval, Alan Joseph decided to accompany Gray down to the Hart ranch. They crossed Crazy Woman Creek and the Lightening River. Rode past an old burnt-out cabin where ten years earlier, a family lost their lives to a Sioux raiding party. Why people came out to this desolate land to make a home for themselves bewildered Wehr. Other than commonly hostile Indians, little was out here. A man could ride for days through nothing except high desert and empty rolling plains. Most summers were too dry for crops to flourish, and most winters brought deep snows and icy winds, threatening the survival of cattle with no shelter.

Another problem was how easily inexperienced homesteaders with flawed senses of direction got lost. Once lost, starvation often lay in their future. Other settlers who tried moving into the area paid a heavy price at the hands of the Sioux, Cheyenne, and Arapaho.

"These burned-out ranches and homesteads always give me a chill," Alan said.

"Homesteads, not many ranches," Gray said. "They should have been smarter than to set up living without a neighbor for fifty or a hundred miles. It was foolish to think the Sioux would leave them alone."

"Our families set up living out here," Alan said.

"Not all alone out in the middle of nowhere. Our families built a town with other settlers in a defensible valley, not in this empty nowhere. And not right in the middle of the buffalo grazing areas. Damn fools if you ask me," Gray said.

"You're always riding back and forth across here," Alan said, prodding Wehr.

"I go back and forth, but I don't plant my hind-end on a cabin porch for the Lakota to shoot at, and I don't generally bring women and children along."

"We take the women clear to Denver every couple of years," Alan said. "Jean and Annie went with us last year, we took Nellie and Millie...she's a child, isn't she? We took Annie and Jean this spring when we took cattle down. The ones we cut the Hart woman cows out from. Have you been havin' problems with your memory?"

Gray preferred crossing the plains alone, in silence, with only a fine horse for company. Especially compared to traveling with a companion who never shut up. Zach Joseph, Alan's younger brother, never shut his mouth. This journey became the first time Gray realized Alan shared the same infirmity.

Thankfully, by mid-afternoon, Alan lost the desire to keep up a continuous conversation. Once again, he became the man Gray trusted to make many of the decisions about the ranch. Alan made the perfect partner since Gray so often wandered off, sometimes for months at a time. Alan never pitched the fits Gray's brother Paxton often threw over Gray's absence. Gray and Alan agreed Gray would not take any share of the profits during his time away. Both men considered the deal fair, never letting Gray's absence interfere with their relationship.

The hot and dry prairie made both horses grumpy as

they put in mile after mile across the barren land furrowed by parched gullies and ravines.

"I guess you see 'em," Alan said, breaking almost two hours of silence.

"Yep," Gray said. "They've been watching us for the last couple of miles. Seven of them."

"Seven is my count, too," Alan said, trying to scan the sloping ridge to the east. "I think that's all, don't you? No place for 'em to hide." Alan spat a stream of tobacco. "Sioux?"

"Arapaho," Gray said.

"Friendly?"

"I doubt it," Gray said, stopping his blue roan and turning toward the Indians. "I suspect they're wondering how well armed we are. Probably figure we'll give them quite a tussle if we have rifles. But they'll work up their courage before long."

"You think we can outrun them?"

"Might," Gray said slowly. "I wish we had that damn Jimmy Hickok with us. Blamed kid's never around when I need him."

"One more man wouldn't be much help," Alan said, studying the terrain around them.

"He's one hell of a shot," Gray said. Gray was still lamenting not having Hickok around when the screaming, painted Arapaho attacked.

"Fight or run?" Alan asked as he pulled his rifle out of its scabbard.

"Never cared for running," Gray said, leveling his carbine and squeezing off the first shot. The Indian farthest out in front flopped off his horse and bounced several yards before landing face down in the dirt.

Alan's first shot also knocked a brave from his paint pony. Gray ejected the spent cartridge and reloaded his Springfield as the first arrow whirred between Alan and himself. Leveling the rifle, he shot a third brave. Alan missed when he fired again. Pulling out his Navy Colt, Gray kicked

Doc in the sides. He charged the Indians, not firing until within twenty yards of the enemy. He hit one of the Arapaho in the chest, flipping him backward off his running horse. Alan took a third rifle shot, killing the lone remaining warrior still charging.

The other two warriors decided to flee. Gray did not let attackers escape. One of the fleeing Indians realized his pony was no match for Gray's horse and turned to fight. He let an arrow fly hitting Gray in the left shoulder, nearly knocking him from Doc's back. Gray fired in haste at the warrior not more than a few feet away. His bullet struck the Arapaho dead center in the abdomen.

Alan's horse almost trampled the Indian as he tore past, pursuing the last fleeing enemy. Alan pulled up and jumped off. Holding his pistol in both hands, he took careful aim and squeezed the trigger. The shot knocked the Arapaho from his horse but did not kill him. Alan swung back on his near-panicked horse and ran down the Indian, now trying to flee on foot. He shot him in the back from point-blank range as he tore past the final Indian.

When Alan got back to Gray, he found him sitting on the ground, his shirt soaked with blood. As Alan got off his horse, Gray yanked the arrow out of his left shoulder. "I ought to listen to Annie and my sister," Gray said as he tossed the shaft on the ground.

"How bad?" Alan asked as he took his canteen off his saddle.

"Jeannie's cut me worse with her tongue," Gray said, pulling his sleeve down from his shoulder. "It burns like hell, though."

Alan pulled Gray's bloody shirt back. "The gash is deep, but the arrow missed the bone. That's lucky."

"I'll thank that Arapaho—if I run across him in the happy hunting grounds."

"You're bleeding like a stuck pig. I'll find something to stop this leak before you bleed out." Alan also brought a bottle of whiskey from his saddlebag and poured some into the wound, causing Gray to wince and comment on his friend's heritage.

"I'm surprised you've not been plugged a dozen times before now as often as you wander around alone on these plains. You ought to stay home more."

Gray often thought about staying home. A soft bed and hot meals seemed like a superb idea, usually after he spent weeks sleeping on the ground while scouting for the Army or traipsing around from town to town. What made him leave friends and family was something he never settled, even in his mind. Still, the wanderlust in him prevented him from settling into a day-to-day existence where little beyond the weather changed.

The uneventful life in High Meadows suited his folks, the Josephs, and Annie. Only Jean understood what pushed him to leave the serene valley. Her opposition to this trip had been the first time she ever expressed anything other than jealousy regarding his wandering ways.

Once the bleeding stopped and a makeshift bandage wrapped his shoulder, Gray was ready to move on. Most men would want to lay up and rest, not Wehr. He was tenacious, stubborn, in Alan's vocal opinion, to a fault. To Wehr, the wound was merely an inconvenience. Unless they ran into more Arapaho, Sioux, or Cheyenne, Gray did not believe they had any more concerns.

The shoulder might stiffen up, but a sore arm would not keep him from riding at a solid pace until they reached the Hart place for a little more doctoring and a decent meal. One night's rest, and he'd be ready to make Dierden Kane answer for any trouble he might be giving Ally Hart.

Once they mounted and started to lope off, three of the Indian ponies, a sorrel, and two paints followed. When Wehr and Joseph stopped, the three Indian ponies began to graze. Gray's throbbing shoulder was no reason to leave three stout horses on the plains. Minutes later, they had the three horses tethered together and headed off to Alice Hart's place with Alan leading the new livestock.

Chapter Thirty-Eight

Ally knew from the way Elijah was walking all slouched over he was going to be the bearer of bad news. She stood waiting for him on the porch, allowing the trouble to come to her, rather than going to meet it. Sam always waited for trouble, hoping whatever evil it was wouldn't show up.

Waiting for trouble wasn't usually Ally's way. She did not like facing adversity as a victim. She believed in going out and confronting a crisis, facing threats head-on before conflicts pounced on her. Since the burning of her barn, Ally had less fight in her. She feared defeat might be inevitable. She made a point of not letting Elijah or Josh know, but she sometimes thought McCormick might sense fear in her.

"Mrs. Hart," Elijah said as he walked up on the porch and removed his hat, "four of our cattle are dead. Their throats are slit."

It never occurred, never occurred, to Elijah to use some etiquette regarding delivering bad news. The faint of heart were at a disadvantage when receiving information from him.

"Where's Josh? He's not hurt, is he?"

"No, ma'am, he's out counting the rest of the cattle. Why would anybody want to slit a cow's throat? I can understand why they would rustle 'em, but why on earth would they kill them and let them rot? Why resent a cow its life?"

"It's not the cows, Elijah. They resent me." Ally and Elijah rode back out to the creek, where the four cows lay bloating and drawing flies in the afternoon sun. Josh had the rest of the cattle in a little ravine about a mile further up the creek.

"Those are the only four we lost," Josh said, anticipating Ally's first concern. "All the rest are gathered up in here," he said, motioning up the gully. "I guess we're going to need to post a twenty-four-hour guard. We sure don't want to lose any more. But, having either Elijah or me here day and night will put a crimp in the barn building."

Building a barn ranked far down the list of Ally's concerns. She worried most about the two men who worked for her. Kane already proved himself willing to destroy her property and livestock. Unless she pulled out, the next step would almost certainly be to kill one of her men or everyone on the ranch. Sitting on her horse in the cobweb-filled ravine, Ally doubted this fight was winnable. She was fighting a killer, and the men on her side were no match for him. Elijah was old, and Josh, despite constant practice, still missed everything he shot at with his pistol.

"One of us needs to ride into town and tell the sheriff about this," Josh said. "I hate to put the burden out here on the two of you, but I think I'm the one to go," he said. "I doubt if Kane'll do anything else for a few days. Probably wait for how you react to this first," he said.

Ally didn't think anything would happen for a while, and she also believed Josh would be the most convincing in getting the sheriff to do something. The sheriff would take some convincing, and Ally figured a city fellow, a numbers man, could outwit a country bumpkin.

"That piss ant sheriff ain't gonna do nothing," Elijah

said. "He's lazy and scared."

"If he won't, I'll go to the fort. The Army's responsible for providing people protection out here," Josh said.

"Let me think for a day or two," Ally said, having second thoughts.

"Ally, there is nothing to think about. I'm heading into town this afternoon. I'll be back tomorrow. Elijah, you stay with the cattle. I'll relieve you soon as I'm back." He waited for her to argue with him, but she didn't.

"All right," she said. "Elijah, I'll go fetch you a bedroll for tonight and make you some supper. I'm going to stay with you, and don't argue with me."

Both men understood arguing with her was pointless. They would let Ally stay out the first night and talk some sense into her after Josh got back from town.

A little before dark, Ally came back with a plate of food for Elijah. "Well, Josh headed off into town with his new gun strapped to his hip," she said. The thought of McCormick riding off healed got a chuckle out of Elijah.

"I hope he don't shoot his foot off. Or shoot his horse clambering on or off." He laughed as he took the plate.

"I don't believe he'll shoot his foot or his horse." Ally laughed. "He may shoot the sheriff, though."

"Only if he aims at the deputy," Elijah chuckled.

"I'm going to walk up the creek a little way and check on the cattle before it gets too dark," Ally said.

"Want me to walk along?" Elijah asked.

"No, you enjoy your supper. I won't be long," Ally said. She walked off into the dusk, thinking she was utterly alone in the world.

Chapter Thirty-Nine

Late in the afternoon, Josh returned from town and found Ally and Elijah sitting on their horses looking out over the cattle.

"The sheriff's not going to do much, if anything," he told Ally when he rode up next to her.

"I told you he wouldn't before you ever left," Elijah said.

"He said we need evidence beyond speculation to prove Kane did it. He says it was just as likely Indians."

"Humph, that fool knows better," Elijah said. "Indians would run the cattle off, cut them up to eat. Not slit their throats and let them lie."

"I better go start supper," Ally said. "Why don't you come along with me?" she said, looking at Josh. "You can eat and come back to relieve Elijah."

Leaving Elijah with the cattle, Ally and Josh rode along together at a comfortable pace. In the late afternoon light, the horizon stretched for miles in every direction. "I sense a peacefulness to this country," Josh said offhandedly. "Especially at this time of day."

Josh regretted what he said almost as quickly as he spoke. After all, she lost her barn and now had four of her cattle butchered. She might not find the land so peaceful.

Ally rode along in silence, her thoughts somewhere else Josh assumed.

Chapter Forty

Two and a half days after the sheriff told Josh he wouldn't help Ally without more proof, Gray and Alan arrived at the Hart place. Elijah saw them riding in and walked out to meet them. "Well, you're a welcome sight," he said, reaching up to shake hands with both men. "What brings you back down here?"

"Brought you some horses," Gray said, handing the rope leading the Indian ponies to Elijah. "Also, wanted to make sure you've not eaten Ally out of house and home."

"Where did you get this bunch of Indian ponies?"

"Arapaho gave them to us. Said they didn't need them anymore."

Elijah knew better, but he wasn't in the habit of looking gift horses in the mouth.

"How are things?" Alan asked.

"Dismal," Elijah said. "Let's walk up to the house. I'll tell you while we walk."

Ally was shocked to see Gray and Alan. She didn't expect them until the cattle sold. She made the men coffee and told them what the sheriff said regarding providing any help.

"The hell with the sheriff," Gray muttered.

"You don't look so good," Elijah told Gray as Gray shifted in his chair and gave a slight grimace.

Ally sneered at her old friend, but Elijah was right. "Are you ill?" she asked, walking toward him.

"He took an Arapaho arrow," Alan said. "He probably needs looking at, but he won't listen to me."

"Where are you hit?" Ally asked as she reached out to touch his face, to find out if he was hot. Instinctively, Gray avoided Ally's touch.

"My shoulder," Gray said, y aggravated Alan told them.

"Take off your shirt," Ally said.

"I'm fine."

"Take off your shirt," Ally said, this time with more authority.

Thinking she sounded like Annie or Jean, Gray unbuttoned his shirt and took his left arm out of the sleeve. Ally unwrapped the bandages Alan put on. She examined the wound and told Elijah to find her some clean bandages and iodine. "And some salve out of the cabinet," she told him as he headed for the spare bedroom Ally now used for a sewing room.

"How bad does this hurt? I've got some laudanum if you want it."

"I don't need laudanum," Gray said. "That stuff makes me half-drunk."

"This is awfully inflamed," Ally said.

"You'd look inflamed too if an Arapaho shot an arrow into you," Elijah said. "You're lucky he didn't hit you a few inches to the right and a little lower. You wouldn't have finished your trip down here."

Ally continued to clean the wound. "I guess you had enough sense to keep it clean, but you need sewing up," she said after cleaning the hole in Gray's shoulder. "Otherwise, you're going to take a long time to heal up. And you won't be worth much until you mend." Surprisingly, Gray did not object to the stitching. "Elijah, why don't you go put their horses up for them? I'm sure Gray doesn't particularly want an audience while I sew."

"I'll give you a hand," Alan said. "I never like seeing a grown man howl."

Ally went and found her heaviest needle and a spool of white thread. "Are you sure you don't want Laudanum?" she asked again. "I doubt if this is going to be very pleasant." Gray still declined. "Suit yourself—it's your shoulder."

Gray cringed when Ally pushed the needle through his flesh the first time. He could feel the thread drag through, followed by a stout tug as Ally pulled the loop tight. After the sixth stitch, Gray asked Ally how many of these she planned to put in him.

"However, many it takes to close you up," she said, with a little bit of a laugh."

"This may be funny to you," Gray said, "but not from my side of your needle.

"Do you want to take a short break?" Ally asked, with some sympathy in her voice while putting her hand on Gray's back.

"No, you're doing fine. Taking a break won't help," Gray said, sounding as if he meant to reassure Ally. "Just keep sewing."

Eleven more stitches, and Ally declared the sewing finished. She made a third offer of laudanum, which Gray again declined. He did accept coffee and Ally's suggestion to lie down and rest.

It took only a few minutes for Gray to be breathing heavily in the next room. When Elijah and Alan came back in, Ally poured them coffee. She made an idle comment about being surprised Gray didn't argue about being sewn up and hoping not too much time passed for the stitches to help.

Alan sneered a little. "Humph, you told him if you didn't sew him up, he'd be a long-time healing. He doesn't want to wait around healing. He wants to go take care of Dierden Kane."

Chapter Forty-One

"You've got a little more color this morning," Ally said when Gray came out of the spare bedroom.

"Where are the others?" Gray asked.

"Out with the cattle," Ally said.

"Why didn't someone wake me?" Gray asked with a slight bit of irritation in his voice.

She took a moment before answering. "We decided anybody sleeping through us having breakfast must need sleep," she said.

Gray glanced up at her. Ally told him to sit down at the table while she got him some coffee and his breakfast.

"I'm going to wash up a little," Gray said, heading out the front door and to the pump in the side yard.

When Gray finished washing and came back inside, Ally cooked ham and fried two eggs over-easy. She poured him a cup of coffee as he sat down, casting a nervous glance at Wehr as he cut into the ham. For some reason, Wehr caused her to worry over little things, which wouldn't concern her regarding others. Now she worried about whether or not he liked eggs over-easy. Ally offered Gray cream and sugar for his coffee, though she knew from his last visit, he drank his coffee black.

A little later, she caught herself looking at Gray as he drank his second cup of coffee. This bothered her. Ally was no daydreamer, never had been, except when she let herself think about living in a city with restaurants and theaters at her disposal. When she sewed up Gray's shoulder, Ally caught herself having what she considered inappropriate daydreams while touching him.

"Are you all right?" Gray asked.

His question startled her. "What?" she said, turning toward Gray.

"Are you all right?" Gray asked. "You appear deep in thought about something."

"Not really," Ally said as she sat at the table with Gray.

"Well, thank the Lord," Gray said with a smile on his face. "I worry when women are deep in thought."

Gray's remark made Ally laugh. "Now, why would a woman thinking worry you?" Ally asked.

Gray smiled a little wider. "Every time I'm around a hard-thinking woman, she wants me involved in something."

"What an arrogant thing to say," Ally said.

"I'm not arrogant," Gray said. "My experience is when a woman goes deep into thought, and I'm around her, she always wants something."

"What does she want?" Ally asked as her interest grew.

"Well," Gray said, looking at Ally with an appealing gleam in his eyes, "I can't say exactly, but it usually leads to trouble."

For some reason, Ally thought back to the night on the riverbank when she asked Gray to help her, and he refused. She wondered what Gray was thinking about now, was he trying to dissuade her before she asked again? Or, like her, was he thinking of something more intimate? A few minutes passed in uncomfortable silence for Ally.

"I'm not sure if I thanked you for fixing my shoulder. If I didn't, I appreciate your care."

Ally smiled. "Can I ask you something foolish?" Gray raised his eyes slightly as if to give her permission. "What does being shot with an arrow feel like?"

"It's unpleasant," Gray said.

"I imagine it is," Ally laughed. She reached out and patted Gray on the arm, something she became immediately concerned about doing. "Would you like another cup of coffee?" Ally asked, feeling a little awkward.

"No, I better go out and join the others, start deciding what we're going to do about those cattle you lost." As Gray started to the coat tree for his hat, he froze. "Where did you get the lance?" he asked, turning toward Ally.

"Cheyenne stuck it in the yard one night. Josh went out to check horses, and when he came back, that was sticking in front of the house. It scared us enough we stayed up the rest of the night, peeking out the windows."

"You're wrong about Cheyenne. This is a Sioux peace lance," Gray said. "A peace lance tells all Sioux you are a friend and to leave you in peace. I guess they've taken a liking to you. You need to stick this back out there."

"We've never had any dealings with the Sioux," Ally said. "Roman Nose told me the Cheyenne would not harm us."

"Roman Nose?"

Ally told Gray about the day Roman Nose promised they would not harm her.

"I guess, he told the Sioux. You must have made quite an impression on him," Gray said.

Chapter Forty-Two

Josh, Elijah, Burton, and Alan stood in the unfinished new barn when Gray walked in.

Alan motioned Gray over. "Josh went and talked to the sheriff about the cattle. He's not going to do anything."

"Ally told me last night," Gray said. "He's likely on Kane's payroll, and if not, he's probably afraid of Kane. Does she have enough money to rebuild this barn?" Gray asked Josh.

"No," Josh said. "But I can help her out."

Alan Joseph shifted from one foot to another. "She best be careful about debt."

"She won't have any debt on the barn," Josh said. "The lumber will be my gift to her. She deserves help."

Alan fidgeted, then said, "From what I know of her, I believe she does, but she's got a lot of trouble. I'm afraid more than you, or your money can help her out of."

Anger started to build up in Josh. Everyone from Burton Brown to the sheriff to Elijah, and now Alan Joseph, doubted she could make her little ranch go. While he understood her trouble, he wondered what they thought the woman should do.

"What about you, Wehr?" Josh asked. "What do you think about all this? Does she just quit? Go to town and beg? Become a prostitute?"

"Don't act like a damn fool, McCormick." Wehr gave him a hostile scowl. "Building her a barn is no answer. Giving her your money is no answer. The woman has two choices: fight Dierden Kane or move somewhere else. If she decides to move, she's got Cheyenne, High Meadows, I guess St. Louis. But you're right about one thing. If she moves, she still needs to make a living. I doubt begging or whoring will suit her much," Wehr said disgustedly.

He paused, frowned at both Elijah and Josh before setting his eyes on Josh. "If she decides to fight, she better understand what kind of fight she'll be in. People are going to die on both sides. I'll tell you this, for your side to win, it'll mean killing Dierden Kane. Killing's the only way you'll beat a man so brutal. Kicking his ass around her front yard and running him and a couple of his lackeys down the road didn't stop him. You'll have to kill him."

For a moment, Josh stared at Gray. Finally, he let out the breath he held since Gray began to speak. "I'll go check on the cattle. I need to think."

Chapter Forty-Three

Elijah swore a little under his breath. "If Kane comes down on us, we'll need thirty men to fight him off. Mrs. Hart is beat, isn't she?" Neither Gray nor Alan responded. "Why did you people give her those cattle if she can't succeed?"

"To be honest with you, Elijah," Alan said in an almost matter-of-fact voice, "Burton wasn't entirely forthcoming with us. He didn't tell us Kane threatened her. When Ally told Gray about Kane, Gray thought it was too late to back out on the deal. But, even then, we didn't know how menacing the threats were."

"Elijah," Gray said, "when McCormick gets back, we're going to sit down with Mrs. Hart and have her make some decision about where she might want to go."

The old man took umbrage at Gray's comment. "You want her to turn tail and sneak off."

Gray held his response for a brief time. "Or be ready to fight a fight she has almost no chance of winning."

"Or, a fella might go over to Kane's place, slip in at

night, and kill him," Elijah whispered.

"You're talking about cold-blooded murder," Alan said. "And his men might come looking for revenge."

Gray expressed doubts Kane's men would come after revenge if Kane were dead. He doubted they were that fond of ol' Dierden.

Chapter Forty-Four

The four men hung around the house for the rest of the afternoon, doing a little work on the new barn, mostly puttering around. Josh brought up the rank horse, drawing a rebuke from Elijah. Ignoring Elijah, he told Gray he wanted to work with the horse, to turn him into a useable animal. Gray liked nothing more than working with a horse. He slapped Josh on the back, suggesting they pay the animal a visit.

When they got to the corral, Gray stopped, telling Josh to stay at the fence while he went in to discover how the horse would react. He slipped between the rails, taking his rope with him. He walked somewhat slowly toward the sorrel, whispering to him as he went. The horse snorted a little and moved away. Gray and the horse repeated the whole scene two more times. Gray moved toward him again, and this time the horse bolted off. He made a couple of circles around the corral. During his third time around, Gray slung a rope out in front of him. The horse lunged back and changed directions.

Gray stood quietly until the animal stopped, turned toward Gray, and snorted a few times.

"Well, that's a start, made him change directions," Gray said. "There's no point in me working with him," Gray said as he climbed up on the fence. "You're the one who wants to ride him. You're the one who needs to gentle him. I'll sit here on the fence and advise."

"How do I start?" Josh asked.

"Walk around in the corral, keep some distance, and don't pay any attention to him. After a while, when he stops watching you, walk a little closer. When he starts paying attention to you, walk a little further away. Walk some more, go a little closer. When he reacts, walk away again. After getting close and backing away, go a little closer, but when he looks at you, you turn sideways and slide toward him. If he starts to paw or throw his head, stop but don't step away, just stop. Turn away, but don't step away."

"What if he charges me?"

"He'll stop," Gray said.

"What if he doesn't?"

"Then I wouldn't want to be you."

"Thanks a lot," Josh said, with a little laugh in his voice.

"It's not a horse's nature to be mean. He's a prey animal. His nature is to flee, not fight. Make sure you give him enough room to move away. Give him enough space so he can't kick you as he goes past you. Now, if he walks toward you, let him come. He'll come at his pace. Let him sniff you, let him nudge you with his head if he wants to. Don't move away, don't try to touch him. Let him look you over. When he starts to leave, let him go. I doubt, though, he'll let you come too close today."

"What if he tries to bite me?"

"Well, I don't think he'll come that close, but if he does, give him a little slap in the mouth. If he tries again, slap him a little harder. Tell him to quit as you slap him."

"How long will this process take?"

"That'll depend on how strong-willed he is," Gray said.

"If he's strong-willed, a little longer. But you'll end up with a fine horse."

Josh stayed out with the horse for more than a half-hour, never getting very close, before Gray called an end to the first day. When he asked for Gray's opinion of the afternoon, Gray laughed and told Josh, "You're still alive."

Chapter Forty-Five

Ally put a fancier than usual dinner on the table. She baked bread, fried chicken, mashed potatoes, made a steaming bowl of gravy, and roasted sweet corn. A pie, still warm from the oven, made a delightful dessert.

While drinking coffee, the after-dinner conversation stayed lighthearted. Alan asked Elijah how long he'd been in Wyoming. The question started him into a long history of his life. He was born in Tennessee sometime in the 1790s, but the exact year was a mystery. An only child, he left home at around thirteen years old, tagging along with a family moving west. He spent a few years in Kansas before wandering up into the Rocky Mountains, where he trapped and hunted to put food on his table. He surprised Ally when he revealed once being married to a Quaker woman named Mary Margaret, who soon lost patience with his unrefined and sinful ways. She left him when he took off on one of his trips into the high country. He later took up with a spoiled dove from Denver. One night when she was drinking heavily, she got mad and took a shot at him. Elijah didn't enjoy being shot at and concluded he wasn't wanted.

When the military came to Wyoming, he found work as a scout, buffalo hunter, and skinner. He scrounged out a living as a bummer until he met Mr. and Mrs. Hart and started to work on and off for them.

After Mr. Hart's tragic end, Elijah, of his own accord, took responsibility for Mrs. Hart and came to her place full-time. For his part, although he wasn't sure how Mrs. Hart felt about Josh, he appreciated him being around. Mrs. Hart needed all the help she could muster, and even if Josh was green and near worthless, he was better than nobody at all. He said he hoped Josh didn't get himself all broke up foolishly messing with that rank horse.

Ally smiled rather sheepishly at Josh, wondering how he liked Elijah's little speech. When he caught her looking at him, he smiled back and shook his head a little; understanding Elijah meant no harm.

When Elijah completed or at least took a break in his story, Gray caught Ally's attention. Not liking unresolved problems, he told her they needed to talk a little. He ran his hand through his blond hair and told Ally he needed to ask her something.

Ally jumped ahead before Gray could say anything. "I'm staying," she said. "And I don't know if I can hold the ranch or not, so don't ask me. I'm going to try." Were she entirely honest, she didn't understand what trying meant. She only knew she wasn't leaving. No one told her what decision to make. If she got killed, she'd just be dead. She made up her own mind, and that's what mattered. No one told her what to do.

Only Gray spoke. "I believe you're in for a rough time," he said. "But, a lot of things are built through rough times. For what my opinion is worth, I think you are doing the right thing." He sat back in his chair and studied Ally. "Then tomorrow, you, me, and Alan will take a ride to Dierden Kane's place for a little talk."

Now wait a minute," Josh said and stood. "I'm going. Ally will stay here."

Gray shook his head. "Since Ally's the one he threatened, she needs to confront Dierden."

"Sit down, Josh," Ally said. "I'm going. You're staying."

The humiliation was evident on Josh's face. He glared at Gray, then Ally. Alan stood and half-glared at Josh. "Gray is right. Ally has to stand up for herself.

"Then one of you stay here, and I'll go along."

"You're missing the point," Gray said. "If Ally stands up to Kane, face to face, he'll find out she's got backbone. With Alan and me there, Kane will see she has substantial backing. He'll think twice about tangling with us. He knows we'll bring a lot of men with us. Worrying about tangling with us may not stop a cur like Kane, but it'll sure as hell give him second thoughts."

"Fine, I've been shown my place," Josh said. He slouched down onto his chair.

Chapter Forty-Six

Alan Joseph and Gray were out on Ally's porch picking up their bedrolls to go sleep out near the cattle when Alan turned to his partner.

"You must be a fool," he said, and not in a friendly tone.

Gray took no time before responding. "Don't go if you don't want to."

"So, you plan on riding right on to Kane's place, with that woman in tow?"

"Yep," Gray said, tossing his bedroll over his shoulder and starting down the steps. He continued across the yard, through the front gate, and over to his horse, where he tied the bedroll behind the saddle's cantle.

He untied Doc and turned toward Alan. "Are you coming?" When Alan started down the steps, Gray stepped up on his horse and waited for his friend to saddle up. Neither man spoke as they rode slowly out toward the gully where the cattle bedded down. For Gray, there was nothing to discuss. He didn't fret about the possible outcomes of his actions. He believed worrying was a waste of time. If a task needed to be done, finish, and move on to the next thing. This needed to be done. Alice Hart had to stop allowing Kane to push her. If she didn't, Kane would destroy her world—or kill her. Kane needed stopping, and Wehr intended to stop him.

Alan Joseph's hesitancy did vex Gray. Alan grew up in this country. He understood the hardships and challenges inherent to this life. Alan also knew Dierden Kane. He grasped Kane would not back down and would do anything to take what he wanted.

Gray and Alan were different. Alan was generally patient, sometimes slow to act. He would measure things out, consider every possible outcome. The way he did when his father died and the families asked him to become the ranch supervisor. Instead of saying yes, Alan told the families he needed to think it over. He thought for almost two weeks before coming back to them, not with an answer, but with a long list of concerns he needed to understand before saying yes.

Gray was not an impatient man. One only had to watch him work with a horse to know that, but he was not a procrastinator. He wanted today's work done today. Zach Joseph, Alan's younger brother, was the opposite. He considered loafing an honest occupation. If there was work to avoid, he avoided it. Yet, other than Annie Laurie and his sister, Zach stayed Gray's closest friend. Something the rest of the Wehr and Joseph families found odd.

Once they arrived at the gully holding the cattle, they circled the herd in opposite directions. Gray found a few head up above the ravine over closer to the creek. He drifted over and rode through the little group, leaving them lazing around. Gray found two cows on the verge of calving. He expected both would calve by midday tomorrow.

"Rustler's moon," Gray mentioned when he and Alan came back together.

Alan gazed briefly at the moon. "Good night to steal

cattle," Alan said. "Be the same for the next few nights. We'll tell those two to be on their toes."

"I doubt Kane's men will come over here to create mischief while we're at Kane's place," Gray said. "He'll want them to stay on the ranch to protect him."

"Just how do you think this little visit tomorrow is going to occur?" Alan asked.

"We're gonna ride over and go directly to Kane. If we don't catch him outside, we'll go up and pound on his door. Ally will tell him she's staying on her ranch and he's going to leave her be. She's not going to bother him, and he's not going to bother her."

"And you think he's going to listen to her and oblige her?"

"Well, he's going to listen," Gray said, "because as soon as we find him, I'm going to shove this forty-four right up under his chin and chuckle when he pisses himself. When Ally finishes, I'll explain to him why he's going to oblige her. I'm going to tell him if he as much as rides across her land again, I'm going to kill him. If anybody else causes her any trouble, whether he's the cause or not, I'm gonna kill him."

"Ally says you already told him," Alan said.

"I told him he'd regret giving her trouble. Didn't say kill him. This time I may shoot his kneecap, so he knows I'm earnest."

"Well, you're an original, I'll give you that," Alan said.

Alan took the bedroll off his horse and bedded down, still peeved at Gray's plan if the way he slammed his bedding on the ground was an indicator. Despite being angry, Alan never crossed Gray.

Alan's being unhappy about tomorrow didn't matter to Gray. Alan was no slacker. When the time came to fight, he would fight. He would not hesitate; he would fight, and he would fight until they won. Like Gray, Alan maintained a stiff sense of right and wrong. Six years earlier, they, along with Zach Joseph, caught three rustlers with about a dozen of their cattle. They hung them from the first tree available, the same way they would hang Dierden Kane if they found stolen cattle on his place.

After Gray and Alan's departure, Josh sat down on the steps leading up to Ally's porch. More than an hour passed, and no one came to join him or to check on his welfare. At first, he wondered why Ally didn't come out searching for him. Then he got mad about her ignoring him. After an hour passed, he decided he didn't care about her. *Go off tomorrow with Gray and Alan Joseph and get yourself killed, or go to hell.* He meant nothing to her, so she meant nothing to him.

For the first time since the lack of whiskey in prison dried him out, he wanted a drink. The darker the night got, the more he wanted to drink, and not only drink, get drunk, drown himself in rye. Drowning in whiskey wouldn't be as painful as drowning in self-pity. The longer he sat on the steps, the more disheartened he became.

For a moment, he thought about how he touched Ally's face the night the Indians stuck the lance in the yard. His thoughts shifted from Ally to Sarah, the woman he truly loved, the one he found beautiful and enticing. Sarah made him meaningful and successful. She made him feel like a good husband and a remarkable lover. She was easy to talk to, easy to be with, but most of all, she made him happy. He remembered their first night together. When he began to undress her, he imagined she would be shy. But she was not. She was slightly demure, but also daring, teasing a little as he took off her camisole. He loved to lie with her, touching her honeyed white body.

A year ago, Josh could not have imagined a life without Sarah. She made him proud of her when they went out to dinner or the theater. She was always the most attractive woman at any gathering, comfortable in all situations, gracious and kind to everyone. Josh once told her he had political ambitions. He thought he might enjoy being governor. However, he preferred being a senator, living in a grand brick home in Washington. He would be a champion of the South, and they would hobnob with Washington's elite. He hoped, eventually, for an ambassadorship, preferably to France.

Sarah laughed at him. She reminded him he didn't speak French or any other foreign language. "And what if I got fat on French cooking?" she asked. "No, I think we're better off right here, at least for now," she said. She advised him to be content in St. Louis, letting life come to them, in its own way and at its own pace.

Ally intended to console Josh and assure him she valued his help, point out there was no insult in staying behind while she made the trip to Kane's ranch. But after an hour, she decided he was not coming back inside, at least not while she was still up.

She went into her bedroom, sat on the foot of her bed, removed her shoes—and ran out of energy. She lay back and let the darkness settle around her. Ally grew downcast, thinking about her life and her future. Over the last few weeks, when alone, usually after dark, she thought about what marrying again might be like. The idea unnerved her. More unnerving, she sometimes wondered about marrying Josh.

Now, Josh sat outside, pouting about a slight no one else considered a slight. If she were so mistaken about Josh's temperament, maybe she'd be mistaken about any man in whom she might become interested. If she made too many mistakes, she would run out of suitors, end up old and alone. Running out of suitors was possible, in fact, probable. Suitors were scarce in this lonely place.

Ally's sinking self-assurance made her wonder if she was doing the right thing, going over to face Dierden Kane.

If he did back down, which she doubted, she might still go broke. Even with the Wehr/Joseph cattle, she could not afford to lose many, a distinct possibility since the cattle would have to survive the winter with no feed stored up. Not only did she have no feed, she had no barn to store it in if she did. Beyond that, her only hands were a somewhat addled aging man and a greenhorn obligated only for three months, half of which were in the past.

She undressed, slipped into her nightgown, and crawled into bed. Despite her troubles, sleep came quickly and deep.

Chapter Forty-Seven

Ally awoke in the dark. Anxious, troubled, fidgety, and four hundred-sheep later, she threw back the covers and got up. She considered taking a hot bath. Even living in the middle of nowhere, Ally took great care regarding her appearance. Before heating the water, she decided being on a horse all day, sleeping on the ground tonight, and repeating the process tomorrow, made bathing pointless. She settled for washing her hair.

Two hours later, Josh sat down for breakfast—grumpy. He wouldn't say what time he went to bed, so Ally abandoned any more attempts at conversation. She made four stacks of hotcakes. As she placed them on the table along with a pitcher of syrup, she asked Josh to call the others. He complied without acknowledging her.

Ally's cooking always pleased Elijah. The hotcakes thrilled him. He put five of them on his plate with a pat of butter between each one. He piled two spoonsful of powdered sugar on them before smothering them in syrup. "I wanted something sweet this mornin', and this sure will do," he said through a mouthful of pancake. Syrup oozed out his mouth, ran down his chin, and dripped on his shirt. Ally patted his shoulder and told him to enjoy himself.

After breakfast, Gray and Alan went out to saddle horses for their trip. Josh left the table and wandered around the corrals and the half-built barn without speaking during the entire meal. Elijah asked what Ally wanted accomplished in her absence.

"Oh, maybe try to do a little on the roof, and be sure to check on the cattle a couple of times a day. Don't work too hard; rest up some." She did not mention it to Elijah, but she suspected with Josh so upset, he would not do much. She would not be too surprised if he up and left. She would be disappointed but not surprised.

Ally excused herself to put a bedroll together. She shoved an extra pair of socks in but otherwise decided to wear the same clothes until she got back. As a last-minute thought, she grabbed a bar of soap and a small box of baking soda for her teeth. In the kitchen, she wrapped a loaf of bread in a towel and stuck it in her saddlebags. She filled her canteen, threw some coffee in a bag with three tin cups and two handfuls of beef jerky, and headed out to the corral.

Elijah sauntered over and shook hands with Gray and Alan before shyly offering his hand to Ally. She put her arm around his shoulder and whispered for him to take care of himself. The whole leaving, though for only three days, made her old caretaker quite sad.

"I suppose I better say something to Josh before we leave," she said, staring at him milling around in the barn.

"Shoulda let the ol' boy pout," Elijah grunted.

When Josh saw Ally, he picked up a hammer and nails and headed over to the lumber pile. Ally thought he meant to discourage her from approaching him. Already aggravated, this little stunt irritated her more.

"I wanted to say something to you before I leave." Ally tried to smile and sound pleasant.

"Well, what?"

Josh refused to look at her. He kept picking up boards.

Angry about his insolence, Ally backed away. "I changed my mind. You're acting like a jackass. I hope you're over it by the time I'm back," she said, quite acerbically.

The first dissimilarity in Ally's demeanor when she came back was the grim and determined, downright gloomy expression on her face. She took her reins from Elijah without saying a word. Mounting, she pulled her hat down. "Are you two ready?"

Neither man said anything. They moved their horses alongside hers and headed out in a slow walk. Ally said nothing to Elijah and certainly nothing to Josh as the three rode away.

Less than a half-mile into their trip, Gray said they needed to pick up the pace a little unless they wanted to take a week getting to Kane's place. "Fine," Ally said, kicking her horse into a lope. Gray and Alan both stopped and stared at her riding away.

"Now, what do you suppose got a bur under her saddle?" Alan asked, flummoxed at Ally's behavior.

"How would I know what a woman's thinking? You're the married one, not me. You're the one who should understand women."

"Reminds me of something your sister would do."

"Well, you're mistaken about Jeannie," Gray said. "Jeannie would make it plain what any bur under her saddle was about."

The two men decided they should catch the woman before she got lost or headed in the wrong direction. Kicking their horses into a lope, Gray pulled up alongside Ally. "I meant a brisker walk when I said pick up the pace, not a damned horserace."

Neither hot nor dry days were unusual during Wyoming summers. Most, like this one, were both. By early afternoon the horses got thirsty and grumpy. Gray's stud began resenting Ally's gelding. He suddenly swirled and gave him a solid kick in the shoulder. Gray dug his heels into the blue roan's flanks, getting him away from Ally's sorrel. He spun the horse around a couple of times and made him back away at a rapid pace, especially for a horse going backward. "Quit! What's the matter with you?" Gray had the animal standing still almost as fast as the horse exploded. "Are you alright? Doc's still young, and he'll surprise you sometimes."

Ally's horse, the alpha among her small group of horses, stood nervously licking his lips, not wanting any further business with the bossy stud. Gray moved his horse back over toward Ally, which didn't work out. The stallion threw his head out and gave Ally's horse a nasty bite. Gray jerked Doc's head around and gave him a sharp slap on the mouth.

"I'm lucky he bit the horse and not me," Ally said good-naturedly.

"Doc's not after you. He's upset at your gelding," Gray replied, also good-naturedly.

"Why's he mad at Cisco? He hasn't done anything to your stallion."

"I guess he expects a little respect," Gray said. "He thinks your horse is acting a little uppity."

"Well, I'll discuss the matter with him," Ally said, a smile crossing her face.

"How come you named him Cisco?"

Ally said he had the name when Sam bought him, and he didn't bother to ask. Sam, she said, accepted things without much interest in the why. Gray decided since Ally brought up the why of things, this would be an excellent time to pursue any why relating to Dierden Kane's aggression toward her.

Ally rubbed the back of her neck, shrugged her shoulders.

Alan asked about any run-ins between her husband and Kane. Ally said Kane bullied Sam a little when they ran into each other at Fort Laramie or in town. She described it as belittling Sam, more than bullying him. She claimed nothing physical ever happened between them. While Sam Hart would defend himself, he had not been a confrontational man. He preferred to reason and negotiate an outcome rather than make specific demands.

"As far as I know, Kane never told Sam to leave. Simply humiliated him in front of others, especially me. Sam believed when someone tried to humiliate a person, they only succeeded in reducing themselves."

Ally did not agree. When her parents died, before Judge Starrett took them in, she and her sister dealt with humiliation. Several families passed them back and forth; none of them able to afford two extra children. A local court decided an orphanage would be the best answer, and that's where they would have ended up, except for the young lawyer and his wife stepping in. Sam simply brushed aside humiliation; Ally did not. Kane didn't care about humiliating her; he wanted her gone.

Ally could see Gray did not believe her when she said she did not know why Kane disliked her. Did he did not think a man like Kane was capable of loathing someone for no reason?

Chapter Forty-Eight

John Coffee Hayes and a small group of Texas Rangers hounded Dierden Kane out of Texas. That took place in 1848, after years of Kane stealing horses and cattle, raping, pillaging, and probably committing at least three murders. Unfortunately, they couldn't gather enough reliable evidence to hang the man. No one caught him in possession of stolen livestock. Two women who accused him of rape refused to testify in court; one testified she never accused Kane. Her story changed after her husband left on an unexpected "business trip," not returning until after the case's dismissal. With no witnesses to the murders, charges were never filed. The brother of one of the murdered men promised to kill Kane, but he either lost his nerve or never found the opportunity.

After fleeing Texas, Kane spent a brief time in Arkansas, where they suspected him of robbing a Fort Smith bank and killing a clerk. A posse chased him for two full weeks before giving up and heading home with, according to the dead clerk's wife, their tails between their legs.

Kane arrived in Wyoming with enough money to build a fine house on the land he claimed and stock his new ranch with cattle. Early on, a few of the smaller homesteaders alleged Kane put his brand on some of their livestock. With no law to help them, their only recourse was branding their calves almost as soon as they dropped. Dierden Kane flourished, while many of the other ranchers struggled and failed. When they went bust, Kane snatched up their cattle and land. Within three years of his arrival, almost all his neighbors, if you called people living ten or more miles away neighbors, gave up and pulled out—or met with an unexpected death.

This afternoon, Dierden Kane stood in the door of his barn, watching the men on his ranch work. Kane did not hire true cowhands. The men he hired grasped how to move cattle around from one place to another. A few of them might throw a lasso well enough to rope a cow. They managed to brand a cow, do menial tasks like repairing a fence or slapping paint on Kane's extravagant house. One or two could shoe a horse. Still, calling them cowhands would have been a stretch. He hired rough men, not necessarily cowboys. His men cared little regarding whether they worked for an honest man or a dishonest one. As long as Kane paid and provided plenty of whiskey, they carried out orders, ready to harm anyone Kane wanted hurt.

Kane's foreman joined him in the barn door. Kane looked over at him. "What'd you say the new fella's name is?"

"Smith."

"I'll bet." Kane spit. "He say where he came from?" For some reason, he couldn't lay his finger on, the new man perturbed Kane.

The foreman sensed Kane's concern regarding the recent hire. "I don't think I asked him. You think you know him from somewhere?"

"I'm not sure," Kane said. "Something about him makes

me nervous. I don't like gettin' nervous." An imperial mustache was his only distinguishing feature. Kane couldn't' pinpoint why the man concerned him. He didn't care. This fella did not sit right with him. "Git rid of him."

Kane headed off toward his house. Behind him, his foreman yelled over to the man Kane wanted gone.

"Mr. Kane doesn't like you, Smith. Pack your stuff and get gone."

"What'd I do?'

"Don't matter. The boss wants you gone. You got thirty minutes."

From a window on the second floor of his house, Kane watched Smith ride off. Then he sat down to nurse a bottle of rye.

As the afternoon stretched on and grew hotter, both Gray and Alan rode in silence. The quiet gave Ally time to think about her life and about being on her own—for the first time. Barely eight when her parents died, her mother first, and her father only weeks later, she was her sister's keeper when Judge Dan and his wife became their caretakers.

The Starretts, both thirty-seven, had an eighteen-year-old daughter. She married only a month after Ally and Ruthie were taken in but never officially adopted. The girls always called them Dan and Mary, never Father or Mother. Dan and Mary always treated them like daughters. Dan occasionally applied a hickory switch to their backsides, but only if well earned. Ruthie earned switchings more frequently than Alice.

Mary showed the girls equal love. Dan also loved them both and did not indicate any preference. Still, Alice recognized he favored her. She and Dan were strong-willed, very much alike.

Dan and Alice engaged in long talks, talks in which Dan praised her for being smart. Zealously curious, she became an avid reader. Alice possessed a remarkable ability to adapt to her situation. Regardless of what boundaries and restrictions Dan put on her, they turned out to be only minor complications, simple snags she quickly overcame to accomplish her goals.

A local boy named Stevens was the first to court her. Though she allowed him to take her to dances, church socials, and other activities, she had no genuine interest in him. At the time, being a wife held no attraction for Ally, especially being a wife to a man who displayed a temper and promptly cuffed a woman when a good smack pleased him.

Finally, Ally declined Stevens' request to take her out. The refusal did not sit well with him. He tried to kiss her, but she turned her face away. Infuriated, he slapped her across the mouth and gave her a shove, which sent her to the ground. Quite a wrestling match ensued. Dan Starrett heard the commotion, pulled Stevens up to his feet, and delivered a knee-deep into the man's groin, a lesson Ally would remember.

After Dan saved her from being assaulted by her former suitor, Ally agreed to allow Sam to court her and eventually married him. They moved from place to place before Sam insisted they should live in Wyoming. She balked at first but gave in, hoping Sam was right.

Then the bull gored Sam. The bull charged Sam's horse, knocking him over. In the horse's wild attempts to regain his feet, Sam lost his seat in the saddle and fell off. The raging animal turned on Sam, picking him up on his horns and throwing him into the air. Sam hit the ground on his head and right side, breaking several bones.

The bull butted him hard, time and again, before savagely sinking a horn into Sam's right side. Sam screamed in agony, trying to free himself of the horn. The beast threw his head back with extreme violence, again throwing Sam in the air. The bull charged, head down, this time driving both horns into Sam. Elijah raced his horse toward the bull while swinging a coiled rope at the animal. The enraged bull retreated to the edge of the river, where he leisurely laid down.

By the time Elijah returned with the doctor, Sam's breathing was shallow, almost undetectable. The physician, an Eastern-educated surgeon holding the rank of major, told Ally her husband was dying, bleeding to death.

Now, with Judge Dan in St. Louis, Ruthie in Texas, and Sam in his grave, Ally found herself for the first time on her own. She half-expected Josh to be gone when she got back, leaving her right where Sam left her when he died, still with only an old man to help, but with more cattle to tend.

Hot and tired, they came to a fair-sized creek. Only an hour or so before they would lose daylight, Gray said they might as well stop for the night, pleasing Ally.

Alan went off to gather up some firewood. Gray went off to scare up something to eat. Ally wandered down to the creek. It was wider than she expected and lined with trees on both sides. Fifteen or twenty yards downstream, she found a deep hole. Hot and sweaty, the creek offered an inviting place for a swim. However, since her two companions might return at any time, she would forego swimming. She settled instead for rolling up her sleeves and splashing a little water on her face and neck.

In only a few minutes, Alan came back with an armful of wood to start a fire. Another half-hour passed before Gray came back empty-handed.

"I guess it's jerky and your bread tonight," he said.

Ally got a loaf of bread and a considerable amount of jerky out of her saddlebags. Alan, fussy about coffee brewing, volunteered for the job.

"There's an art to making good coffee," he said, "and Gray's no artist."

"I make good coffee," Ally said.

"Well, I tasted yours, not bad," Alan said. "But brewin' coffee over a fire, *that* takes a particular skill. You must be meticulous. Most women never master coffee over an open flame. A man, although Gray ain't one who's learned, a man makes better coffee over a fire. Adding the right amount of chicory, which I happen to have, right here in my pocket, that's the secret."

Alan rubbed some chicory between his hands and dropped a few pinches in the steeping pot. "You'll notice I let the coffee start to brew before sprinkling in the chicory. And the perfect amount of chicory, not too little, not too much. We'll let this boil a bit. You're in for quite a treat."

"A bunch of horses, unshod ones, crossed the creek," Gray said, casually pointing down the creek as Ally handed him a piece of bread. "They're heading west, the same as we are. Don't know how long ago. I might have some idea if I checked the tracks on the other side, but I didn't want to wade across."

"How many?" Alan asked.

"Eight or ten, I don't think more than a dozen," Gray answered. "Likely a hunting party. I don't think we need to worry. My guess is Cheyenne or Arapaho. I think most of the Sioux are a little to the northeast."

Alan poured everyone a cup of his coffee. Ally and Gray sipped theirs without saying anything. "Well?"

"Well, what?" Ally asked.

Chapter Forty-Nine

Gray was sitting by the creek, tossing pebbles in, when Ally came up behind him. "Can't sleep again?"

Gray glanced at her. "Too hot and muggy."

"I've been hot and miserable all day," Ally said.

"That why you couldn't sleep?"

Ally sat beside him and paused before answering. "No. I'm concerned about tomorrow."

"You'll be fine," Gray said.

Try as she might, Ally could not quite come to grips with her upcoming confrontation with Dierden Kane. From what little Gray said, they would ride up to Kane's house, knock on the door, and she would simply tell him to stay off her land, stop harassing her, that would be that.

"Gray," she said, unsure and nervous about how to make him talk about the next day. "You don't think he's going to leave me alone because I ride on his ranch and tell him to, do you? Be truthful with me."

"Well, to begin with, the first thing you're going to tell

him is you know he burned your barn and killed four of your cows. To ensure he's listening, you're going to tell him while gouging him in the chest with my spare pistol. While you're poking him, tell him to leave you alone."

"I can't aim a gun at a man!"

"You pointed one at his men the day he came on your porch," Gray said. "You're not going to point at him anyway. You're going to jab this ol' Navy Colt right into his breast bone. Do it hard enough to make it hurt."

"You have lost your mind!"

"That may be true." Gray half-laughed. "But if you don't toughen up, you're going to lose everything."

Ally leaned back and stared at Gray. He seriously expected her to stick a gun in a man's chest. "Fine, but what if he refuses? What if he tells me to clear out of the territory?"

"Pull the trigger." Gray didn't even glance her way. He just sat tossing pebbles in the river.

"I'm not going to plain murder a man. What kind of person do you think I am? What the hell kind of person are you?" Ally moved beyond disbelief to anger. Tomorrow instead of going to Kane's ranch, she would turn back and go home. If Wehr and Joseph wanted their damn cattle back, fine.

The only thing Ally did not understand was why she was still sitting on the bank. Why didn't she walk away? Yet, Ally sat next to him, staring off across the creek, angry at the man, as mad as she ever remembered being. The longer she stayed, the angrier she got at herself for not leaving. Never a person not to act on her feelings, she was upset and disappointed in herself.

Gray was not sympathetic or kind; his tone bordered on harsh. "Ally, you don't seem to get it through your head. You are not dealing with a normal man. You're dealing with someone who is barely human. The man burned your barn, killed your cattle. There's no guessing how many people he's murdered, and he's going to kill you unless you run or stop him."

His eyes burning down on her, Gray made his thoughts very clear.

"If you think for one minute Kane's going to back down, you are mistaken. The Army won't consider this as their matter, and there is no real law out here. You'll stand up for yourself, or you'll die. Your only other choice is to run."

An awkward silence came—and went.

"You don't strike me as a runner." Gray scowled at her. "Don't kill him tomorrow, fine, but you listen to me, sooner or later, you'll kill him because if you don't, he'll kill you."

Gray abruptly stood, got more intense, actually began to shake.

"When he kills you, he'll also kill that ol' man of yours when Elijah tries to protect you, and then, just for the hell of it, he'll kill that greenhorn working for you. Your choices are damned limited! You better understand them."

Gray turned and stomped off in the dark. Alice Hart sat quietly, watching him walk away. Frustration started her crying. Crying made her frustration worse. She was lost, with no rational resolution left. She hated everyone. Elijah, because she felt obligated to protect him. McCormick because she thought he'd be gone when she got back. She loathed Sam for putting her into these circumstances. Gray for being so heartlessly blunt about everything. She hated herself for blaming others for her problems. Most of all, Ally hated Kane for being the cause of everything.

Ally regained her composure and followed Gray into the darkness. She found him standing by the creek. He turned toward her but did not say anything. He looked too outraged to speak. "I'm sorry," she said, hardly loud enough to be heard. "I understand it's my best interests you're thinking about." She stopped looking at him and gazed off across the water. "Are those antelope across there?"

"I think about a dozen."

Gray still sounded mad. Ally turned back toward him and touched his arm. "Gray, I can't shoot a man like that. I can't." She waited only briefly for an answer before continuing. No reply was coming anyway. "I'll fight, and if I'm forced to kill him in a fight, I will, but I can't shoot him in cold blood."

Gray exploded. "Damn it, woman! It won't be in cold blood. Cold blood would be if you walked up and shot him without a word. You're going to confront him. When you brace him, do you think he's going to give you a sweet smile and agree? He won't. The man is deranged, wicked. He's pure evil." Gray shook his head and turned away.

Ally suddenly understood his reputation, the hushed rumors, and harrowing tales she had been hearing since he brought the cattle to her ranch. Stories of a hard man, a gunman with no compunction about blowing a man all over a street. A man as barbaric as this wild land.

Gray's temper pacified as quickly as it flashed. He turned back toward Ally, his anger gone. His calm demeanor unnerved her. He was an absolute contradiction.

"All right, Ally, we'll do this your way. I still want you to take my spare pistol when we confront him. If his men start shooting, Alan and I will want all the help we can get."

Ally sat at the edge of the water. After a minute, Gray sat beside her, and they both watched the antelope drinking across the creek. "I'm surprised they don't run," Ally said. How immediately she became comfortable with this man concerned her. She was totally at peace with Gray. Just who was the contradiction?

"I wouldn't be surprised if elk stayed around, as long as we're on this side of the creek. Antelope, though, are usually pretty jumpy," Gray said. Several minutes passed in silence.

"Ally," Gray said, turning to look at her, "maybe instead of shooting him in the chest, shoot at his feet, don't hit them, just make him dance."

Ally laughed a little at this bewildering man. A short time later, she surprised herself again by laying her head on his shoulder. Gray stiffened a little. She was embarrassing him, at least a touch, but she left her head resting on his shoulder. After a time of sitting, a time Ally enjoyed, she sat up straight. "Sam used to tell me I can tell what other people are thinking," she said. "I don't think so, but when I told you this afternoon, I don't know why Kane dislikes me. I don't think you believed me." She started to wait for an answer, decided not to.

"Gray, I don't. Kane's always been aggressive, telling us to leave. After Sam died, he got meaner, more personal. He told me he's going to kill me if I don't go. He never threatened that before. That's the only thing I didn't tell you. I don't understand why he holds such hatred toward me."

Gray did not speak. He shook his head a little. Without thinking about how the man might respond, she touched his face. "Would you hold me? I'm so tired of being alone." She did not make him hold her long, although she wanted him to, his arms were comfortable and warm. "We should head back to camp."

As Gray stood, she mentioned being hot and tempted to take a dip in the creek. Gray laughed and told her if she wanted to skinny dip, he'd be happy to watch. She jabbed him in the ribs, saying, "I don't swim alone," as she headed back toward their campsite, a little disappointed.

Chapter Fifty

At least an hour before daybreak, Gray restarted the campfire. Even though Alan would be unhappy and complain about its quality, Gray made coffee and then saddled the horses. He sliced some bacon off a slab that he and Alan had left over from their ride down from High Meadows. They had the bacon because Jean insisted they take it along, contending that it was preposterous to shoot something for every meal. Not that he would ever admit it to Jean, but Gray was grateful she had been so persistent about the bacon. After all, just last night, he had found nothing to shoot, and eating jerky could get tiresome.

Only a few minutes later, the smell of breakfast cooking woke Ally. Gray had to roust Alan, who had not as much as twitched in his bedroll. "There's not much to throwing some bacon over a fire," Gray said when Ally told him that he should have awakened her to cook the breakfast.

"I wish you'd have got me up too," Alan said. "Now, I've got to drink your rotten coffee."

"I don't know that anybody's forcing it on you," Gray said.

"Do you have a watch?" Alan asked Gray. "You are aware that it's still pitch dark, aren't you?"

"What I'm aware of," Gray said, "is that I want to get to Kane's place as early in the day as possible."

Gray ignored Alan's suggestion that maybe they should have just ridden all night if that was so blamed important. Alan then told Gray that he could shoot Kane in the afternoon just as easily as he could shoot him in the morning.

"I'm not shooting him at all," Gray said. "Ally is."

"I'm not going to shoot Kane," Ally snapped, biting her words off, but clearly in good humor.

"I thought we decided you'd shoot him."

Ally just shook her head. She cut everyone a slice of bread and put three strips of bacon on each. Then she sat down next to the fire with her two companions. Alan poured a cup of coffee and handed it to Ally, who blew on it and took her first drink. "Oh my, that stuff is awful!"

Gray argued with Ally that his coffee was just fine, excellent, in fact. Alan maintained that they would have had better coffee if Gray had warmed up the dregs of what he'd made yesterday.

Gray announced that he wanted coffee when he drank coffee, not some vile potion concocted with chicory. Ally claimed that if she had a fork with her, she could stand it straight up in that thick goo. Gray told her that she should add some water or cream if it was too strong for her delicate mouth. "Well, I don't have any cream," Ally said. "Besides, adding water or cream, or sugar for that matter, is no cure for bad coffee. Once coffee is too strong, there's no fixing it."

Gray drank another cup before telling the others he was going to throw the rest on the fire, and they could climb on their horses. Ally said there wasn't enough coffee left to put the fire out. She added, "I'm surprised there is so little left, considering the quality of it."

Gray told Ally about his dear mother, how she said, "If

you can't say something, nice, you shouldn't say anything. Since I built the fire, it's you folks' responsibility to put it out."

That was Gray's final word on coffee, breakfast, and fires.

"If we're still following those pony tracks after it gets light, I guess we ought to take a closer look at them," Alan said. "If they turn off in another direction, I guess they won't matter.

"If they could smell that coffee this morning, I'm sure they've gone in another direction." Ally laughed, getting one last jab in.

While breaking camp, the reality of what lay ahead later in the morning started to weigh on Ally. When Gray asked her if she was ready, Ally simply said she was prepared to go, but not sure she was ready for what could happen once they made it to Kane's place. She surprised Alan, but especially Gray, when she told him that she might as well take his spare pistol now. He unbuckled his saddlebag and handed her a Navy Colt.

"I've got a holster for it if you want it," he said, giving her the pistol.

"No, I'll just stick it in my belt," she said. For the next hour, Ally rode in silence, her thoughts taken up by what might happen later. What troubled her most wasn't facing Kane; she knew that was something she'd have to do if she had any hope at all of staying on her place.

What troubled Ally was her lack of experience in confrontation, at least in a confrontation like this. She had confronted Sam on occasion, standing her ground in arguments. Simply because she wanted it, she forced Sam to add a wrap-around porch onto their house, even though it served no real purpose and stretched their financial means. She had no misgivings about confronting the storekeeper in town, telling him his prices were nothing more than robbery. She once demanded that Burton Brown improve the price he was offering for some of their cattle. But, in truth, the consequences of those minor skirmishes were trifling. Little in her life would have changed whether she triumphed or lost.

This time, however, winning or losing would make a difference. The hitch in this situation was that if she won, nothing changed. She really wouldn't gain anything that she didn't already have, not unless she counted peace of mind, and peace of mind in her world was a tenuous thing. It was dependent on cattle prices, weather, the Indians' mood, and how many hands she could hire.

Conversely, if she lost, she would most likely lose everything: her stock, her home, and probably even her life. It wasn't only her life that might be at stake. It was Elijah and Josh, and now Gray and Alan, she was putting in danger.

Gray spotted a lone rider heading in their direction. "Who do you suppose that is?" he asked.

"Probably one of Kane's men," Alan said. "I wouldn't think anybody else would be out here. He doesn't seem to be in any hurry," he said.

A few minutes later, they stopped alongside the man, who was riding a nice-looking paint horse. "We're a little surprised to come across somebody all alone out here," Gray said, extending his hand to the man wearing an imperial mustache. Something that made him look like a shyster or knave, at least in Gray's opinion.

"Hal Smith," the man said. "Headed for Fort Laramie. I've got a brother in the Army there."

"I have a little ranch a few miles from there," Ally said.

The happy-go-lucky expression that Smith had been wearing faded a little. He twisted in his saddle and looked like he might have something to say that was going to cause him a little uneasiness. "Ma'am, your name wouldn't be Hart, would it?"

"Ally Hart," she said.

Smith rubbed the back of his neck. "This makes me feel

a little awkward, Mrs. Hart. I worked for Dierden Kane the past four days, 'til he ran me off yesterday."

"We're on our way to pay him a little visit," Gray said. "I'd say you're not too particular about who you work for."

Smith laughed just a little about that. "Well, normally, I try to be. But, in this case, I can't argue with you." Smith tapped his reins on his chaps. "He offered me the job in that little town there just outside the fort. A couple of soldiers at the fort told me not to take his job. My brother told me I was a blamed fool if I did. But I needed a job, and there didn't seem to be too many around."

"Four days," Alan noted. "I'd say it didn't last long."

"Worse yet, he didn't pay me. Jist told me to git. I'd already decided that I'd work through a week, and then when I got my pay, I was going to take off. I'd settled it in my mind that I didn't need a job bad enough to stick with that outfit."

Smith seemed honest enough in what he was saying.

"You should know something, Mrs. Hart. I heard Kane talking to some of his men about you. He's planning on doing you some harm. The point Kane made was that you don't learn. I don't know if you know, but he burned your barn down and killed a few of your cattle. In the next week or two, he plans to burn your entire place down and take the rest of your cattle. Kane knows he can't sell those cows you've got with that outfit from up north's brand on 'em, but he says he can use them for breeding stock and make plenty of money off their calves." Smith took his hat off and hung it on his saddle horn. "Worse yet, ma'am, this time, he plans on killing you and those men you've got working for you."

Gray stiffened in his saddle. "What were you going to do with this information?" he asked. "Were you gonna let this woman get killed?"

"I ain't such low scum as that," Smith said. "I told you as soon as I collected a week's pay, I was pullin' out. I'd have told the military and then found her place to warn her."

Gray still wondered why a man wouldn't move on when he found out the man he worked for was planning a murder.

He wondered enough about it that he confronted Smith.

Smith was a bit piqued at Gray's allegation and pointed out that he could have kept his mouth shut, not said anything about Kane's plans.

Gray didn't respond. He just stared at the man.

Alan did ask how many men Kane had working for him.

"Thirteen at the ranch. Some don't like that 'cause they think it's unlucky," Smith said. "Supposed to be two more out at a line camp. I guess that's true—never saw 'em myself." Smith took a flask out of his shirt pocket and took a long, slow drink.

He offered it to Gray and Alan, but both declined.

"He likes to bluff people that he has twenty-five or thirty, but it ain't the truth."

Smith and Gray continued to stare at each other.

"How much further is it to Kane's place?" Ally asked.

"Around three hours, more or less," Smith said. "There's a creek about an hour from here. I spent last night there. Figured I could make the fort if I pushed hard today."

"You can make it, but it will be after dark when you get there," Ally said.

"Why does Kane hate Mrs. Hart so much?" Gray asked.

"Don't know, you'd have to ask Kane."

Gray was not happy with the answer.

Smith said he needed to be on his way and headed off to the east. Before he did, he warned them about Cheyenne moving around in the area.

Alan stared at the man as he rode off and then looked over at Gray. "You think he's lyin' about Kane kicking him off his place?"

"No, I don't think he's lying about that. I'd run off anybody wearing a mustache like that myself," Gray said. "I don't quite trust a man that would stay around when he knew Kane was planning a murder." Gray, although he didn't know for sure that he was right about Smith, was correct in his judgment.

Less than an hour after riding off from Smith, they reached the creek that he'd mentioned. Ally's mood had been gloomy since the meeting with Smith. She was tired of sweating. Her hair was damp and limp, her shirt was clinging to her wet body, and she was just overall miserable. Neither Alan nor Gray were talkative, which made the ride seem even longer. Gray had not smiled since they broke camp and mounted their horses, something else that worried her.

She was distraught over Smith's statement that Kane intended to kill her. She had *thought* he might try to kill her. Now, she had corroboration. Ally tried to shut it out of her mind, but she couldn't. Worse yet, she kept thinking about how Kane might do it. Shoot her, stab her, hang her, maybe even burn her. Ally believed he was capable of all those things. Burning scared her the most, and it seemed the most likely. Kane hated her enough to kill, so he probably hated her enough to want her to suffer and die in pain.

Pale and quivering, Ally reached for Gray. "I'm afraid of Kane. I can't do this," she whispered so that only Gray would hear. For whatever reason was in her head, she didn't want Alan to know.

"You'll be fine," Gray said, but he couldn't relieve her distress or soothe her agitation.

"Kane and his men, they'll kill us. Take me home."

"Ally, you're fretting yourself sick for nothing," Gray said. "If we don't confront him, he'll never leave you alone."

"Take me home!" Ally screamed. She didn't care if Alan heard. She didn't care who heard.

Suddenly Gray turned impertinent. "No."

Ally was stunned by his spitefulness. "You bastard!"

"Maybe so, but we're not going back without facing Kane."

Biting at her bottom lip, her chin trembling, tears started to run down Ally's face.

Alan took Gray by the arm. "If she doesn't want to go, we don't have any right to force her."

Gray's eyes narrowed, his jaw clenched. Now he was scaring her.

"I never took you for a coward," she heard him snap at Alan. Ally shied away from the men, positive there would be a fight.

"Stop it. I don't want to cause a fight between you two."

Gray turned away from Alan, back toward Ally, pointing his finger at her. "We're not going back."

"You can't stop me." There was no fight in her voice. She was defeated. Going home was the easier of two bad alternatives. Maybe it was weak, but it was better than facing the fear of the other. Because of the look Gray was giving her, she thought she was going to vomit.

"No, I suppose I can't," Gray said. "But if you turn back, I'll start for High Meadows, right now."

Ally climbed off her horse, ran her hand through her sweaty hair before slumping down to the ground. A small scorpion caught her eye. When he started toward her, she picked up a stick and swatted him away. Truth was setting in. She could smell her fear, and it had a terrible stench. For some reason, she pushed her hand down into the dirt. When she raised her hand, the imprint seemed too small. It made her feel small. She shook her hand as if she could shake off her fear, along with the sand. The fear had to go. She had to swat that scorpion Kane away. She just needed a bigger stick. "Alright, I'll go." She didn't look at Gray or Alan, Merely brushed off her pants and stepped up on her horse. Gray walked over to her, so damn casual about it.

He patted her knee. "Trust me," Gray whispered as calmly as if he was merely telling her to believe he could saddle her horse.

Ally had stopped being surprised by people, but Gray frequently surprised her—when he shot ol' Satan, when he refused her request for help that night behind her house, when he came back to help her, and especially now because she did trust him.

Ally's chin was quivering again. "Protect me."

"Depend on it."

Ally would. Her other choices weren't that good.

Two hours later, they came up the crown of a rise, and Ally got her first look at the Kane ranch. "That's quite a house," she said. A fresh coat of white paint made the house shine in the bright sun. The black shutters added to its sophisticated-looking exterior, something that Ally mentioned to her escorts.

"The house may be sophisticated," Gray said, "but the man who lives in it isn't unless you consider a hog wallowing in the mud sophisticated."

"You see Kane anywhere down there?" Alan asked.

Ally looked carefully at the porch on the house, around the barn and corral. None of the three men milling around was Kane.

"He's in the barn," Gray said.

"I can't see anybody in the barn," Alan said, squinting to see into the dark barn.

"You should have been paying more attention. Kane just walked past the doorway," Gray said. "He's in the left side of the barn."

"I sure didn't see anybody walk across that door," Alan said skeptically. "I hope you're right. I'd hate to think we rode this far for nothing."

"I'm right," Gray said.

For the next few minutes, they stayed on the ridge, watching the limited activity down around Kane's corrals and house. Ally wished that Kane would come out of the barn to settle it in her mind that he was, in truth, on the place. She also wished that they would just start down the hill. The watching was making her nervous and was serving no point that she could grasp. Gray barely moved. He simply sat on his horse, studying the area below him.

Five more minutes passed before he muttered, "Let's head on down there."

Ally's apprehension returned as they rode down the hill. She tried to look over the entire area, wondering how many of Kane's men might be in the barn with him or behind the barn, any place they might be out of sight. Back on the top of the rise, she'd wanted to get this over. Now that they were almost to the first corral, she was so frightened she felt she was going to be sick. If she was going to be sick, Ally hoped she could put it off long enough that she could retch on Kane's feet.

As soon as Kane's men noticed them, all three ranch hands came out to challenge them. The oldest of the three demanded to know who they were and what they were doing riding onto Kane's property. Without uttering a word, in one motion, Gray yanked and cocked his pistol. Pointing it right at the chest of the man who had been talking, he told them they were here to see Kane, but to assure a safe visit, he wanted all three to hand their guns up to his partner.

"Much obliged," Alan said when each handed him their pistol.

Gray asked if anybody was in the barn with Kane, to which one of Kane's men said no, that he was alone. Gray tapped the man on the head with his pistol. "If that turns out not to be true, you're the first one I'll shoot. Now all of you turn around and start walking toward that barn. If any of you as much as open your mouth, you'll find out how hot hell is."

Once they were at the barn, Gray had the entire group stand off to the side of the door where no one inside the barn could see them. He leaned over and whispered something to one of Kane's men. "Now," Gray yelled when the man didn't do anything.

"Kane, you better come on out here. You've got some visitors that you'll want to see."

Kane hollered back, wanting to know who it was.

"You better come on out here and see," the hired man yelled back.

Kane came out of the barn carrying an armful of harness. As soon as he saw Gray, he tried to drop the harness and grab at his gun.

"Bad idea," Gray said, pointing his pistol at Kane.

It was a bad idea. When Kane dropped the harness, a good part of it hung up on his pistol. Ally could have taken the spare pistol Gray had given her out of her belt and emptied it into his fat belly before Kane could have freed his revolver from the harness.

Ruined by his predicament, Kane asked what the hell they were doing on his land.

"Just your lucky day, I guess," Gray said in a brazen tone.

"You better hope the rest of my men don't come back."

Gray laughed at him. "That's no way to treat guests, Dierden." Gray took his right foot out of his stirrup and laid it across his saddle horn.

"You're a damn casual fella, ain't you?" Kane snorted.

"Why wouldn't I be?" Gray said. "It's a beautiful sunny day. I'm surrounded by friends, had some crisp bacon for breakfast this morning. It was a nice leisurely ride over here. Why it's been a fine day. So far, anyway."

Alan was irritated by Gray's demeanor. He always had to be so cavalier.

Gray pushed his hat up off his forehead. "You don't seem happy to see us," Gray said. "So, let's get down to business, Dierden. If it gets much hotter, I might start to get less agreeable. Mrs. Hart here wants to have a little discussion with you." Gray looked over at Ally. "You might as well go ahead, Alice."

Surprising Gray, Ally stepped down off her horse and handed him the reins. More surprising, she took the pistol out of her belt, cocked it, and pointed it at Kane. "You burned my barn. You killed four of my cows, and I found out this morning you plan to kill me."

"You're crazy," Kane said.

His denial enraged Ally. "Don't you lie to me," she shrieked in a nervous rage. "Don't lie to me!"

Kane tried to look up at Gray and Alan. "Git this lunatic

away from me," he said. Neither Gray nor Alan said a word or even moved. Kane erupted in a profanity-filled rage aimed primarily at Ally but including Gray. He screamed at his men to do something. One of Kane's men did ask Kane just what he wanted them to do with three people pointing cocked guns at them. Kane, shrieking like a madman, swore to kill Ally and then told Gray that after he finished with the Hart whore, he'd gut him. Gray laughed at him.

Ally didn't laugh. Her face flushed with anger as fury overcame her. For the first time in her life, she utterly hated another person. When Stevens was courting her, especially after he hit her, she was afraid of him. She certainly never wanted to be around him again. Ally didn't like him, but she wouldn't have said she hated him. Kane was different. She hated Kane. She hated him because he had bullied her, burned her barn, killed her cattle, and now was threatening to kill her. However, those things, as horrible as they were, weren't the real reasons for her loathing the man. The real reason was that he did not respect her; he considered her less than human.

Suddenly, without one word of warning, Ally rammed her knee hard into the man's groin, quite the surprise to both Gray and Alan. Kane was likely surprised as well. Gray probably would have enjoyed asking him if he was surprised. It seemed likely that he was, but right now, Kane was too busy rolling around in the dirt and groaning to respond to any questions.

Gray laughed. "Damn, woman. My sister couldn't have done that better."

One of Kane's three men took a step toward Ally.

Gray waved his gun at the man. "Not a good idea."

Some of Ally's composure returned, and she bent down over Kane, lying in a fetal position swearing at her. She poked him with the pistol. "You listen to me. If you think I won't stand up for myself and fight back, then you've damn well underestimated me." Looking down at the man, she again lost her composure. Shaking with anger, she screamed at him that she wasn't going to take any more bullying from him. "You've pushed me far enough. I'm not some animal, and you're not going to treat me like one. I'm tired of it, and it's going to stop." Satisfied with Kane writhing around in the dirt, she turned her attention to his three men. "You should find yourselves a better place to work. This pig is going to get you killed."

A slow learner, Kane moaned something about sending Ally to hell, causing Gray to step off his horse and kick him in the face, rendering him unconscious. Ally briefly resented Gray interceding, telling him she could take care of herself.

"I can see that," Gray said. "I just didn't want you to kill him."

"I wasn't going to kill him," Ally said somewhat mildly and almost smiling. "I was going to kick his nuts again."

"I hope I never make you mad," Gray laughed.

Ally,. embarrassed by her statement, at least mildly embarrassed, gave Gray a self-conscious smile. "Well, you better not," she said. "As you can see, I have hard knees."

Alan Joseph, who had almost seemed removed from the events of the last few minutes, started to laugh. "You remind me a little of his sister," he said, smiling at her, "except Jean would have shot him."

Gray looked hard at one of Kane's men. "Where are your ropes?"

"What do you want with a rope?"

"I need them to hang you with," Gray said.

Alan protested the idea of hanging them. Gray laughed off Alan's uneasiness, indicating that maybe tying them up might suffice. He told Alan to look in the barn for ropes and a bridle.

"What do we need a bridle for?"

"Dierden's going with us. I'm not sure Dierden is quite convinced yet about our message."

On his way in the barn, Alan asked one of the men where he'd find a rope, and bridle, and a saddle.

"No saddle, just a bridle," Gray said.

Once Gray had Kane's men trussed up to his satisfaction, all three hanging over the top rail of the corral with their hands and feet tightly tied to the bottom rail, he delivered quite a sermon on how they would not be wise to follow after them. If they did, he promised to shoot Kane as soon as he saw them coming.

They left with Kane flopped over the horse's back, like a dead man. Before they reached the top of the first rise, Alan was questioning why they brought Kane along.

Ally thought the reason should have been apparent. Gray thought the question idiotic. By the time they covered about four miles, it was noon, and the day was brutally hot. Kane, who swore like a drunken trooper for the first two miles before begging to be untied, had at last shut up.

After another thirty minutes or so, Gray decided they'd come far enough to cut Kane loose and let him ride the horse in a usual manner. Periodically over the next two hours, Kane would launch into a new cussing fit, threatening what he was going to do once he got free. After one intensely blue outburst, Gray cuffed him across the mouth and told him that if he didn't shut up, he'd break his jaw. The rap in the mouth split his lip, and Kane spat blood for the next twenty minutes.

The heat grew so intense that Ally wished they had stopped for the day at the creek where they'd camped the previous night. The problem was that the temperature had slowed their travel so much that it had taken them ninety minutes longer to get to the creek than it had taken to go from the creek to Kane's ranch. Both Gray and Alan wanted to get closer to Ally's place before they stopped. Finally, Gray decided that they needed to give the horses a rest, which they did under a group of cottonwood trees.

After he stepped off his horse, Gray gave Kane an annoyed look. "Dierden, I'm tired of your company. It's time for you to head back. But, before you do, you better understand something. I told you once that if you gave this woman any more trouble, I'd kill you. You're lucky I haven't. You won't get lucky again. You or any of that worthless bunch of yours cause her any more trouble, and you're a dead man."

"You can't take all my men and me," Kane said, still defiant.

The insolence of the remark set Gray off. He hit the man square in the face, knocking him flat on his back. Gray put his foot hard on Kane's neck while pointing a finger at him like it was a gun. "You harm Mrs. Hart, her or anything that's hers, and I'll come down on you with every hand that works for us and half the men in our valley. Now get out of here!"

Kane managed to get to his feet and reached for his horse's reins. "Leave that horse here. You're walkin' back."

Ally stepped over and took the reins from Kane. He started to grab them back but caught a look in Gray's eyes that made him change his mind.

"Damn you, you'll pay for this," he snarled at Gray. "And so, will you, you whore!" he bellowed at Ally.

"I'm not a whore," Ally screamed.

Kane grabbed the sleeve of his shirt, pulling it up to his elbow, revealing a ghastly scar. "No? Then who slashed my arm in that whorehouse in Texas? Remember that, you whore!"

Kane spat in her face before giving her a violent shove. Gray started after the man, but Ally pulled the navy colt and shot before he got to him. Shot in the foot, Kane screamed, hollered, and jumped up and down on his remaining foot until he finally fell over and rolled around on the ground, shouting and cussing even louder.

Gray found the absurdity of the whole thing funny and started to laugh. He swung up on his horse and told both Ally and Alan to get mounted.

He moved his horse over to Kane and looked down at him, still laughing a bit. "If I were you, Dierden, I'd use that kerchief you're wearing around your neck to wrap that foot up. You might want to break a limb off one of those trees to use for a crutch. You've got a long walk home."

Gray gave Kane's horse a sharp slap on the rump, and

the animal took off in a dead run back in the direction of Kane's ranch. "Maybe, you can catch him before he gets all the way home." Gray turned and rode off, with Ally and Alan following behind.

For some time, they could hear Kane screaming and swearing at them as they went. They knew Kane had pulled his boot off because he kept screeching that she had shot his damn big toe off. Alan, succumbing to a minor feeling of guilt, occasionally glanced back, the last time seeing Kane with his boot off, struggling to wrap up his now four-toed foot.

Chapter Fifty-One

Ally's disposition improved as they rode. For a moment, she even chuckled. When Gray quizzed her about what she was finding funny, she confessed that she hadn't intentionally shot Kane. "Well, who were you intending to shoot?" Gray asked. "Surely, not me. Must have been Alan."

"I wasn't trying to shoot anybody," Ally said with some mild fun in her voice. "I wanted him to get away from me. I meant to pull the pistol and point it at his face so he'd back up. As I pulled it, I cocked it in the same motion, just the way you told me to," she said, looking at Gray and laughing. "As I was pulling and cocking at the same time, the damn thing went off and shot him in the foot. Goodbye, big toe," she laughed.

Ally also admitted that even though she had not meant to shoot Kane, she was not sorry about it. She wanted to ask Gray if he thought their morning's efforts would stop Kane's harassment. Since she sensed that Alan did not believe that, she decided not to ask Gray until she could talk to him alone.

Ally thought that Gray had been and would continue to be honest with her. Alan, on the other hand, baffled her. He seldom spoke directly to her, and she was unsure how much of an ally he would be if things turned rough. Alan had not participated in the tying up of Kane's men. When Gray told Kane that he would come down on him with every hand working for him and half the men in their valley, Alan had remained silent. He even seemed a little resentful when Gray ran Kane's horse off and left the man on foot. Why he would have resented that, Ally didn't know.

The day was now pitilessly hot, and Ally wondered if the heat might be contributing to the fretfulness she was having about Alan. After all, he had been willing to give her cattle, and he had come down with Gray to check on her welfare. She had to acknowledge that he hadn't said or done anything that should cause her concern. But she had once heard a preacher, a Methodist hellfire and brimstone preacher, preach on the sins of omission. That was what worried her about Alan, not what he had done, but what he had not done, the sins of omission. She decided that she would simply ask Gray about this when she got the chance.

After the talk about Ally shooting Kane's toe off ended, they again rode for a time in silence. Riding in silence never bothered Gray, and it did not seem to bother Alan. While it didn't bother Ally—in fact, she perhaps slightly preferred silence to Elijah's constant banter—she did enjoy some conversation mixed in with the quiet. Mostly when she was in a good mood, and after she forced herself to stop worrying about Alan, her mood improved considerably.

As a result, she began a new conversation by asking Gray if he would put his spare pistol back in his saddlebag. She told him she'd stick it in hers, except they remained filled with bread and jerky. As she handed Gray the pistol, Alan took a watch out of his pocket. "Twenty 'til four," he said. "Why don't we stop and give these horses a rest? I wouldn't mind one myself."

Chapter Fifty-Two

As much as Josh thought about leaving the Hart place, it was not an option. He had nowhere to go. St. Louis was certainly not a possibility. If Judge Starrett found out he'd fled, he'd probably send marshals and even bounty hunters out after him. Josh mostly moped around and accomplished nothing the first morning Ally was gone.

He had spent most of the morning trying to clear his head of Alice Hart. He was still insulted that she had not taken him along. He did not care what Gray and Alan had said; she should have intervened for him.

When he first came to help her, she was rude to him. When he was thrown from a horse trying to work her cattle, she laughed at him. When he purchased a gun to protect her, she had been critical of him. When she wanted to talk with someone, if Gray was there, she chose him. Making matters even worse, he had been having some mildly erotic thoughts about the woman.

That upset him because it made him feel disloyal to

Sarah. When Sarah was alive, he never as much as glanced at another woman. She was the love of his life. Nothing in his life had compared to Sarah's embrace. Sarah made him feel complete, alive, and excited about life. Yet, he had imagined himself with Ally, a woman who didn't care about his feelings and had humiliated him.

Even Elijah possessed enough intuition to know that Josh was sulking about being left behind. Fed up with Josh's demeanor and behavior by noon, he tore into him, calling him a greenhorn and telling him he didn't have enough good sense to know when he was well off. Elijah let Josh know again that Gray and Alan were men of influence in these parts, while Josh, himself, still couldn't tell a cowy horse from a jackass.

"Kane wouldn't give you any more concern than he would a damn mosquito. If you rode on his place wearin' that new pistol of yours, he'd take it away from ya and shoot you in the hind end with it, if not in your fool head." He told Josh that he might be able to add numbers together, but he wouldn't be worth spoiled milk when it came to defending Mrs. Hart. "You can't count Kane to death, you know. Elijah picked up a hammer and tossed it at Josh. "If you want to help her, you skin your backside up on that barn and go to work on the roof."

Josh was hotly insulted by Elijah's rant. Nevertheless, he got a ladder and started to lug lumber up on the half-finished roof.

"Why, you damn fool," Elijah yelled. "Is that how we hauled lumber up there before?"

"Well, I can't pull two ropes up at the same time," Josh yelled back, referring to how they had tied two ropes, one on each end of some stacked-up boards, and then pulled them up on the barn.

"Well, of course, you can't," Elijah bellowed back. "That's why they left two of us here." Elijah, muttering the whole time, stacked up some boards, got the two ropes, tied one around each end of the stack, threw the two ropes up to

Josh, and then climbed up the ladder with a bucket of nails.

After Josh stopped sulking, the two men made considerable progress with the roof until Elijah whacked his thumb with his hammer. That set him to squealing like a stuck pig. Elijah's squealing set Josh to laughing, and between the squealing and the laughing, any desire to keep roofing died.

"Lordy, that hurt," Elijah moaned. "This poor thumb is gonna swell up like a poisoned dog."

"Well, you ought not to whack it with a hammer," Josh said.

"You sure take pleasure in another fella's misery," Elijah said.

Josh tried, with some success, to curtail his laughing. He judged they could finish the roof with two more hours' work and suggested they put it off until morning when it might at least be a little cooler. Elijah, wanting a spoonful of laudanum and some axle grease for his thumb, was happy to get off the barn.

While Elijah plastered his thumb in axle grease, Josh went back to the well and pumped a fresh bucket of water. Then he unhooked the dipper hanging from the pump spout, filled it, and poured a dipper full of the cooling water over his head. He took the bucket of water up to the horse trough, only to be discouraged when he found the tank to be more than half-empty. It would take about fifteen trips back and forth to the well to fill the tank.

Sam Hart had contrived an ingenious contraption for hauling water when he took an old worn-out buggy and hung a big washtub from a couple of ropes tied to the top of the buggy. You could harness a horse to the buggy, and in three trips, haul enough water to fill the horse trough. Unfortunately, the buggy burned in the barn fire. After Josh's third trip to the well, Elijah, who was no shirker, saw what Josh was doing, grabbed another bucket, and helped finish the filling.

"How's the thumb?" Josh asked.

"I ain't forgetting it's there," the old man replied. "Not throbbing like it was, though. I'll be able to swing a hammer in the morning. Mrs. Hart will be pleased when she sees the roof on."

Josh was watching the horses out in the corral and didn't respond about the roof. "I think I'll go out there and work with that sorrel a little," he said, taking the lariat that Gray had used off the fence post.

"That rank devil? You want to git yourself killed?" Elijah asked while waving his hand in the air.

"Gray says he ain't rank. He just needs to be worked with," Josh said, slipping between the rails of the corral.

"Then I'd let Gray work with him if he's that blame stupid," Elijah said in a frustrated voice.

Josh stood for a minute, looking over the coiled rope. "Has he got a name?"

"A name? Hell, no, he ain't got no name. He's too mean to give a name to." Elijah stepped up on the bottom rail and leaned over the corral. "Just what am I supposed to tell Mrs. Hart after that horse stomps you into jelly?"

The remark again made Josh feel inadequate. "Tell her you were right. The horse was rank," Josh said, sounding wounded. "And bury me up on that little rise over by the creek, not next to her husband."

The sorrel was on the other side of the corral and paying no attention when Josh started to ease toward him. As soon as he noticed the man, he tossed his head in the air and snorted at him. It didn't seem to be a very friendly snort. Josh hesitated for a moment to see if the horse was going to have any other reaction. The horse threw his head a couple more times but otherwise seemed unconcerned. He took a few more steps, stopping when the horse pawed at the ground and made a short lunge in his direction.

"What's the matter, don't you like people?" Josh whispered. The horse gave him a long hard look but didn't move. When Josh took a couple of steps closer, the horse broke into a run, hugging the corral. He went about halfway around, causing Elijah to back away from the rails. The animal spun around to face Josh. He again threw his head up and down and loudly voiced his displeasure. Josh stood still and spoke to the horse in a voice too low for Elijah to hear.

He then took a few steps forward but didn't get nearly as close before the horse again bolted. After the animal stopped, Josh turned sideways to the horse and sidestepped without looking him in the eyes. Gray had told him that if he sidestepped toward the horse, the animal would have less reaction.

Gray had been right. He stopped, probably twenty feet away, and stood still for a little while. The horse wasn't taking his eyes off Josh, but he was standing quietly. Josh turned and faced the horse and then took one step toward him. When he did, the sorrel spun his backend toward Josh and kicked out with both feet. Fortunately, Josh was out of kicking distance. He remembered that Gray had told him to throw the rope at the animal if he kicked at him, which he did. What he didn't do was hold on to one end of the rope. Josh did fret for an instant about being ropeless. He waved his arms, causing the horse to move away far enough that he could retrieve the rope.

Josh worked with the horse another thirty minutes, never getting especially close, but also without being charged, kicked, or stomped into jelly. Overall, Josh felt he had accomplished something with the horse—maybe not a lot, but something.

Chapter Fifty-Three

Dierden Kane had been able to break a limb from one of the cottonwood trees to use as a makeshift crutch. After crippling along for less than a half-mile, he knew he was going to miss his toe. Kane had been successful in wrapping his newly acquired stub, mostly stopping the bleeding. He could not get his boot back on, which had him now hopping clumsily across the plains. Thorny bushes, goat heads, and every imaginable type of stickers covered the ground. Snakes and scorpions were all over the place.

Kane was a pathetic figure—stumbling, tripping, and sometimes crawling along his way. It would have been difficult to decide as to which was worse, his pain or his rage. Another soul would likely have pitied him, at least until they heard all the cussing and screaming about what he was going to do to Alice Hart, Gray Wehr, and even to his hired hands for not coming to get him.

The truth was that his men had not even started to look for him. Almost four hours passed before another hand showed up at the ranch to free the three draped over the corral rails. All three had headaches as bad as any a whiskey hangover could have caused, two were so stiff and sore they could barely move, and the third man had heaved his breakfast. None of the three were anxious to climb on a horse and go looking for a miscreant like Dierden Kane, who they doubted would come looking for them. Their general feelings were that they didn't much care what happened to Kane.

Even though there were two creeks between him and his ranch, Kane was a long way from the first one, and the lack of water was adding to his wretched state. He relentlessly mumbled to himself about the revenge he'd take. Alice Hart was his chief target. He would kill the woman, but first, he would hurt her, hurt her bad, use her for his personal pleasure, maybe more than once. Before killing her, he would make her beg to die. The idea of cutting her and burning her amused him.

After another hour of cussing and limping along on his makeshift crutch, the wretched thing snapped, sending him sprawling onto his face. He stubbed his toe, well, the place where his toe once was, during his fall. That started blood shooting out from the wound again. His foot felt like it was on fire—no more limping along today.

Chapter Fifty-Four

Ally looked over at Gray. "Good Heavens, Mrs. Hart, you shot his toe off," she said..

Since he wasn't with them when Gray shot Satan, Alan didn't quite get the joke. Gray considered leaving Alan in the dark, something Gray personally would have found humorous. If it had been Jean with him, instead of Alan, he would have, she would have gone mad from not getting the joke.

"Ally is gifted at predicting Elijah's responses," he said.

"I see," Alan said.

Ally sensed Gray still doubted that Alan got the joke. Alan was a serious man with little sense of humor. Ally found that odd since Gray had told her the rest of Alan's family; parents and brothers had a sense of humor. Gray said Alan's brother Zach laughed and made light of everything. Zach didn't take anything seriously, notably, not work. He would have gotten a good laugh out of Ally's comment. Alan was just the opposite. He believed in working and thought humor to be a tremendous waste of time.

Over the next hour, Ally and Gray engaged in frivolous dialogue. By the time they made it to a medium-sized creek, Alan was tired of the meaningless talk and suggested that they stop for the day. He untied the shotgun from behind his saddle and headed up the creek, hunting something to shoot for supper.

Ally sat down next to Gray. She looked at him and, in a whisper, asked, "Am I doing the right thing?"

"Why the whispering?" Gray asked.

"It's a secret question," Ally said, laughing slightly. "Well, am I?"

Ally often thought Gray tried to avoid eye contact with her, but this time he looked at her and smiled. "You're the only one who can know that."

And therein was Ally's real problem. She didn't believe that she could have what she wanted. Ally wanted to live in a city—St. Louis, Chicago, or even Houston or Austin, although Texas heat did not have a great deal of appeal to her. She just wanted to be free of isolation. To be somewhere she could visit with neighbors, have a meal in a restaurant, attend church services with someone other than soldiers. She also wanted someplace not so dominated by men.

In her world, there were only three or four other women, unless you included a handful of saloon strumpets, whose lives were even drearier than her own. The three or four other women lived with their families on ranches no more successful than hers. They were even more worn down by their lives than she was. They all looked older than their age and were generally too tired to socialize with other women.

So, there was no answer to her question about doing the right thing. If it was her only choice, it didn't make any difference whether it was right or not. She had made a mistake marrying a man whose dreams didn't align with her own. Even though she had loved him, what they wanted out of life was very different. At present, she was still stuck in Sam's dreams, feeling hopeless about escaping.

It bothered her that she had, alone in her room at night, thought about a life with Josh. Nevertheless, she knew she would not go there, at least not unless he entirely convinced her that he wanted the same dreams she did. Ally remained far from convinced that Josh had any dreams at all; he was too full of regrets.

Since Gray had confirmed what she already knew, that she alone could decide her future, she moved on to the other two things on her mind. She asked first if Kane would now leave her alone. Gray's response was simple and to the point.

"No."

Ally knew that would be his response. "So did today achieve anything?" she asked.

Gray took the bandana from around his neck and wiped his face. "We put a scare into him. He'll think twice before he comes after you. He'll still come, but he'll think twice. We put some doubt in his mind and maybe in the mind of some of his men. It won't stop him, but a man with doubts is more likely to make mistakes. And he'll have to heal up," Gray said with a laugh. "Kane thinks he's tough and figures that gives him the right to run over other people. He has no morals. The only way to stop men like him is to crush them. We hurt him today, but he's not crushed."

Gray shifted a bit and told Ally that her real decision was going to be whether she wanted to stop Kane or whether she wanted to leave it up to someone else. He added that if she wanted to leave it to someone else, she would have to move because Kane was particularly after her.

Ally asked Gray if, by crushing Kane, he meant killing him.

"Yes," the always direct Gray said, "unless someone else does it first."

"Who else would do it first? He doesn't seem to be after anyone but me."

"You're in a bind, that's for sure," Gray said. "The easiest thing would be just to leave."

Ally thought about Gray's advice. "If I do that, I'll have

nothing," she said. Her life here was difficult, but there were no guarantees that it would be better anywhere else. At least she had her own home, a few head of horses, and enough cattle to make a modest living. Her existence was lonely, but it did offer some slight security.

If it wasn't for Dierden Kane, she could get by. While she had never said much regarding the local sheriff refusing to help her, it upset her. He always claimed there was no proof that Kane was behind anything that had happened to her. It wasn't a lack of proof; Ally didn't think that sheriff would recognize evidence if it were biting him on the hind-end and left a welt. Proof had nothing to do with it. The man was afraid of Dierden Kane and wasn't scared of her. He'd never arrest Kane, but he might arrest her. It was probably not legal to shoot a man's big toe off.

How could she beat such a brutal enemy? Ally didn't know. But, sitting on that creek bank, she had decided she was not running. Now the only thing she was unsure about was whether Alan Joseph was on her side. Maybe it didn't even matter. She had no idea how Gray would respond if asked, but she wanted to know, so she just straight out asked him if Alan was on her side.

Gray didn't ask why she wanted to know.

He just laughed and said, "Alan's not necessarily socially accomplished."

Ally didn't see what that had to do with her problem.

Gray hesitated. "He prefers to keep to himself. His wife is the same way. A couple of years ago, our folks decided that we should pick someone to sort of put in charge of the ranch after they pass. Course, everyone has a vote, but they thought there were too many of us kids not to have one person in charge of the day-to-day operations. We picked Alan, partly because he's the oldest, but mostly because he has good business sense. He's worn it like a burden ever since." He assured Ally the man was on her side and would be a formidable friend when things got rough.

"But you probably won't be here when things get

rough," Ally said.

"We've talked about that. When we get back to your place, Alan will go back to High Meadows. He'll come back with four or five men. I think that'll be enough to put an end to Kane and his bunch. It'll take them a couple of weeks to get back, but it'll take Kane at least that long to heal up."

"I know," was all Gray said when Ally told him that she was grateful.

Ally again started talking about hating the fact that this kind of fight was coming. Gray took both of her hands and told her that she had to stop thinking like that.

"Right now, this is a hard land, Ally. It still tolerates men like Kane."

When Gray took her hands, she felt a tenderness in his touch. It was a feeling that she had not sensed from a man in a long time. She wished him to put his arms around her, comfort her, perhaps even kiss her forehead. Instead, his grip on her hands got tighter, his voice grew more intense.

"Men like Kane will be tolerated until people start standing up to them. It's unlucky that it's fallen on you, but it has. You heard how he threatened you."

The tone of his voice now sounded like he was issuing her an order.

"You're the one in the right, Ally. You need to start thinking that way. You're no coward, but life has been unkind to you. Don't let it tear you down."

Ally let his words sink in.

"I swear, you need a little fun in your life," Gray said, abruptly changing the subject. "What do you do for fun?"

Ally laughed at him. "It's been a while since I had any fun," she said, thinking it was a silly thing for Gray to ask but happy that he'd made her laugh.

"Well, what were you doing the last time you had fun?"

"I can't remember." She laughed nervously, feeling a little odd that she couldn't remember her last fun. She stood and looked around. "I don't see much around here that looks like fun."

"Not any trees around here large enough to make you a swing. I guess you wouldn't consider mumblety-peg much fun."

"I cut myself once trying to do that."

"Right now, our options appear limited," Gray said. "We'll have to be creative."

There was a glint in Ally's eyes when she pointed at a deep, wide spot down the creek.

An hour or so later, Ally's hair was still damp when Alan came back carrying three medium-sized sage grouse. He seemed rather proud of himself, announcing that they'd have a good supper. He was right; the young hens made an excellent meal. "I meant to tell you," Alan said, looking at Gray, "after I shot my second bird, I ran into a fella that says you owe him a buffalo robe."

"What the hell is he doing down here?" Gray asked, clearly surprised.

Alan poured himself a second cup of coffee. "He asked me that very same question about us."

"I know why we're here," Gray said. "Why is he here? And don't say to collect his buffalo robe."

"Sioux and Cheyenne have been in some big counsel," Alan said. "The Sioux intend to move against the Crow and wanted to warn the Cheyenne in case the Crow move onto their land. Paints His Horse's father sent him to speak for their band. He's got seven braves with him."

"You were talking to Indians?" Ally asked, wanting to make sure she understood what was going on. Despite living her adult life in the Indian territory, Ally's actual dealings with Indians numbered only three. None had been hostile. She had seen them at Fort Laramie, once Spotted Tail, himself. But she didn't consider those genuine encounters. She didn't believe all the ghastly stories about their cruelty. Still, they were so different. Their skin was dark. Their language was unfamiliar, their spiritual beliefs were different. Ally didn't loathe them the way other whites did, but they did disquiet her.

Very casually, Alan acknowledged that yes, he was with Indians, one to whom Gray owed a buffalo robe. Gray explained that Paints His Horse was the son of the chief of the band of Teton Lakota, who lived most of the time at the far end of their valley. He told her they grew up playing with Paints His Horse, that they'd been lifelong friends. Alan added that Gray's mother taught Paints His Horse English, and his mother had taught them Lakota.

"I told him they could camp with us tonight," Alan said. "They turned me down."

Dusk comes slowly during Wyoming summers. By Alan's watch, it was eight-thirty, still light, and still hot. Ally was the first to notice the Indian sitting on a horse on the other side of the creek. "I hope you two know him," she said.

Gray looked across the creek, waved, and yelled out, "Are you comin' across, or are you just gonna sit there watching us?" The Indian started across the creek. As he crossed, Ally looked him over. He was wearing fringed tan pants that she assumed to be deerskin. Raven black hair hung halfway down his bare chest. Two eagle feathers were hanging down on the left side of his head. He was a very handsome man, high cheekboned, and smoothly muscled. Still, the lance he carried in his right hand made him look fierce, not someone she would want as an enemy. When he got close, she was struck by his piercing eyes.

"That's a fine-looking paint horse your riding," Gray said while looking the animal over. "You steal him from Annie?"

"Annie doesn't raise paint horses," the warrior said. "You would know that if you came home more often." The Sioux slid off his horse. "You have my robe?"

"Why would I be hauling a buffalo robe around on a hot day like this?" Gray asked.

"How come he owes you a buffalo robe anyway?" Alan

asked Paints His Horse.

"I told him I could split an arrow with another arrow," Paints His Horse said. "He laughed at me. Bet me a robe."

"I'd say that was a mighty fine shot," Alan said. "How far away were you?"

"There wasn't anything fine about it," Gray said. "He just took one arrow and jammed it down into the string notch of another one, then pounded them on the ground splitting the bottom one. He's nothing but a blame mountebank...a charlatan."

Paints His Horse laughed. "I didn't say I'd shoot at the arrow. Only a fool would have tried that. You should have asked how I was going to do it."

"Oh, you'll get your robe, soon as I find some mangy old buffalo to shoot."

Gray motioned for Ally to step closer. "Ally, this is Paints His Horse. It's hard to believe, but he's the son of a Lakota chief. This is Ally Hart," he said, looking at Paints His Horse. "She owns a ranch not too far from Fort Laramie." Gray told his friend that they still had some coffee and asked if he wanted a cup. Paints His Horse asked who made it.

Gray tossed a hand in the air. "Ain't you the persnickety one," When told Ally made it, he accepted the offer. "You want some grouse? I didn't cook it either."

Paints His Horse said he had eaten antelope before he came to see them. "I was afraid you might be cooking over here."

After Paints His Horse, in answer to Alan's question, told them about the counsel with the Cheyenne, under Dull Knife, Gray told him that a small band of Arapaho had attacked him and Alan on their way to Ally's place.

Paints His Horse said the Arapaho were angry over so many whites crossing their land. He talked about the Lakota and Cheyenne agreeing to allow white men to pass through their land, but only to pass through, not stop or build homes.

The Arapaho had refused to agree and were now raiding not only homesteads but also the wagon trains. He also said

Red Cloud, Man Afraid of His Horse, and Roman Nose were starting to talk of war because white soldiers were building forts on the Lakota and Cheyenne land.

Alan mentioned planning to go home the day after tomorrow. Paints His Horse shook his head and said that was not a good idea. He told Alan if he wanted to go home, he should go with him and the other Lakota, not alone.

That news complicated Gray's plans for Alan to bring back help. When he told Paints His Horse about Ally's problems with Kane, and their intention for Alan to go home and bring help, Paints His Horse said that by the time Alan could start back, the land between the Powder and the Tongue Rivers would be swarming with Lakota, Cheyenne, and Arapaho.

He said that most of the bands would probably scatter by late summer, the Oglala and Hunkpapa going to the Paha Sapa, the Brulé, and Minniconjou moving to the Big Horn and Greasy Grass, the Cheyenne and Arapaho going south of the Powder.

"I think you should go with Paints His Horse," Gray said, surprising both Alan and Ally. "We've found out what we wanted to know. We should probably get word back to our families before they worry themselves to death." Before Alan asked about coming back with more men, Gray put a stop to it. "Hickok said he was going to scout for the Army. Maybe I can find out where he is and get his help." Gray also tried to convince the others that since he knew several of the officers at Fort Laramie, he might get their help. "We'll make do."

It only took Alan a few minutes to saddle and pack his gear. He told Gray that he'd let Annie and Jean know that he was fine and would be back at the end of the summer. Then he laughed a little and said, "Maybe I should be honest with them and tell them you'll be back in your own good time...just like always." Alan leaned over and whispered to Gray to keep the others from hearing. "Protect that woman, if you're determined to, but nothin' else."

"Nothin' else?" Gray asked.

"Damn you. You know what I mean." Alan spat a stream of tobacco and rode slowly away.

Paints His Horse put his hand on Gray's shoulder. "Keep a good watch, Graham." He swung on his horse and smiled down at his friend. "Don't get yourself killed. When your sister finds out I was with you, she'd probably blame me."

Ally and Gray watched the two men ride away. "Did he call you Graham?"

"He always does," Gray said. "My mother hates the nickname Gray. Paints His Horse admires her, so I think he calls me Graham to please her."

"I like Graham. I might start calling you that myself, except it would baffle Elijah beyond explanation." The friendship, which was evident between Paints His Horse and Gray and Alan, surprised her. He'd been nothing like the tales about Indians. He smiled easily, was amiable and friendly, and honestly, Ally thought, he was also a rather magnificent-looking man. "Paints His Horse seemed to have quite a sense of humor," she mentioned.

"Well, he's a storyteller," Gray said. "Once in a while, his stories wander into the neighborhood of truth. Course, he doesn't stay there long," Gray laughed.

The response amused Ally. She asked Gray if all the Sioux were like Paints His Horse.

"Not any more than all white eyes are like you or me." He told her that the Lakota, the Cheyenne, even the Arapaho were just people. "Some are good, some aren't so good." He also said that he didn't have a more genuine friend in this old world than Paints His Horse.

"Their way of life is different than ours," he said. "Still, in many ways, they're the same. They love their families, and they want to protect what's theirs. Just like you do," he said, looking directly at Ally. Gray talked for a while about believing that the whites had caused most of the problems. "The Indians were here first. Unfortunately for them, there'll eventually be more of us than there are of them. The Lakota took the Crow land, and the whites will slowly take theirs. Manifest Destiny, I suppose, is how it will be justified."

"It does seem unfair," Ally said.

"The worst of it is that they've been lied to in every treaty we've made with them."

"Does Paints His Horse feel that way?"

"He'll never make war on us in High Meadows. But, when things get bad enough, he'll leave our mountains and fight the whites. When it's over, I hope he comes home."

"What will you do?"

Gray looked away. "I wish I knew."

A nearly hour-long silence followed in which Ally started to think about riding back to the ranch alone with Gray. It had not occurred to Gray that the two of them spending a night alone together might not be comfortable for Ally. For her, it was an unexpected change of circumstances. She wasn't worried about her companion behaving gentlemanly, it was riding into the ranch the next morning— alone with Gray—that she felt might be uncomfortable.

Neither Ally nor Gray were tired, which made for a bit of a clumsy time, putting Ally a bit ill at ease with the normally untalkative Gray.

The night air was starting to get a slight chill in it, and Gray built up the fire they had cooked their meal over earlier, providing heat and a lovely glow. Ally sat on the opposite side of the fire from Gray, but in a few minutes, the light breeze changed directions, sending the smoke into her face. "You better switch sides," Gray said, "otherwise, you're going to suffocate in the smoke."

"We should have brought a couple of good books to cut our boredom," Ally said.

"A book would certainly cut the boredom," Gray said.

Ally was somewhat stunned by Gray's response. "Are

you a reader?" she asked.

"Is that hard for you to believe?"

"No, of course not," Ally said, denying the truth of being surprised.

"My mother forced it on us when we were young. The habit just kind of stuck. I even read a little poetry."

Gray's nose may, or may not have, moved higher in the air, but he suddenly did look more scholarly.

"Poetry!" Ally exclaimed.

"Last winter, I read *Leaves of Grass*," he said, prompting a blush from Ally. "Annie's folks sell novels in their mercantile, but they can be a little slow to get them. I just read *Moby Dick* but didn't like it much. I also read *Uncle Tom's Cabin.* That lady convinced me to fight in a civil war if one comes." In his best literary elegance, Gray asked Ally what she had been reading.

"Judge Dan, my friend in St. Louis, the one who sent Josh to me, sent me the first chapters of a new story; it's going to be a serialized novel by the English author Dickens. It's called *A Tale of Two Cities.*"

"Well, aren't we the literary intellects," Gray said. "Yet, neither one of us has brought a book along." He laughed. "I guess we'll have to come up with another way to pass the evening."

Ally had concluded that she liked Gray, although she was not sure she understood him, at least not entirely. "You're quite the enigma," Ally said, smiling broadly.

"That's what Annie and my sister say," Gray laughed.

Ally suggested that they could take a walk but then decided it was getting a little too chilly to leave the fire. Gray said that he was a little hungry and suggested heating the sage hens they had leftover from supper. Ally warmed them while Gray checked on the horses. The reheating dried the birds out a bit, but they were still satisfying. Gray poured them what coffee was left and got another pot ready to put on the fire in the morning.

Ally brought up the fact that Gray told her earlier in the

day that she had to stop worrying about whether or not she was doing the right thing. She knew Gray was right and told him that she had decided there would be no more second thoughts. She then revealed that she was not sure Josh would still be there when they got back.

"Why do you think that?"

"You saw how upset he was about not being brought along," she said.

"Then he gets his feelings hurt too damn easy," Gray said, showing no sympathy for the man.

"Maybe so," Ally said.

Gray indicated that he fully expected Josh to be there when they returned. He was sure the man had some feelings for Ally. Gray also believed that love was a complicated thing, and from what he knew of Ally and Josh's backgrounds, a romance between them would be even more confounded. His sister was once engaged, but the man drowned during a flash flood, and since then, Jean had rejected every man who attempted courting. He fully believed that he would marry Annie Laurie, but *when*...that was the great unknown. Gray was sure that he sometimes noticed a little loneliness in Ally, and occasionally an innocent flirtation. However, he didn't think Josh was what she needed.

While Gray had been contemplating the fluctuations of romance, Ally had started humming a song unfamiliar to him. He was enjoying it when she abruptly stopped.

"I'm not a whore." Ally looked straight at Gray to make sure he was listening. "I've never been a whore."

"I never thought you were," Gray said, averting his eyes.

"Good. I'm glad," Ally replied smartly. Gray thought that would be her last word on the matter. He hoped so. It wasn't.

"I have a sister that lives in Texas." Ally moved over and sat next to Gray.

Now where is this going.

"We're not twins, but everyone mistakes us for twins."

She paused to see if Gray would say anything. He didn't.

"A few years ago, well, several years, I suppose, Judge Dan sent me a letter about Ruth. He said if I heard anything unpleasant about Ruth, not to let it bother me." Ally reached down and poured herself some coffee. "Ruth lives in Texas. She looks just like me." She looked Gray right in the eyes. "Do you think Ruth could be a whore?"

"That's some question. Besides, how would I know?" Gray half-laughed, hoping to make the conversation end.

"You move around a lot." Ally laughed. "I know she's not one now. She's married and has two kids. Still, I wonder if she used to be one. If she was and sliced Kane's arm, I suppose he could mistake me for her." Ally tossed the coffee out. "If that's true, he's sure made a blunder."

Gray mentioned the late hour and suggested they turn in.

Chapter Fifty-Five

When Gray woke smelling bacon frying, Ally was sitting on the other side of the fire, sipping coffee and looking down at him.

"The sun's only been up about ten minutes," she said. "The bacon will be ready soon."

Gray stood and tried to stretch the kinks from the hard ground out of his back. He asked Ally how long she'd been up.

"Not long, less than an hour," she answered, handing Gray a cup of coffee.

"I'm normally the first one up," Gray said, bumbling around the camp to find something to do.

"You might as well sit and relax a little. Everything is ready to go. Just have to throw the saddles on the horses."

"I'm not used to having someone do all the work. I carry my share."

Ally found Gray's comment amusing. She said it didn't take much effort to stick a coffeepot on the fire or slice up some bacon.

"You can fetch a loaf of bread out of my saddlebag. We'll consider that your contribution."

Gray followed instructions while Ally poured them more coffee. After breakfast, Ally mentioned being home in about three hours.

Gray was quick, saddling the horses. Faster than Ally hoped. While she was not sure she should admit it, she enjoyed her little trip. Well, except maybe shooting Kane's big toe off. She didn't regret that too much, at least not after Gray told her he doubted Kane would die from having a toe shot off.

Ally was throwing one last coffeepot of water on the fire when Gray came over, leading their horses. Ally took her sorrel's reins, but instead of mounting, she stared out across the creek. Gray sat on his blue roan.

"Something wrong?"

Ally looked up at him, smiled, and sighed. "To tell the truth, I enjoyed our little adventure. It's been a bit of a break from the ordinariness of my life." She laughed a little at Gray's suggestion to spice her life up a little by shooting one of Josh's toes off. "Gray, what do you think about Josh?"

"Well, I haven't thought much about him."

His answer disappointed Ally.

Gray must have recognized the disappointment on her face. "Why would my opinion matter?"

"Oh, I guess it doesn't," Ally said.

Gray stepped off his horse and suggested they wait a little while if Ally didn't want to start back. "I'm pretty sure he'll still be at your place."

Ally didn't say anything. She kept staring off at nothing.

"He'd have been jealous of our swimming," Gray said.

Ally shook her head, stared at the ground, but didn't reply.

"I guess I'm not sure what you're trying to find out," Gray said.

"Nothing," Ally said, abruptly looking away.

Gray led his horse down to the creek. Doc took a short drink but mostly splashed around with his nose. After a while, Gray looked back at Ally, sitting on the ground looking despondent.

He walked his horse back up to her. "I think Josh might be a little smitten with you," Gray said.

"That's what I was afraid of." She sighed. "I'm not interested in being courted," Ally said in a blunt tone. The truth, however, was slightly different. Courting did appeal to her. So did something physical. She swam with Gray, initiating that caper. While the brazenness of skinnydipping bothered her a little, it didn't bother her much.

She also wanted an emotional relationship with an emotionally healthy partner. At times, Josh seemed helpless, wallowing in self-pity. Even Elijah dominated him. She did not need or want a weak-willed man. Josh might do for a casual fling, but choosing another husband was something more complicated.

"Tell him you don't want to be courted." That was too simple and straightforward to satisfy a woman.

"He hasn't been open yet about trying to make overtures to me. I can't tell him to stop something he hasn't started." Ally knew from the expression on Gray's face he was going to be worthless. "You're no help."

"I'm helpful. My help is just too logical for a woman."

Chapter Fifty-Six

For a while, they rode in silence, causing Gray to wonder if Ally was sulking a little. The silence didn't bother Gray. Ally sulking did. "Why so quiet?"

"I can't chase Josh out of my head. He made me mad when we left. I didn't care until this morning. Now I can't free my mind of him."

Women were like that—constantly fretting about something not worth worrying over. The man had been acting like a child when they left, moping about the entire morning. Ally told him, so that should have been the end of her problem, in Gray's opinion. It wasn't, and now Gray was going to have to listen to the woman nitpick, probably all the way home. Hoping to put the whole topic to rest, Gray asked her what, to him, was most logical. "Why can't you rid your mind off him?" Gray couldn't decide whether he had irritated her or baffled her.

"Haven't you been listening?"

"Of course, I'm listening. What else is there to do out

here?"

Ally stopped her horse and stared at Gray.

He found the befuddled look on her face so humorous he almost laughed. "Well, exactly what about Josh can't you get off your mind?"

Ally shook her head a little and looked astounded.

Gray went through a whole list of possibilities, including, is he too thin-skinned, too self-pitying, too lazy, too dumb, too smart, too useless, too smitten with you?

Ally continued to stare at Gray. "I don't know...for sure."

"Well, kick my butt and call me Charlotte," Gray said. He frequently used the phrase to express frustration. Of course, the term was pointless because no one had the slightest idea what it was supposed to mean, which didn't bother Gray in the least.

"What does that mean?"

"Means you're not making any sense," Gray said tartly.

"Me? You're the one not making any sense. And, who's Charlotte?"

"This entire conversation makes no sense," Gray said. Ally agreed, although she thought only Gray's part made no sense.

Gray nudged Doc forward, and Ally followed along. A little way on, she put her hand on Gray's arm. "He gets insulted too easily," she said.

"Then stop insulting him."

"All right, I will," Ally laughed.

"Well, I'm glad we got that resolved," Gray said, holding back his laugh.

Chapter Fifty-Seven

Dierden Kane's night alone on the high desert had not been pleasant. His foot burned and throbbed all night, denying him any sleep. The morning didn't improve anything. The heavy morning dew made him damp and cold. He was hungry, and as soon as the day heated up, he would be in for a good sunburn and terrible thirst.

Kane lost his hat while draped over the horse, and his abductors didn't bother to pick up the damn thing. With little hair, his white head would probably blister by mid-afternoon. The bandanna he wrapped his foot with was crusted with dry blood and so stiff and rough it was irritating his stub. Since the makeshift crutch broke, he hadn't been able to walk, limiting his progress to a slow crawl.

After the sun came up over the horizon, Kane sat on his hind end for another hour, cursing everybody and everything. Wallowing in self-pity and anger, he started crawling toward home, creeping only a couple of hundred yards before coming up on a small nest of hornets in moods as bad as his own. Two of them stung him, one under his eye and the other inside his ear. His day couldn't be much worse.

Chapter Fifty-Eight

An hour from her ranch, Ally told Gray she would prefer saying Alan started for home this morning rather than last night. Gray was indifferent, but he did understand why Ally might be concerned. Five or six miles from home, they reached the Platte River. When they did, they found Hal Smith, or at least what there was of him to find.

He was naked, lying face-up with a Sioux arrow between his feet. He was disemboweled, with his privates cut off, his eyes plucked out, and missing his scalp. Even the ridiculous mustache was gone. His skin had a bluish cast, what skin he had left.

Ally became sick. Gray stepped off his roan to help her down. He led her away from the mutilated corpse and held her up as she continued to throw up. She dropped to her knees and leaned on both hands. Gray knelt beside her and rubbed her back.

Sam didn't look good after the bull finished with him, but Smith's body was worse. Flies swarmed over him, fighting for bites of flesh, buzzing in and out of his nose and mouth. He not only looked grotesque, but he also smelled—

stank of rot and decay.

Her throwing up was short-lived, and Gray helped her back to her feet.

"I've never seen anything so gruesome," she whispered.

"I hope you never do again," Gray said.

"Which Indians killed him?"

"That's a Sioux arrow." Gray examined the body, trying to judge one vital issue: how long-ago Smith died. The blood was dried, but blood drying wouldn't take too long since the entire morning had been hot and dry. "I'll go find some stones to put over him." Gray started down to the river but turned back toward Ally. "Why don't you stay here? Kind of keep your eyes open. I'm not sure how long ago this happened."

To appease Ally, Gray stacked rocks on the body for over an hour. It was not a good idea. If the Indians came back, they would know someone had been there. That might set them on their trail.

Ally came over, leading both horses. "Why would they do this to one man alone? He wouldn't have been any threat to them."

Gray, not a speculator, simply shook his head. He took Doc's reins and stepped up on his horse.

"We better go," he said. "With this many hoof prints around here, there were at least a dozen braves." Gray sensed Ally might be a little concerned for her home and told her tracks were heading off to the north. She asked if they might have come from the east, the direction of her place. Gray pointed at the river. "They came across right here." Coming across the river didn't prove her home was safe, but it did seem to reassure her.

Not long before the newly roofed barn came into view, Gray stopped and asked Ally how she was doing.

"All right, I suppose. But I'm afraid I'm going to have nightmares about his body."

The woman was pale and still shaken. Gray pulled his horse right against Ally's. He reached over and took her hand. She leaned against him, making Gray uncomfortable, but he put his arm around her shoulders.

"Why would anyone mutilate another person? Would your friend do something so horrible?"

"No," Gray said, although it was conjecture. As far as Ally's questioning the why, Gray didn't spend much time considering the *why* of things. The *why* rarely made any difference in outcomes.

The Lakota, Cheyenne, and several other Indian Tribes mutilated enemies because they believed they would enter the next life in the condition they left this one. Anger likely played a role in these particular actions. The solution was rather obvious, at least to Gray: don't make Indians mad. Gray believed anyone wanting to understand many Indians' anger for white men needed only to look at how white men treated Indians.

"Smith did something to provoke those Sioux," Gray said. He told Ally such a level of mutilation implied revenge.

When they returned, Elijah asked about the absence of Alan Joseph, but Josh was more curious. A blind man would have seen the jealousy in him.

Gray described how earlier in the morning, they came across the Sioux band who lived in their mountain valley. He justified, neatly, he thought, how he and Alan believed one of them should go back home to update their families. The Arapaho's attack on the way down made it sensible for Alan to travel with friends. Elijah found the logic reasonable. Josh gave the impression of only being disturbed over Ally and Gray being alone, while more or less being uninterested regarding the reason. Ally wanted a change in the subject, which Gray provided by bringing up Kane's toe.

"You shot his toe off? Good heavens, Mrs. Hart!" Elijah's response, though predicted, made Ally smile.

"His *big* toe!" Gray elaborated. "She yanked my ol' Navy Colt out of her belt and blew his big toe right off—slick as a whistle." He went through the motion of drawing a pistol. "Boom!"

Elijah was impressed. Josh, judging by his appearance, not so much. Ally, somewhat mortified when she shot him, now, a day later, was laughing and proclaiming to be quite a marksman.

Josh remained the only one failing to find fun in the description of the incident about her shooting off Kane's big toe. In her mind, Ally thought of several reasons Josh didn't enjoy the story, each one foolish. Either he did not like the idea of her shooting Kane based on what the consequences might be, or he envied her marksmanship. Or, Ally returning alone with Gray annoyed him so much he didn't care about anything else. Whatever his issue, Ally didn't care.

After Elijah's excitement over Ally's big toe shooting waned, she expressed surprise and gratitude about the progress made on her barn. Elijah said, except for the blamed heat, they would have accomplished more. He said they checked the cattle twice a day, and they were doing fine.

"Josh's been tryin' to work with that rank horse," Elijah said.

"How'd you do?" Gray asked.

Before Josh could respond and maybe gain a little respect from Gray, Elijah butted in. "Well, Josh ain't dead, yet."

Elijah meant the remark as a compliment, but Josh had become so thin-skinned he took it as an insult. He decided he'd endured enough impertinence, especially from Elijah, and planned to stop the nonsense if he had to take a swing at the old buzzard. Fortuitously, for one of the two, Gray stepped in between before Josh reacted.

He put a hand on Josh's back. "Let's go see what you've been doing," Gray said. "As soon as you gain his trust, you're going to have yourself a real solid horse."

Once Gray and Josh got to the corral, and out of earshot, Ally slipped an arm around Elijah's shoulder. "I think we should go ahead and let Josh work with the sorrel," she said.

"It'll be good for Josh and the horse."

"I suppose you might be right, Mrs. Hart," Elijah said before adding, "if the blame fool don't end up dead." Ally almost scolded Elijah, except she doubted Elijah grasped he offended Josh. She let it pass, not wanting two men moping around with their tails tucked between their legs.

The sorrel didn't pay much attention to Josh walking around in the corral. When Josh walked toward him, the horse moved away but didn't snort or throw his head. Gray told Josh he achieved something, a decent beginning for two days' work. Josh sort of doubted Gray's sincerity, but he appreciated the compliment.

"You mind a suggestion?" Gray asked.

Josh's shoulders slumped. Of course, advice. Josh sighed, turned toward Gray, and agreed to hear his suggestion, another pointing out of his failures.

"Let's take those other horses out before you work with him tonight. Force him to focus on you."

What? No criticism? No, here's why you're a failure? A simple idea to give him more control? Josh stood a little straighter. Someone had confidence in him.

Gray complimented him a second time. "How well do you throw a rope?"

Josh's mood improved enough because of Gray's compliments that he grinned. "Not worth a tinker's damn if you're asking if I can rope a horse."

"Well, we'll work on your roping," Gray said in a lighthearted manner. "Pretty soon, you'll be roping antelope."

After a few more minutes of Josh working with the horse, the two men headed back to the house while Gray told Josh about the discovery of Hal Smith's body. Josh asked how Ally reacted.

"Not real well," Gray said. "Nobody would. I'll go over

to Fort Laramie in the morning and tell the Army about Smith. Supposedly, Smith has a brother in the Cavalry. But whether he does or not, they need to be told what happened."

He told Josh he wanted to tell Ally about his plan at dinner.

Elijah was shocked about Gray and Ally finding a man killed by the Sioux.

Josh sometimes wondered how a man could be shocked so frequently without having his heart give out. Yet, here was Elijah Yancey, still in good health.

When Gray, halfway through dinner, brought up going to Fort Laramie the next day, Ally had little reaction. She said she and the others would go along. Elijah became mildly concerned about leaving the ranch all alone. Ally reminded him of how recently she separated Kane's toe, his big toe, from the rest of his foot. She assured Elijah they didn't need to worry about Kane for at least two or three weeks.

Chapter Fifty-Nine

Kane could not hear anything out of his left ear, now looking more like cauliflower than an ear, or see through his swollen shut eye. His right foot was already infected. Everything together limited his crawling to less than a mile's progress.

As miserable as he was, it galled Kane most knowing his attack, his revenge against Alice Hart, would be delayed. The shrew who put him in this wretched state remained unscathed, probably crowing about what she did to him while he crawled around like a filthy crippled dog. "By hell, you may be laughing now," Kane screamed, "but you won't be for long. Not long, you whore."

Chapter Sixty

Before heading off to Fort Laramie, Josh gave his pistol a thorough cleaning while Elijah gave Josh his constant reminder about how the gun didn't need daily oiling.

Gray went outside where he saddled horses for him and Josh, hitched up the wagon for Ally and Elijah, all to avoid the absurdity of Elijah's humor, which he found fatiguing. He was amazed at how Ally good-naturedly tolerated the shortcomings of her two hands.

When the other three came out, Ally walked up right next to Gray's blue roan stud. When she did, Doc reached around and bit into her shoulder. Ally yelped and slapped the horse across his jaw. "Damn you!" she screamed as she landed another slap. She turned away from him; when she did, the horse rammed into her, slamming her arm into the fence. For a moment or two, she was not sure she would be able to keep standing. "Oh, that hurt," she moaned, bent over and grabbing her shoulder.

Gray was trying to help her stand. "Your horse wants to

kill me," she said, poking Gray. "Lord, I ought to be smarter than to walk past a stud's mouth. Damn you, Doc." She gave the horse another dirty glare. "I think you broke my arm against the fence rail." Gray put his arm around her waist to hold her up. "Am I bleeding?" Struggling with lightheadedness, she appreciated Gray's support.

"How would I know."

"Well, look and see," she demanded with some hint of humor in her voice as she pulled her dark blue shirt down at the shoulder. Gray peeked down the sleeve of her blouse.

"Well, a little. Not much, but there's a deep set of teeth marks. You might want to use something to keep the skin soft," he said.

"I'll be right back," she said, walking off with Gray's assistance while the other two men stood there. Gray walked about halfway to the house with her, holding her arm. "I think I can walk alone now."

"You want any help taking care of that?"

Ally fancied Gray's flirtatious smile. "I can do my own doctoring," she said good-naturedly. "Well, maybe you should help me up the steps," she said, realizing she was still unstable. As they started up, Gray told her she was walking like a drunk. "The bite is bad enough, but I think my arm may be broken. He rammed me hard into the fence rail." Gray stayed on the front porch after helping her through the door, just in case.

She threw her blue shirt on her bed. Ally expected to find teeth marks, but not as distinct as they were. She washed off the blood, more than Gray led her to expect. She put some salve on the wound and tried to bandage her shoulder. The bite area was burning like Hades, and her arm ached from her shoulder clear down into her fingers. The arm hurt so severely from banging into the rail, lifting her arm was impossible.

Fumbling left-handed, she dropped the roll of gauze. She picked it up, dropped it again, and then a third time.

Giving up, she opened the door slightly, whispered at

Gray, still standing on the porch. When she got his attention, she motioned for him to come in. "I can't wrap this myself. Help me, will you? And no peeking down my camisole."

Gray gave her a wink. "No, ma'am."

He was quite adept at the bandaging. Ally struggled with getting a clean shirt on and ran into another problem. "I can't button this left-handed." Gray made some silly remark, either trying to be amusing or out of being self-conscious about never helping a woman button her top before. "Well, no one's ever helped me before, so I guess we're quite a pair."

"We better put you in a sling."

Ally did not disagree. "Grab the blue shirt I tossed on my bed." Gray tied the sleeves together, hung them over her head, and helped put her arm in the makeshift sling. He asked her if she had any of those cinnamon rolls from breakfast left. "Why?" Ally asked, laughing a little.

"I don't want them for me," Gray said.

"Well, Elijah doesn't need any more," Ally said. "He's already eaten three of them."

"I want you to eat them," Gray said. "Something sweet and sugary can help an injured person perk up a little."

"You don't find me perky enough?" Ally laughed.

Gray brought back a cinnamon roll and a cup of milk. "You'll feel better, or at least a little stronger. We'll let the fort physician check your arm."

Back out with the others, she patted Gray's stud and rubbed his neck. "You can't play so rough with a girl."

"Are you all right, Mrs. Hart?" Elijah was distressed by seeing her in a sling. He helped her into the wagon, repeatedly apologizing for possibly hurting her as he tried to help.

"Not the first time I've been bit by a young stud. I hope it's the last, but probably not."

She caught Josh looking at her, wanting to say something. "I'm fine," she told him. "Don't blame the horse. A wise person would pay a little more attention to stallions."

Ally's arm was better, when less than halfway to Fort

Laramie, Gray spotted a small military detachment headed toward them. Josh set off on a wild path of guesses about reasons they were out on the plains.

"Josh," Elijah said, "the difference in a man experienced, and a newcomer like you is an experienced man wonders things to himself, but an inexperienced man asks out loud."

Gray pointed out they would find out soon enough.

The group included a second lieutenant, the sergeant who brought Josh out from St. Louis, and five cavalrymen. The lieutenant, a talkative fella with what sounded like an Irish brogue, was somewhat acquainted with Gray. He said he wished the Army had known Gray was down their way because they needed a capable scout. "Sioux, under Dull Knife and Little Wolf, are raiding wagon trains and farms."

"Lieutenant," Gray said, "Dull Knife and Little Wolf are Northern Cheyenne, not Sioux. Even if they join forces, the Sioux won't ride under Cheyenne chiefs."

The sergeant leaned over and whispered to Josh, "I told the damn fool that—twice."

The officer mumbled something about only repeating what he'd been told.

"Who told you something so foolish?" Gray asked.

"My major told me," the captain said, before realizing the risk of blaming a superior and adding he believed a scout told the major.

"If he did, I'm afraid you boys have yourselves a useless scout, or major, one or the other. What's the scout's name?"

The sergeant helped out the lieutenant. "Hickok."

"Yes, Hickok," the young officer said. "Never heard of him. He's probably incompetent."

Gray laughed. "J. B. Hickok?" He laughed a little more. "Kick my butt and call me Charlotte," he said, laughing still harder. "James Butler Hickok may be a lot of things, but he's not dumb enough to think Dull Knife and Little Wolf are Sioux. Nor is your major, unless Major Lewis is no longer in charge."

Elijah twisted in his saddle, without a doubt, stunned by Gray's audacity. "Isn't Hickok the fella who was with you when you beat...er, bought the horse from Kane's man? I never heard of him either." Elijah never quit when he was ahead.

"Well, you're out of touch as this lieutenant," Gray said, although good-naturedly to Elijah. "Where's Hickok now?"

The lieutenant said Hickok, a captain, and a corporal broke off from them about fifteen minutes back to head north looking for the hostiles while the rest searched to the west.

"You're too short on men to tussle with the Indians, Sioux or Cheyenne. I advise you to turn around and go back to the fort."

"My orders are to proceed," the insulted lieutenant said.

"You'll turn right back to the fort if you're smart," Gray said in a mocking voice.

"I have orders!" The officer said insolently.

"You ever fight Indians, lieutenant?" Gray asked in an ill-mannered voice. Insolence always aggravated Gray, especially coming from a man he thought might be an ass. The lieutenant didn't answer. "How about the rest of you men?" Except for the sergeant, the other men sat with blank looks on their faces.

"I fought Kiowa and Pawnee," the sergeant said. "Had a couple of brief tussles with some Utes."

Gray said he didn't have much experience with Utes, but he knew the Sioux and Cheyenne. "How many men did you have with you in those fights?" Gray asked. The sergeant said fifty or sixty. "How would you have done with five?"

The sergeant grunted, "We'd be dead men."

Gray again told the lieutenant to take his men back to the fort.

The lieutenant responded in anger. "There are settlers to protect."

"Oh hell, man. What's wrong with you? You couldn't protect yourselves, let alone a bunch of sodbusters. Turn your asses around and go home. Major Lewis didn't send you out here to be slaughtered."

"I'm an officer in the United States Military. You'll talk to me with due respect."

"I'll talk to you any way I damn please. You're a fool." Fed up with the lieutenant, Gray turned to the sergeant and asked him what Major Lewis ordered this shave tail.

"To search for Indian sign," the sergeant said.

The lieutenant flushed a deep red. "Hold your tongue!"

"Well, sergeant, I can give you the answer." Gray completely ignored the lieutenant. "Yesterday, we found a man, not ten miles from here, been killed by the Sioux. We ran into him the day before, and he said he had a brother at Fort Laramie." He looked back at the lieutenant. "If you've got any sense at all, you'll bust your hind end back to the fort." The officer did not reply. "Suit yourself," Gray said. "Luck to you, Sarge. You're gonna need some." Gray rode off with Ally and the others trailing along behind him.

"He sure lit into the lieutenant," Elijah said to Ali as they drove off.

"He needed lit into," Ally said. "He'll lead those men into a massacre."

About fifteen minutes later, Gray stopped and turned to look at the others. "This should be about where Hickok and those other two turned north. I'm gonna go find them. Go ahead to the fort, and I'll arrive late tonight or in the morning." He told them he doubted they'd run into any trouble going back home. But if they were uncomfortable making the trip to wait for him and go tomorrow. He focused his attention on Ally.

"With any luck, I'll talk Jimmy Hickok into coming back to your ranch with me. From what we found out yesterday about how many men Kane has, I expect he'll only have around ten men with him when he hits you. Jimmy gives us four, five if we count you," he said, smiling at Ally. "Jimmy's a solid man in a fight. I'd be comfortable with those odds."

Ally said she wasn't worried about getting home and

would rather stay at the fort than travel after dark. "Then I'll take Josh along with me," Gray said. "Let him gain a little experience." Gray didn't want to take Josh. He was trying to give the man's frail ego a boost.

"That would be fine," Ally said. "You don't mind, do you, Josh?"

"No, not at all. Two of us will be safer than one."

"Well, 'til tonight or tomorrow," Gray said, waving his hat.

As soon as the two men were out of earshot, Elijah told Ally that Gray needed him instead of Josh. Ally found Elijah's statement amusing, although she hid her amusement from him. *You men— such egos.*

"True, Gray would be better off." Ally enjoyed stroking Elijah's ego. "But Josh needs to gain some experience out here. And, I feel a little safer with you," she said.

Elijah smiled at her. "Mrs. Hart, you're sort of fond of Gray, aren't you?

Elijah rarely surprised Ally. This time he did. His comment threw her. Gray did appeal to her. He was wild, self-assured, and little influenced by the opinions of others. Gray, in her view, was warm, funny, and plain enjoyable. He was also physically pleasing, which did not hurt. She liked his strength and character. He inspired her to resist Kane and to make a go of her little ranch.

Despite all those attributes, he was flawed, unsettled, a rogue, a bit of a renegade with feasibly a little outlaw in him. For all virtues in him, he was still just a man. Her immediate problem was how to answer Elijah and how to make him drop the subject. She did not want him to play Cupid.

When Ally stayed quiet, Elijah went right ahead and asked again. "Well, are you, Mrs. Hart?"

Frustrated with his persistence, she said briskly. "Aren't I what?"

"Fond of Gray?"

Knowing the man wouldn't let go of the notion, she decided to put the meddling old-timer in his place. "That is none of your business!" She paused, letting her somewhat harsh response set in. Her bluntness didn't do any good.

"Well, I suppose not," he said, his etiquette clumsiness on display. "But I can tell you Josh is getting jealous."

That was too much. "Josh? It's less of his business." She turned toward Elijah, fire in her eyes. "Who I'm fond of is of no concern to either one of you. Certainly not to Josh," she added. "And both of you need to stay out of my doings."

"Yes, ma'am, stay out."

Chapter Sixty-One

Ally's anger with Elijah didn't compare to the rage Dierden Kane was screaming at the hills and plains. He wanted revenge. Nothing else mattered. Right now, though, he was too angry to plot out any plan. Nothing he conceived was brutal enough.

Alice Hart and that damnable Gray Wehr were initially the targets of his vengeance. However, as the day edged past mid-morning with the sun blazing hotter, his men were becoming a focal point of his wrath. He couldn't walk without some kind of crutch to lean on, and there was nothing here in this awful forsaken land to use as one. "Where are you, you bastards?" Kane screamed at the top of his lungs. He laid still for a few minutes listening for horses or voices in the distance—nothing.

He tried again to stand and maybe hop along. He failed. He was blind in his left eye and deaf in his left ear. Crawling required every bit of his strength. Twenty or thirty yards at a time necessitated stopping for rest.

Finally, four of his men rode up on a nearby bluff with the noon sun burning down. They stopped their horses and looked around without seeing him. Kane would die if these fools didn't help him. One of the men stepped off his horse and walked partway down the hill on foot. He looked right at Kane, nothing. Kane could see them plain enough with only one good eye. With eight good ones between them, why couldn't they spot him?

He struggled to his knees, waving his arms and screaming at the top of his voice. Two of the mounted men turned their horses in his direction. One of them pointed toward him.

Kane let loose a profanity-laced rant when his men got to him. "Where the hell have you been? You better have food and water for me."

"We came lookin' when your horse showed up this morning," the foreman said, a bit too impertinent for Kane's liking. "We thought you might be dead," he said, drawing an ugly frown from Kane.

Another man handed Kane a canteen. "You better go a little easy," he said when Kane started guzzling the water.

"You go to hell."

"You'll be the one who gets sick," the man said.

"What happened to you?" a third man asked.

"Damn Hart woman shot me in the foot." The hate on Kane's face prevented any of the men from saying anything about a woman shooting him. "I'll kill that whore," Kane snarled.

"What happened to your face?"

"Hornets."

The third man, the only one with much actual concern about their boss, said he didn't think they had anything to treat the stings with, but he would wash up the foot. He used his bandanna and almost a full canteen of water, trying to clean the wound. "This is gonna need some more attention and a doctor." One of the other cowboys provided another kerchief for a bandage. "We've got some jerky and bread with us. Do you think you can eat something?" the man who did the bandaging asked.

Kane cursed at the man about not eating since breakfast yesterday. The jerky was leathery, and the bread nothing but dry hard tac. Kane complained the whole time he ate. Demanding whiskey, his mood got uglier. The man who did the doctoring said if they had any alcohol, he'd have poured some over Kane's toe to stop blood poisoning.

Kane rested another hour before telling his foreman to find him a pistol and help him up on a horse.

"We didn't bring any spare pistol, but there's a rifle in the scabbard on the saddle of the horse we brought you."

"Gimme yours. I'm tired of being unarmed." He handed over his gun, an old 1848 Colt Dragoon. After being helped on a horse, Kane checked the Colt to make sure for ammunition, cocked it, and shot the foreman in the stomach. He waved the pistol at the other three. "Nobody leaves me out here this long." He pointed at the man who bandaged his foot. "You're the new foreman. Now, all of you mount up."

The man Kane shot was sitting up, moaning, his shirt soaked in blood. "Ain't you dead yet?" Kane nudged his horse closer while glaring at the pathetic man.

The dying man was staring at his hands, covered in sticky red ooze bubbling out of the gaping hole in his belly. He gave the impression of being in awe of his situation. With some great effort, he managed to glare up at Kane. "You gut-shot me, you son-of-a-bitch" He tried to spit at Kane. "I hope that woman shoots your balls off."

Kane laughed, cocked the pistol again, and shot him through the forehead.

Chapter Sixty-Two

Josh had no desire to ride off looking for two soldiers, and this Hickok fella, whoever he was. He would have much rather ridden on to Fort Laramie with Ally. Lately, Ally gave the impression she was happy to be rid of him at any opportunity. Before Gray came back, he believed Ally was pleased to have him at her ranch and might be growing fond of him. But, since their return, she seemed to view him as an annoyance, maybe worse.

"You think we can find three men out here? Josh asked. "They may be miles from here."

Gray's expression dulled. He rolled his shoulders and rubbed the back of his neck. "You must be the most doubtful man since Thomas."

Josh resented the comment. Nevertheless, self-doubt had become his constant and inescapable companion. The reasons for him to doubt himself were plentiful. One could fill a book with his failures since Hanna's death. He failed Sarah the night Hanna died, and although she might have denied it, he failed in attaining her forgiveness. The marriage might have continued, but he had lost her love. Josh failed to protect her when their house was broken into. He failed at being a man when he lost her. He even failed at being a successful drunkard, getting himself thrown in prison. Most recently, he had failed at wooing Ally Hart.

"Those fellas aren't more than a quarter-hour ahead of us, a half-hour at the most. Let's stretch these horses out a little," Gray said.

"How do you know we're on the right path? I haven't seen any tracks."

"Because I know Hickok," Gray said, then took in and let out a deep breath.

"All right, Josh, listen to me," he said in a calmer voice. "These soldiers want to find out where the Sioux and Cheyenne are moving. There were only eight of them, to begin with, enough to beat back a small hunting party, if lucky." He told Josh to think about the situation, pointing out the Army wanted to locate Indians, which was why they broke off in two directions to cover more ground. "The bad part," Gray said, "was splitting up, made them too weak to handle more than a half–dozen braves, and only if the Indians had no guns. Now, if you wanted to divide a group of men that small, wouldn't you want to divide up someplace where anybody tracking you wouldn't see tracks split off? A place they wouldn't realize you reduced your force?"

Josh conceded Gray's logic made sense.

"Most of these plains out here are easy to track a horse over," Gray continued. "This outcrop of stone, though, you couldn't follow an elephant across this. So, if Hickok was going to break off from the others, this is the place." Gray paused. "Add the fact the lieutenant told us they split off about fifteen minutes back from where we talked to them, and the timing is right."

"Wouldn't Indians understand about this stone outcrop?" Josh asked.

"Jimmy's counting on them not expecting such a small

group to separate. He's taking his best gamble. That's what I would do."

Gray and Josh ran their horses for a little over a mile before coming up on a slight rise. Gray told Josh to head over to the left while he went to the right. He told him to keep in sight, but by spreading out, they'd be able to view a lot more ground. Before they got any distance between them, Gray hollered for Josh to come back. He pointed a little to the right and three bluffs out front. "I don't see anything," Josh said.

"Look for movement, not quite halfway up."

"Nothing," Josh said, shaking his head in disgust.

"It's them," Gray said. "Let's ride a little closer, and I'll fire a shot to catch their attention." They ran their horses down the slope, across a wide arroyo, and up the next rise. "See 'em now?"

Much to his relief, Josh did. Gray decided not to shoot and chance bringing a large group of Sioux or Cheyenne down on them. Instead, they rode within yelling distance. Hickok and the two soldiers stopped and headed their horses back toward Gray and Josh as soon as they heard them.

Hickok had grown the scraggly mustache of a young man. He was wearing an open crown, flat-brimmed silver belly colored hat, "Where's your sister?"

"She's at home, staying clear of you," Gray said.

"She's a beautiful woman. Is she fond of the little black pup I gave her?"

"The dog's a blamed nuisance," Gray said before extending his hand to the captain, an overweight man with bushy mutton chop sideburns. "Tom, we ran into your lieutenant. He didn't tell me you were the captain out here." Gray glanced at the corporal. "I'll swear, Tom, how'd you sober this scoundrel up enough to bring along?"

"A full day's work," the captain laughed.

"Somebody has to keep these officers safe," the corporal replied, sticking his hand out to Gray.

"Weren't you a top sergeant the last time I saw you?"

"Oh, hell, they make rye whiskey to keep me from being

a general."

"What was my lieutenant up to?" the captain asked.

"Being a damn fool, near as I can tell," Gray said. "You better hope he doesn't come anywhere close to Indians. If he does, he's gonna get your men killed." The captain shook his head. Gray pointed at Josh. "This is Josh McCormick. He's working out at Alice Hart's place."

"I understood she had a new man." The captain shook Josh's hand. "How's she doing?"

"Well...she's getting by." Josh didn't want to paint too bleak a picture, but he did want to be honest. "She got some new cattle from Gray, which helped her. But," he said before hesitating for a moment. "She's had her struggles. Dierden Kane has been threatening her. Somebody burned her barn and killed four of her cows."

"Kane did it. Hell, he admitted it. But there's no proof," Gray said.

"Someday, somebody's going to prove something on him, and when they do, we're gonna hang him," the captain said somberly. "I hope I'm still out here to put the rope around his neck."

"Where else would you be?"

"A war is comin' back east, Gray. Within a year would be my guess." The captain hesitated before clarifying his answer. "Well, at least if Lincoln gets elected president. The southern states will be unhappy about a Lincoln presidency. Except for the Army leaving this wilderness, a fight in the East might not be of much concern in the West, not past Kansas.

Gray nodded. "Ally, Alan Joseph, and I went over and had a talk with Kane about leaving her alone."

"How did that go?" the Captain asked?

"Ally shot his big toe off."

The once top sergeant, now a corporal, laughed. "I'd of give up drinking to of seen that."

Captain Douglas changed the subject—to Indians. The captain described the upsurge in attacks on wagon trains and homesteaders. "The day after tomorrow, there's a plan to send about seventy-five men out to hunt for Indians. "We could sure use another scout," he told Gray. Gray's first concern was why they wanted to find Indians; his second was how long they would be out.

Captain Douglas told Gray what he was sure Gray wanted to hear: they didn't want a fight, only determine where the hostiles were and how strong they were in numbers. To Gray's other question, he replied, "Ten days, no more." He validated his answer by adding, "The post commander doesn't think we can have so many men out any longer and keep the fort safe. Ten days, I give my word."

"Is Jimmy your only scout?"

"They sent a dispatch rider to the North Platte for Jim Bridger. If you want my honest assessment, I doubt they'll find him. So yes, Hickok is most likely the only one."

The adventure of scouting always appealed to Gray. He wouldn't admit it, at least not to anyone who cared about him, but the unknown, especially coming with risk, tugged at him. In truth, danger and hazard played a significant role in why he regularly left his valley. It wasn't so much wanderlust, as Annie and his sister believed; it was the charm he found in danger, plain and simple.

He wanted to go, but he had made something of a promise to Ally Hart, at least he was sure she considered it a promise—to help her face Dierden Kane. "Tom, I need to talk to Ally Hart before I agree. I need to be there with her when Kane comes calling."

"Hell," the captain half-laughed, "if she blew his toe off, Kane needs more than ten days before he bothers her. Besides, since you and she lacked the kindness to help him home, he's likely as not bled to death by now."

"I'll talk to her," was the only commitment Gray would give.

Chapter Sixty-Three

Dusk settled over Fort Laramie before Gray, Josh, Hickok, and the two soldiers arrived. Eventide was Ally's favorite time of the day. Things got less troubled. Struggles eased. Beautiful sunsets turned skies red, pink, and a mysterious lavender. Ally could slow down and release the day's burdens. She believed she could be content if days only consisted of sunrises and sunsets.

When Gray, Josh, and Hickok walked into the cafe where Ally and Elijah were eating, Josh asked about Ally's arm before Gray did.

"The doctor didn't think my arm's broken," she said. "Nevertheless, it hurts. He said I wouldn't be able to use it much for a couple of weeks." Ally could see it irritated Josh when Gray expressed sympathy first. Josh was thinking, *damn him*, Ally could see it in his eyes.

Gray told them they had no trouble finding the three men they went looking for. "You two remember Jimmy? You met him in our cow camp when you got the cattle," Gray said.

"I prefer James." Hickok shook Ally and Elijah's hands. "Or, J.B. is fine." He flicked his hand, dismissively toward Gray. "Gray and his sister are the only ones who call me Jimmy. He calls me Jimmy to annoy me. I think he pays Jean."

"You see any Indians?" Elijah asked.

"Not one," Gray said.

A blond girl with a missing tooth came over and asked the three newcomers if they wanted to eat. Hickok said along with his meal he'd like a shot of smooth Tennessee sipping whiskey. "We've only got one kind," the girl, no more than fifteen or sixteen, said. "You can sip if you want to. Most people guzzle the stuff."

"If you only offer one choice," Hickok said, "I better have two shots. It's probably not fine whiskey. The first shot will be to accustom me to the taste, so I can enjoy the second shot."

"Anybody else want whiskey?" the girl asked.

"I drink whiskey every Tuesday," Elijah said.

"Today's Thursday," the girl said.

"Today's Thursday?" Elijah tried to appear stunned. "That's something different," he said. "On Thursdays, I only imbibe with strangers." He smiled broader. "Josh is stranger than most. I'll have two, too."

For the first time since his last drunken state, Josh craved liquor. However, because of Ally's presence, he restrained himself, still hoping to regain his standing with her. Josh begrudged Gray over what he saw in Ally's eyes when she looked at Gray. He saw a gleam not there when she looked at him, although he thought he used to see a slight glint before Gray showed up.

Josh plucked at the cuff of his shirt. "Gray, when the captain brought up the subject of a possible war between the states, you didn't want to talk about which side you favor."

Josh's tone was condescending.

"What was I supposed to say?" Gray asked, every bit as condescending.

"Say which side. I went across the Mississippi River and listened to Lincoln and Douglas debate when they were in Alton, Illinois," Josh said. "I have to say I sided with Douglas." Josh's comments reeked of self-righteousness. "I favor the south. I believe in states' rights."

"States' rights? What a pile of horse manure," Hickok said as he leaned over toward Josh. "The only right those states are concerned with is their right to hold human beings in slavery for their greedy financial gain. It's morally indefensible." Hickok slammed his fist on the table and shoved a finger in Josh's face. "I've seen the backs of black men after the beatings they endured—men, women, and children half-starved. Such cruelty is reprehensible."

Josh scooted his chair back and shut up, letting the divisive issue drop.

They sat in awkward silence until the girl came back with the four whiskeys. Hickok was the first to take a sip. "This is poor whiskey," he said, whacking the glass down on the table.

Elijah guffawed and slapped his knee. "Most whiskey drinkers out here would barely know whiskey from coal oil. Bringing in quality whiskey would be a waste."

"Well, I appreciate good whiskey," Hickok said. "And this sure ain't." He took a second sip, and for an instant, appeared about ready to spit. "Hell, coal oil might be an improvement."

Elijah laughed a little harder. "You ain't supposed to sip. Sipping lets the taste linger in your mouth too long. Whack whiskey down in one gulp...like this." Elijah picked up his first shot and slammed the amber liquid down while tilting his head back. "That, my friend, is how you drink whiskey."

Dinner's arrival interrupted the whiskey discussion, giving Gray the chance to breach the scouting subject. While

Josh favored Gray departing, it irked him Gray would consider abandoning Ally. They all knew Kane would retaliate for what Ally did to him. He thought Gray leaving was no more than desertion.

Ally, on the other hand, remained unfazed. She agreed Kane would be no threat in the next ten days.

Josh chaffed about Ally believing Gray going on a scout being a positive thing, something to benefit those living out here. After listening to several more minutes of Ally and Elijah praising Gray, almost crediting him for preventing any Indian hostility, Josh, still ruffled over Hickok's criticism of his war views, had enough. He wanted a confrontation. "I think you're leaving Ally in a considerable amount of jeopardy."

Gray remained calm. "If I thought she was in danger, I'd stay with her."

"A lot of help, you'll be if Kane attacks her place while you're out glory hunting."

Ally leaned forward and put her good hand on Josh's forearm. "Joshua," she said.

Having her call him Joshua only irritated him further. "I think you're damn cowardly." Josh leaped to his feet.

Elijah jumped up and stepped in between Josh and Gray. "Josh, you better let this dog lie," he said, nudging Josh back several feet.

Although Gray remained seated, he glared at Josh.

Ally pushed her chair back and stood. "Stop it, Josh. Nothing will happen before he gets back."

Gray stayed restrained.

Josh kept trying to get loose from Elijah's bear hug but without much success. He kept running his mouth until Gray stood. Josh worked an arm free and pointed at Gray. "I'm tired of you making a fool out of me in front of Ally!"

"The only one making you look like a fool is you," Gray said.

Josh stomped on Elijah's foot and charged Gray, who let go a straight right, hitting Josh smack in the face. Josh's eyes bulged, his head snapped back, and he staggered briefly before falling backwards...out cold.

Elijah bent over and looked down at Josh. "I swear this old boy ain't never gonna learn nothin'."

Ally shook her head before telling Gray the scrap wasn't his fault.

"I doubt if he's hurt much," Gray said.

A stocky man, the restaurant's owner, scurried over and motioned at the unconscious Josh. "Drag him out of here. I don't want any more trouble."

Elijah and Hickok obliged.

Gray and Ally sat back down. "What am I going to do about him?"

"I wish you would stop asking me things like that." Gray smiled. "I doubt he's going to change much," he said.

"I doubt it too," Ally said. For quite some time, they sat without talking. The quiet time was comfortable. "When he first came out here, I wondered if I might find something decent in him. He was so broken. Still, I thought there was something in him, something worth saving."

Gray sipped his coffee while looking kindheartedly at Ally. "Do you think a man can be so ruined he's beyond hope?" she asked.

"I don't know, Ally. Might depend on what he was before he broke."

Ally thought about that. After all, she had no idea what kind of man he had been before his daughter died. When Judge Dan vouched for him, she didn't pursue the issue. Still, in her original letter back to the judge, she told him not to send the man. The judge persisted and sent him anyway, insisting she needed help.

"If you liked him when he first came, what changed about him?"

Ally had to think; it was hard to put her finger on an answer.

When Josh showed up, she purposely took about two weeks to observe him before making any judgment.

Afterward, she began to admit to herself she rather liked him. He was smart, in book knowledge anyway, had some sense of humor, and made her believe he wanted to help her. He started out being willing and anxious to learn.

After she got the new cattle, he started to change. He became thin-skinned, sometimes possessive about her. Most of all, he resented Gray, which puzzled Ally. She wondered if he was jealous of Gray, or if it bothered him that Gray might be the stronger, better man.

As far as her feelings about Gray, she made sure they stayed causal. At least she tried to keep them casual. She enjoyed his company, found him unassuming, felt comfortable with him, and appreciated his protection. She hadn't trusted anyone for a long time, not the way she trusted Gray. In a short time, she'd come to consider him a dear friend. She engaged in a little harmless flirtation with him. She might like a night with him, but nothing more.

Gray was too wild to want a future together. The Laurie girl was welcome to take on that task. Regarding him being a better man, Gray was who he was, indifferent about what others thought of him while making no judgments about other people. He minded his own business and expected the same in return.

"Ally, you worry too much."

Gray's statement did not surprise her, coming from someone who didn't worry at all. Ally rested her chin on her palm. "Sounds like advice is on the way."

"I don't give advice. I only make observations."

That was true enough, something else she liked about him. She had been given enough advice in her life, especially from men.

"And my observation," he said, much to Ally's delight, "is you should find yourself a man who does not need reforming."

"We can agree on that." Ally's eyes lit up. "Do you know any?"

"Not one," he said as he waved the blond girl over to

ask for more coffee. "Every man I know is beyond reform. They're too long unreformed."

"Are you too long unreformed?"

"Me? I'm the worst of the lot. I imagine you'd shoot my big toe off within a month."

"Maybe more than a toe." Ally ducked her head and stared at the floor. "I love your company, but we'd be a curious pair."

"I suspect you're too much for most men. I suggest you hold off for someone who might become a governor, or at least rich."

Ally enjoyed sitting with Gray and carrying on a pointless conversation. There had not been enough pointlessness in her life, and a little more was welcome.

Chapter Sixty-Four

The next morning, when Gray asked Hickok to help Ally Hart against Dierden Kane, Hickok reminded him of his employment by the Russell, Majors, and Waddell Freight Company. He was merely on a brief leave to go on this scouting mission. Hickok said his next job was to drive a freight team from Independence, Missouri, to Santé Fe, out in New Mexico. After a bit of persuading regarding how his sister might appreciate him helping her brother, Hickok decided to give Gray a short time.

Before Gray and Hickok rode out with the troops, Elijah came sauntering up. "You look stymied," Hickok said.

"Josh must have gone to one of them saloons after we dumped him off last night. He's still drunk." Elijah's mouth was set in a hard line. "Mrs. Hart is not going to be happy about this."

Gray turned to Hickok. "If the major shows up, tell him I'll catch up with you. I won't be far behind." He left with Elijah to find Josh. When asked how often this was happening, Elijah said it never happened before.

"Up 'til the last couple of weeks, Josh has been a decent fella. Something has sure changed him."

Gray didn't much care. The man was becoming an annoyance. They found him half-asleep in one of the barn stalls, just awake enough to start swearing at Gray. Gray yanked him to his feet and threw him out the front door, where he bounced into a corporal coming for his horse. Gray dragged him, brutally, to a nearby horse trough, and down he went. Josh came up, gasping for air. Gray shoved him right back under the water.

When Gray decided he'd had enough and dragged Josh out of the trough and to the ground, Josh coughed, hacked, and rolled around in the dirt, trying to breathe. Gray gave him a solid kick in the ass, sending him sprawling on his face in the mud. He grabbed him by the collar and the belt and yelled at him to get on his damn feet. When he did, Gray slammed him into the side of the barn.

A few cavalrymen gathered around to watch. One of them asked Elijah what the fella did. "He got drunk," Elijah said.

"Where's your stockade?" Gray asked one of the soldiers.

"Down there," a young private said, pointing to the left.

Gray half-led and half-dragged Josh to the jail. After a few words to the jailer, he tossed Josh in one of the dirty, rotten-smelling cells.

Gray found Ally, told her he'd be back at her place in about ten days. "Oh, by the way, Josh is sobering up in the stockade. In my opinion, you should leave him there."

Chapter Sixty-Five

Ally did a little shopping and waited another four hours before going to check on Josh in jail. When they took her back to his cell, she found him sprawled out across a filthy-looking bunk, sound asleep. "Would you wake him up for me?"

A jailer picked up a bucket of some kind of liquid. Ally didn't know what, but he threw it on Josh.

Seeing the look on her face, the jailer's mouth turned up into a wide grin, "Water, ma'am. We already took the other stuff to the latrine ditch."

Josh started cussing whoever threw the water.

"Are you sober?" Ally asked in an unpleasant voice. There was some hesitation before he answered her.

"I suppose so," he said.

"We're ready to leave," Ally said, void of any emotion. "Elijah is going to ride your horse. You'll be better off in the back of the wagon."

No one uttered a word on the entire six-mile trip back home or while unloading the supplies.

"Elijah, I need a minute with Josh."

"Yes, ma'am," Elijah said while backing out the front door.

Ally turned to Josh. "Didn't I tell you I wouldn't abide a drunk? Wasn't that almost the first thing I said to you?"

"I believe right after you asked if I was the criminal Judge Dan sent you," Josh said in a smart-assed tone.

"I'd be careful, Josh, especially if you have any aspirations to stay here."

Josh asked to sit, saying he was still a little shaky.

"I don't care what you do." Ally meant what she said. When he sat, she went to the kitchen and pumped two cups of water. "I didn't make any coffee," she said, placing one cup in front of him and sitting across from him with the other. Another long silence. "Are you just going to sit there?"

"What do you want me to say?" He tapped on the table, ran a hand down his chest. His sarcasm and defiance disappeared.

Ally frowned at him, her brow knit. She was debating whether to give him another chance or send him away. Sitting across from her, he looked beaten down, pitiful. But she did not pity him. She was not overly angry. Honestly, she did not feel anything.

"What has happened to you?" she asked.

"What do you mean?"

"You're not stupid. You know, what I mean," Ally yelled.

Josh jerked up straight. His eyes tightened. "All right," he said, "I'm tired of being treated like I'm valueless." His face turned red. "I'm the butt of every damn joke. I get all the menial jobs. My opinions are ignored or laughed at. Do you want me to go on?"

"Yes, why don't you?"

"The hell with you!"

Ally threw her cup of water in his face, stood, and tore into a harsh tongue-lashing. "Go ahead, hit me if you want to," she screamed. Josh leaped up. Ally thought he was going to hit her, but he did not move toward her. "Why don't you whimper to me about how you lost your daughter and your wife? Cry about not being strong enough to stand up to such a tragic loss."

"You…witch."

"That is rich," she laughed at him. "You don't have the guts to call me what you're thinking." Ally picked up her cup. She waved it past his face and got louder. "Nobody feels sorry for you. They don't need to. You handle pity all yourself." She turned her back on him and went to the kitchen.

Josh spun around, slamming the door behind him. He grabbed a lariat off the corral and darted between the rails, grumbling something about teaching a rank horse a lesson.

Over and over, Josh flung the rope at the animal, repeatedly missing. When the horse turned his backside to him, he rushed up behind, thinking he would get close enough to toss the rope over the horse's head. He got close—a flawed idea.

The hoof smashed into his thigh, right above his knee. His leg flew out from under him while the dull thud echoed through the air. He hit the ground face down and swearing. The kick did not break his leg, but the horse made his point.

Elijah rushed toward Josh. "You need help?"

"No," Josh bellowed. Elijah raised his hands and backed away. Josh scooted and crawled but mostly scooted over to the fence and pulled himself up.

"I told you to leave the rank devil alone," Elijah said.

"Sure, you told me." Josh moaned. "Everybody tells me."

"Well—you oughta not to ignore such good advice."

Ally came out to find out if Josh was hurt. The kick took the fight out of him, and he supposed he was fine when Ally asked about his welfare. Elijah said he had a lot of chores to do, adding it didn't appear he would have any help with them. Josh, too unstable to stand, let alone walk, continued to lean on the fence. Ally asked him a second time if he was hurt. He again said he didn't think so. Neither said much for quite some time.

"Josh," Ally said before hesitating. "Don't give up on working with the horse."

His eyes widened.

Ally rubbed her palms together. "You need to succeed at something. The horse might be your opportunity." She took a couple of steps toward him. "I didn't need to be so hateful in the house," she said. "I do have compassion for you losing your family."

Josh didn't consider the apology sufficient but kept quiet.

"I've never lived in a city as large as St. Louis, not even as a little girl with Judge Dan, so I may not understand what it is to be a city man." She put her hand on his arm. "But out here, you can't quit the way you do. Not if you want anyone to respect you." Ally leaned back against the fence. "As I say, I'm ignorant about cities, but out here, you have to earn things to prove yourself."

"You're giving me a rough damn judgment," Josh said.

Ally brushed her hair away from her face. "No, Josh, not rough. True. When things are hard, or look like they might get hard," she said, "you quit."

Joshua clamped his jaws together. He disagreed.

"You said you wanted to learn to work cattle, but when Gray was more skilled than you, you gave up. You went and bought a pistol to protect me, but after you didn't become a crack shot after a couple of days of practice, you quit. When we didn't take you to Kane's place, you pouted like a child." Ally's voice got more assertive. "But, most of all, when you wanted me, you gave up."

Josh wanted to deny any interest in her. When he turned to face her, a surly "What?" was the only thing he could mutter.

"If you want me, you better work a whole lot harder at getting me."

"Well, you're sure full of yourself," Josh said.

"That might be," Ally said, "but it doesn't change the truth." Ally licked her lips. "You touched my face the night the Sioux left the lance. When I opened my eyes, you started apologizing. You wanted to kiss me. Why didn't you? The next morning in the kitchen, I gave you the opportunity. Instead of kissing me, you ran away. Think about that for a while." She headed off toward the house.

Chapter Sixty-Six

Josh stood around in the corral for another thirty minutes, mad, feeling like a jackass, not ready to admit to himself he wanted Alice Hart.

He tapped on her door. "Ally?"

"In the kitchen."

He awkwardly started to tell the woman what he'd been practicing for the last fifteen or twenty minutes. "I wasn't sure how you feel about me."

"That's fair," she said without turning around. "Neither am I."

His planned speech squelched, he felt utterly asinine. With five little words, Ally wrecked his plan to woo her. After a few minutes of gaping at her, Ally turned and walked toward him.

"Some reason you came back in?" she asked.

"To talk to you."

"Go ahead," she said, sitting across from him and staring.

He didn't. Less than an hour passed since Ally castigated him about being so hangdog, and here he was—again acting whipped.

"What were you going to talk about?" she asked, this time sounding impatient.

Josh gawked around the room, still not saying anything. "Have you gone, mute?"

"No, I haven't gone mute!"

"Then talk."

Ally could be intensely frustrating. Something about her destroyed Josh's ability to talk, at least to say anything sounding halfway intelligent. She was beautiful, but Sarah had been beautiful, and he never had trouble talking to her. Not until Hannah died. Hannah's death destroyed everything else in his life, maybe even his ability to speak to a woman. Or, maybe talking to another woman made him unfaithful to Sarah. Whatever the issue, it ruined his life, not only his life but his future.

"I wanted to talk about you and me," he managed to mutter, making himself sickeningly vulnerable.

"Fine, let's do," Ally said.

Josh couldn't tell whether the woman was sincere or sarcastic. She did possess a sharp tongue.

Ally asked him if he wanted her to start. Embarrassed, he told her yes.

"I don't want to be alone for the rest of my life," she said. "Everything else I'm unsure of." Her eyes drifted away from him. "Let's take a walk along the river."

Jealousy burned in Josh every time Ally walked with Gray. He planned to make the best of his opportunity. Ally put her arm in Josh's.

"I enjoy walking along the river," she said. "If you like to fish, the Platte is full of trout."

"I've never done much fishing," Josh said.

Ally pulled her arm away. "I'll say one thing about you, Josh, you're a hard man to drag into a conversation."

"You should have waited for Gray and taken him for a

walk."

Ally laughed at him, but not in a good-humored way. "If Gray were here, I'd do more than walk with him." There she said it.

Josh didn't even respond.

"Your problem is you spend all your time worried about what somebody else is doing but don't pay enough attention to what you're doing."

"What's that mean?"

"I would think it would be obvious," she said, snapping her words. "You pout if I go for a walk with Gray, but you never ask me to go with you." She laughed at him again. "I guess you're afraid he's going to sweep me off my feet. But you never try to do any sweeping of your own."

For some reason, Ally began a detailed explanation about her feelings for Gray. She started with how he became a good friend, how much she trusted him for advice, and continued with how, in her opinion, he was what a man should be. Yet, she concluded that nothing romantic would come from their relationship as dear as he was to her.

"I guess you find nothing romantic about me, either."

"I don't know," Ally said. She stopped walking. "I don't know what I want from you."

Her honesty didn't resolve anything. "I guess we're right where we started," Josh said. The whole time couldn't have gotten any more uncomfortable. With nothing to lose, Josh put his hand under her chin, raised her face slightly, leaned over, and kissed her.

Chapter Sixty-Seven

The closest doc did not give Kane good news. He told him it would likely be a week before he'd see much out of the eye the hornet stung. He wouldn't speculate on when the swelling in Kane's ear would go down enough to hear. He used a stiff brush to clean out the stump and a scalpel to scrape—unbearably—some infection out.

Kane bellyached to the doc about how rough he was being. The physician told Kane if he didn't clean this infection out, treatment would be a lot rougher when he cut off his foot or the leg clear up to the knee.

The doctor predicted a week before he could walk. Walking then would depend on the unlikely possibility of getting a boot on. Kane's revenge on Alice Hart would be served cold, at least two weeks cold.

Chapter Sixty-Eight

A week later, romance had not advanced far. Josh was so clumsy in his courting Ally wasn't sure she could endure the ordeal. She did not understand how a man with so little passion in him ever wooed a woman into marriage. Being a gentleman, or timid, his hands never wandered anywhere beyond her arms or back. Even though she would have stopped such nonsense, she thought he should at least try. Any thoughts in her mind about lovemaking didn't include Josh, probably never would.

One positive thing came out of the failing courtship— remarkable progress on the barn. By the end of the week, barring a severe storm, Indian raid, or Kane attack, both the barn and new living quarters for Elijah and Josh would be complete.

Ally took some pleasure in Josh making progress with the rank horse. It was a little slow but more than with her. She was also pleased that Josh took Gray's earlier advice about taking the other horses out of the corral. At first, the rank horse used the space to his advantage, keeping more distance between himself and Josh. However, after a couple of days, the sorrel decided it took too much effort to keep running from the man. Now, for the most part, the horse ignored Josh. Occasionally, Josh might touch him, although the horse always moved away, which amused Ally.

Ally told him he needed to rope him, put a halter and long lead rope on him, and start some groundwork. After an hour of missing the horse, Ally suggested he try roping a fence post. She pointed out being right-handed, the rope would drift to the left every time he threw it. He needed to adjust for the drifting. Soon, Josh was proficient at roping— a fence post. At roping a moving horse, not so much.

Chapter Sixty-Nine

"The village on this side of the river is Sioux," Gray said. "The one on the other side is Cheyenne." A half dozen Cheyenne warriors were crossing the river to join the Sioux waiting on their side. "Soon as the Cheyenne cross, let's ride down."

Four Indians rode out to meet them. Gray said they had some good fortune and some bad. "The two on the left are Lakota: Spotted Tail, we've met several times, that's good fortune, the other is Red Cloud...bad fortune. The Cheyenne are Roman Nose; I know him a little too, and we have a mutual friend. The other Cheyenne is Dull Knife. I was at a counsel with him once."

"You make a positive impression?" Hickok asked.

"He probably won't remember me. I wasn't involved in the talks, just a bystander," Gray said. "I don't recall Dull Knife being friendly," he said. "I suspect they'll stop before we get much closer. Making us come to them makes them superior. When they do, we need to stop, raise one hand in acknowledgment, and ride on over to them."

The Indians did stop, Gray raised his hand, and they rode the rest of the way to them. Gray held up his right hand to show a scar across his palm. "I'm brother to the Lakota Paints His Horse, son of Old Crow Dog."

As boys, he and Paints His Horse cut their hands to mix their blood. Gray's mother scolded them over how dangerous the stunt was. They were lucky they hadn't cut their hands off. Both boys laughed at her concern. Old Crow Dog called the blood mixing childish silliness. Jean had been impressed with the boys' bravery, so much so, she got herself a whipping for insisting she was going to have a blood brother too, or sister.

Spotted Tail did know Gray. He was friendly enough, saying he liked both Old Crow Dog and Paints His Horse. Roman Nose was also sociable, talking with Gray about their previous meetings. When Gray brought Ally up, Roman Nose talked about promising her peace and having the Lakota put a peace lance in her yard. Gray expressed Ally's gratitude and said the Cheyenne would always be welcome at her ranch. Dull Knife said nothing.

Red Cloud was not friendly. He demanded an explanation of why the military was on Lakota land. None of the three Wasichu had an answer acceptable to either the Sioux or Cheyenne. Because only Gray spoke enough Lakota to carry on a conversation, the responsibility of answering fell on him. Gray told the truth, aware it would not be well received, but at least he'd be telling the truth.

"We came out this far to see how many Lakota and Cheyenne joined together." The answer was both short and truthful—things to his advantage.

His answer satisfied Spotted Tail and Roman Nose, not Red Cloud. He asked why the Lakota and Cheyenne were concerns of the Wasichu.

"More and more wagon trains are being raided. We wondered why," Gray said.

Red Cloud's jaw tightened; his mouth drew into a snarl.

"They are our enemies."

"We have a peace treaty with you." Red Cloud did not respond. He glared at Gray. "It was signed almost ten years ago," Gray said.

Red Cloud became more belligerent. "You Wasichu broke the treaty."

"The Lakota and Cheyenne broke the treaty first by attacking the Crow on the land given to them," Gray said.

Red Cloud nudged his horse forward and spat on the ground. "Crow," he growled and spat again. "All Wasichu lie. You promised your people would only cross our land. Lies. You kill our buffalo. You caused war between the Lakota and the Assiniboine because you killed our meat, and there is not enough for both. Your soldier Gratton entered our land and killed Conquering Bear. You are building bridges against your promises. The soldiers do not enforce the treaty as promised. They allow hunters on our lands. Your army provides them protection and gives them guns. Your treaty lies."

Hickok leaned over to Gray. "Quite a speech."

Gray kept the conversation in Lakota. "What you say is true, Red Cloud. But your raiding of the wagon trains and killing of the settlers will only make things worse."

Red Cloud jerked his horse to the left, kicked his flanks. He was within inches of Gray's face, his hot breath stinking. "For who? Not for the Lakota." Red Cloud spun his paint horse and galloped toward the Indian camp, an insult.

"Red Cloud and many others want war," Spotted Tail said. "Those of us who want peace are now few."

"True also of the Cheyenne," Roman Nose said. "Your woman friend will be safe, but the raiding will not stop."

"If you turn your soldiers and leave, we will not attack you," Spotted Tail said in English. With Dull Knife never saying a word, the three remaining Indians turned and went back to their camps.

"I think we should take his advice about leaving," Hickok said. The captain agreed.

As they turned back to the troops, Gray told them Red Cloud would be a problem. "He's growing in influence, and he's not happy."

Chapter Seventy

Eight days after Ally Hart shot his big toe off, Kane still couldn't pull his boot on. He could see out of his eye and hear some out of his ear. He was hobbling around on two crutches and constantly swearing about what he would do to the Hart woman.

Four days after he sent the two men to recruit more men, they returned with one. Kane flung one of his crutches across the porch, bouncing it off his white picket fence, breaking two slats. "I told you I wanted four, damn you."

One of the two recruiters said they were lucky to hire one. Kane screamed and hollered about Alice Hart having Gray with her. "He'll kill half of you before you fire a shot."

"Hell, he's only one man. There'll be more than a dozen of us," one of the other men answered. "Unless you ain't goin' along," he added, looking at Kane.

Dierden Kane did not take insults from hired men. "What did you say?"

"Well, I wasn't sure you'd go with your bad foot," the

man said.

"Kane's right about Gray," one of the other men said, joining in the conversation. "He's tough as they come. We'll want to kill him quick."

"I'll kill him and piss in his mouth," another man said.

"You better be soberer than you are now," Kane shot back, aggravated by the man's drunken bragging. "I don't give a damn which one of you kill Gray or any of the others, but the woman is mine. I'm gonna gut her while she's still alive. You can all have your way with her first, but I finish her." Kane hated Gray Wehr, but he despised Alice Hart. Killing Gray would be enough, but the woman deserved more. She would beg to die.

Kane spent the rest of the afternoon and early evening sucking down whiskey and contriving brutal ways to hurt Alice Hart.

Chapter Seventy-One

Ten days after leaving with the soldiers, Gray and Hickok rode back to Ally Hart's place, where they found Ally alone brushing a horse. "Well...Kane's not burned anything down," Gray said as he dismounted. Ally laughed a little and walked over to hug Gray. After glancing around the area, Gray asked where Elijah and Josh were.

"They're out with the cattle. They should be back in an hour or so," Ally said.

Ally, like his sister and Annie Laurie, always knew what Gray was thinking.

"I wouldn't worry about Josh," she said, smiling. "I don't think he's one to hold a grudge. And I'm sure he doesn't want some kind of blood feud with you," she said.

Gray laughed.

"I see you were able to talk your friend into coming with you," she said, grinning at Hickok.

"I hope I brought enough ammunition," Hickok said.

"I hope you don't need any," Ally said. "How'd your

scouting go?" she asked, turning back to Gray.

Gray told her they found Sioux and Cheyenne, more in fact than he expected to come across. He said Roman Nose had been with them and repeated his promise she would be safe. "I did tell him the Cheyenne would be welcome to water their horses here." He also told her to offer them a cow occasionally. The rest of his description of the meeting with the Indians wasn't encouraging. He described Red Cloud as unfriendly and confrontational. He said Dull Knife did not say one word but wore the sour disposition of a man wanting war.

"Do you think there will be a war?" Ally asked.

Gray was honest in his answer. He was always honest with Ally. "I do. There are too many immigrants. Too many of them are squatting on the Indian land instead of passing through." He talked about the immigrants killing too many buffalo and said the Indians, not just the Sioux and Cheyenne, but the Arapaho, Arikara, and Shoshone, are fed up. The Sioux, he told her, are at war with the Crow and are pushing them off the Crow land. "The whole situation is touchy," he said.

"This will upset Elijah," Ally said. "He worries about Indian raids."

Gray reassured Ally about being safe from Cheyenne, probably from Sioux, as long as the lance stayed in her yard.

Ally took them inside, promising to make them some coffee. Hickok asked her if she might have anything more potent, like whiskey. She told him she had only a little for medicinal purposes, cleaning out cuts and wounds. She said she used half a bottle on Gray's shoulder, leaving none available for getting drunk on, or for any drinking at all.

"What are you, a Mormon, or something?" Hickok asked.

"I'm a Baptist." Ally laughed. "And a teetotaler." She poked Hickok in the chest, "and so are you while you're around here."

When Josh and Elijah came in, Gray wasted no time

before speaking to Josh. "You appear sober."

"Somebody damn near drowned him the last time he drank." Elijah hooted. "You wouldn't have a cookie, would you, Mrs. Hart?"

"They're under the blue towel," Ally said, pointing at the counter next to the pump. "Go, help yourself."

"Why they're ginger. I swear, Mrs. Hart, did you make those because they're my favorite?"

"Whatever I bake are your favorites."

"Well, I do enjoy your cookies," Elijah said, coming back to the table with the whole plate. Ally told the others if they wanted one, they better be quick; they didn't last long with Elijah around.

By the time the cookies and coffee disappeared, the cookies eaten mainly by Elijah, Josh had not said anything. Gray rubbed his three-day beard. "Ally says you're making progress with the sorrel. Let's go see how he's doing."

"Ally says I need to start groundwork with him, but I can't throw a rope on him."

Gray didn't look at Josh but answered casually. "Roping a horse can be a little tricky. I'll toss one on him for you today if you want. Once you rope him the first time, you'll improve pretty quick."

Gray grabbed the lariat, and he and Josh slipped through the rails. Gray told Josh the same thing Ally said about the rope drifting to the left. "He's not going to be happy about this," Gray said. "Watch yourself when I catch him."

When the sorrel saw the rope, he started to run hard around the corral. Gray swung the rope twice and threw the loop over the horse's head. The speed with which Gray threw astounded Josh. His attempts were slow and awkward. Gray was fast and graceful. He held the rope behind him and leaned down on it, almost as if sitting in a chair. "Don't fight him any more than you have to," he said as he turned with the horse while he charged around the corral. After a dozen or so trips around, the horse started to slow down some. Gray pulled the rope a little tighter but still let the horse run.

Finally, the horse stopped, turned, and took two steps toward Gray. "That's what we want," Gray said. "Now comes the part where we stand and stare at each other 'til he decides what he wants to do."

The staring contest lasted longer than Josh expected. The horse pawed at the ground a little. When he did, Gray gave the rope the slightest tug, starting the whole process over again. This time, however, the horse didn't run as long. When the sorrel stopped, he turned toward Gray, and this time licked his lips.

"Good boy," Gray said quietly. "He's thinking things over. Deciding if he's gonna let me be boss." After more lip licking, the horse took a few steps toward Gray. He tossed his head a little and took a couple more. A few more steps and he was close enough for Gray to reach up and rub his jaw. "You're a sweet boy," Gray whispered. "You're not rank, are you? You're a sweetheart."

After a little more rubbing and whispering, Gray told Josh to walk over sideways to them. He said if the horse became bothered, stop and wait a little while. After stopping twice, Josh stepped up next to Gray, who handed him the rope. "Give him plenty of slack, and I'm going to move away," Gray said. "If he wants to go, let him. He's going to make you go through the same thing I did."

The horse did go, and Josh did a top-notch job of letting him move. He stopped once, briefly before charging off again. The second time the horse stopped, he licked his lips and came toward Josh.

"Reach up and rub the side of his face," Gray told him.

After a while, Gray told him to try and take the rope off slowly. The horse stayed calm, quietly stood next to Josh after the rope was off. When he left, he didn't charge off. He walked off.

"Do the same thing for the next couple of days," Gray said. "Go slow and easy, and you'll win yourself a lifelong pal."

Josh's attitude toward Gray was changing. Josh could

not deny Gray being a friend to Ally. He basically gave her the cattle to put her back on her feet. He gave her those Arapaho ponies, and he was protecting her from Dierden Kane. Honestly, Gray treated him decent. If they met under different circumstances, they might have been friends. Perhaps, they still would be.

It didn't dampen Josh's mood when Gray and Hickok talked rather somberly over dinner about the scouting trip, about possible Indian trouble coming.

After the meal, Josh asked Ally to go for a walk along the river.

At the river, he turned Ally toward him and gave her an enjoyable kiss.

When he finished, she was smiling at him. "That was different," she said. Josh didn't say anything. Instead, he took her hand and led her down the riverbank.

"You're quiet."

"Thinking about things," Josh said.

"What things?"

"Life. I guess."

"You're doing a good job with the sorrel, you know."

Lately, Josh had become a man unwilling to take a compliment. Especially if he could use the opportunity to complain—whine, in Ally's opinion—about how life had been treating him. This time, he accepted the praise. "I shouldn't say this," he began, "but I am kind of proud of myself."

"Well, you should be," Ally said. "Everybody's been scared of that horse. Not even Sam would go near him. I'm proud of you too." She slipped her arm through Josh's. "It's been a while since I've seen you smile," she said.

"I'd like to kiss you again." Ally didn't respond, not in words. She did allow him to kiss her. "Ally, do you ever get tired of being alone?"

She cast her gaze to the ground. "Sometimes." The question made her look sad. Josh might be getting serious about her, but she wanted things to go gradually between them. In some ways, she felt she made a mistake marrying Sam. She didn't want to make another one. Too many mistakes might cause a person to give up. Giving up might cause a person to die.

Josh turned her toward him. He had a lopsided smile. "Would you ever consider marrying me?"

Would you ever *consider* marrying me? What kind of question is that? Ally had been afraid Josh would ask her to marry him. But she did not expect to be asked if she would *consider* marrying him. Ally didn't know much about gambling, but she was familiar with the term hedge your bets. She didn't want a man who hedged his bets. She was sure of that, if nothing else. Despite being piqued about Josh's inept proposal, if he was proposing, she didn't say no. She didn't say yes. She hedged her bet.

Chapter Seventy-Two

The following morning while finishing their living quarters on the side of the barn, Elijah could not have been more surprised when Josh said he and Ally had discussed marriage.

"We haven't made any firm decisions," Josh said.

Elijah's jaw dropped. "Married?"

"I said we haven't decided yet," Josh said.

"Marry Mrs. Hart? Preposterous, you can't marry Mrs. Hart."

"Why not?" Josh asked.

"Because she needs a man who can work cows...and run a ranch."

"We might go back to St. Louis."

St. Louis? That had never, never occurred to Elijah. Thinking about Ally, leaving gave him a headache. It made no sense. It wrecked Elijah's world. No news could have been worse. He frequently worried about all the bad things threatening their lives here, but never Mrs. Hart marrying and leaving. In less than five minutes, Josh downright ruined

Elijah's life.

Once quite a drinker, Elijah hopelessly racked his brain for where he might have hidden a whiskey bottle. Getting drunk seemed like a reasonable solution. Desperate to stop this nonsense before it went any farther, Elijah decided to use Gray as a threat. "When Gray hears about this, he's likely to tear a hole in you."

"Why would Gray care?"

"Because him and Mrs. Hart fancy each other," Elijah said.

Josh shook his head. "We talked about Gray. There is nothing between them," Josh said.

Much to Elijah's relief, Josh said they would talk about this later and left.

Gray and Hickok had ridden out to check the cattle, leaving Ally alone in the house. When Josh went in, he went straight to the point. "I told Elijah we discussed marriage."

"You what?" Ally's reaction stunned Josh. He expected she would be pleased. She wasn't.

She hadn't said yes. She didn't even consider it an earnest conversation, just idle talk, a one-sided conversation, not to be taken sincerely. Ally Hart was not a romantic, sometimes, not very affectionate, which bothered her a little. Ally was practical and proud of being realistic. Being practical meant she might consider marriage someday. Still, there was the issue of love. Not so much being in love, but whether the emotion held a role in her life anymore. And if love did carry a part, was Josh McCormick the right man?

"You were serious about marriage?" As far as Ally was concerned, this was a topic requiring more thought, considerably more.

When Josh went back out to work, Ally slipped out the back door and started on foot to where she thought Gray and Hickok might be. Beet red and smelling sweaty, she finally found Gray, thankfully by himself.

"You lose your horse?"

"No, I felt like taking a walk," Ally said.

"I enjoy a walk once in a while. But generally not in the heat of the day. A cool evening suits me better." He took his canteen off his saddle and offered water to Ally. "You better pour some of this over you. I expect a person could fry an egg on your forehead."

Ally soaked her head and took a long drink. "Come sit by the river with me," she said, handing the canteen back.

"Your eyes look like you're coming off a six-day drunk."

Ally, too tired to get into foolishness with Gray, sauntered off toward the river with Gray following along.

"Ally, you look forlorn."

"I have a problem, Gray."

"Most of us do," Gray smiled.

"Last night, Josh asked me to marry him...well, sort of, he asked if I'd ever consider marrying him."

Gray laid back and closed his eyes. "I've thought about asking Annie to marry me. But in all my worldly adventures, I made a few enemies. I wouldn't want her to end up a widow."

Ally had no idea how to respond. So, she stared at him, waiting for him to open his eyes. It took long enough. "I was going along fine in my daily routine."

Gray sat up and interrupted her. "And Josh shows up and spoils everything."

"Exactly," Ally said. "I guess I'm in a predicament." Ally shrugged.

"Too bad Elijah's not younger. He'd make you a satisfactory husband."

Ally chuckled. "He's fond of me. And he's kind to me. Course he might fall over dead any day."

"Then you'd be a widow again. Right back where you are now," Gray said.

Ally brushed some ants off her arm after a red one bit

her. "I'm not sure I want to be married again." Another ant crawled up her neck and over her chin. "Let's walk; there are too many bugs here."

"You're sitting next to an anthill."

"Why didn't you tell me? You jackass." She laughed, giving him a sharp poke in the ribs with her elbow.

"I thought maybe you liked ants."

Ally finished shaking and brushing her skirt. Gray stood and suddenly gave her a quick hug. It was brief, but a shock. "What was that for?"

"Figured you needed a hug."

Ally did need a hug—a hug, with no hidden scheme, no plan to use her. Just a simple hug to make her feel better, and it did. "I'm not going to marry Josh." She put her arm around Gray's waist. "I don't want to be alone forever, but I sure want the right man...this time."

Chapter Seventy-Three

Dierden Kane, helped by a woman of ill repute, not the consumptive one he lived with, another one he passed around to keep the disreputable ranch hands happy, got a boot on.

His foot hurt like hell, but the boot was on. Without the aid of a crutch, he limped out the door of his ostentatious house and down the front steps. His new foreman, the one Kane picked when he shot the previous one, asked about his foot. Kane growled about hurting before calling the man a damn fool for not knowing. "I want every manjack in before dark to meet with me in the bunkhouse."

"Two men are out at the line shack," the new foreman said.

Kane snarled while pointing to a red-haired cowboy coming out of the barn. "Put his ass on a fast horse and send him after them. You go round up the ones out with the cows. I want every man here tonight. We're leaving early in the morning."

The new foreman asked where they were going.

"That damn Hart woman's place."

When the two men rode off to bring in the rest of the crew, Kane went into the barn and found a long skinning knife. He spent the next several minutes honing a sharp edge. He hit the edge on the grindstone a couple of times to put some nicks in the blade. He wanted the edge sharp, but he also wanted the blade a little jagged, so cutting Ally Hart would inflict more pain. He wanted Alice Hart to hurt when he cut her. He planned to slice on her for a while and then gut her as he would an animal. "I'll make you sorry you bucked me, you bitch."

Kane limped over and stuck his foot down in a horse trough, soaking his boot. He figured the leather would stretch and conform to his foot and, with any luck, ease some pain. By Kane's timing, Alice Hart only had about forty-eight hours to live. That pleased him. It pleased him more that two or three of those hours would be torturous and agonizing.

Satisfied he would soon have revenge, plus forty head of cattle with that damned W/J brand on them, he lumbered back up to the house, where he poured himself a nice glass of brandy. Sipping brandy would be a pleasant way to pass the day.

By mid-afternoon, when the first of his men started to come in, Kane staggered down the massive stairway into his ornate entryway. Half-drunk, but still sensible enough to put the cork back in the brandy and sober up before he met with his men, he poured himself a cup of strong coffee.

Shortly before dark, the red-haired man who went to fetch the two men at the line shack rode in alone. Seeing Kane hobbling in his direction, he walked over to meet him. Kane was angry. "Where are the other two?"

"Dead," the man said. "Shot full of Sioux arrows. They burned the line shack down too."

Kane went into a cussing fit about having only thirteen men to attack the Hart place.

"How many does she have?"

"Two work for her, but Gray and Joseph may still be

around."

"I doubt he's still around," the other man said. "Gray, he doesn't stay anywhere long." He spit tobacco. "Hell, if those two are around, counting you, there'll still be fourteen of us, to four of them. The odds are still way in our favor.

"Gray Wehr balances out a lot of odds," Kane said.

"I guess a bullet kills him, same as anybody else."

The man's response further irritated Kane. "Well, maybe you ought to head on over and kill him before the rest of us ride in."

"I ain't afraid of him," the man said.

"Humph." Kane limped toward the bunkhouse to meet with his men.

Kane started the meeting off by kicking a yellow barn cat for rubbing against his leg. The cat rolled across the floor, jumped up, and escaped through an open window. Kane asked where they kept the whiskey. As soon as a cowboy produced a bottle of rye, he took a deep drink. He passed the whiskey around, making clear this would be their last drink until they got back from the little trip.

None of his men appeared surprised or alarmed about his plan for Alice Hart and her ranch. He offered a one-hundred-dollar bonus to the man who killed Gray Wehr but made it plain Alice Hart belonged to him. He told the men they could take anything they wanted from her place before they burned everything down.

One man asked if that included horses. Kane said to take anything they wanted, but there probably wouldn't be enough horses for every man to take one. He decided the man who killed Wehr would not only win the hundred-dollar bonus, he'd also get the first pick of the horses.

"We'll leave as soon as the sun comes up. And no more damn whiskey. No more drinking." Kane limped off to his house.

"A hundred-dollar bonus," one cowboy said. "That Wehr must be one tough fella."

Chapter Seventy-Four

"Last board," Elijah said as he overlapped the one below and nailed it down. "I guess we're done," he said, glancing at Josh nailing the other end of the last board on their newly completed living quarters.

"Done? Don't you want a floor?" Josh asked.

"Why would we need a floor?"

"To keep us out of the dirt," Josh said.

"Walking on a little dirt ain't gonna hurt you none. You're sorrier than a prissy little girl or starchy old woman."

Elijah grinned and took off for the other side of the barn. Josh grunted and followed.

Ally and Gray were watching Hickok shoe one of her horses, watching and listening to him complain about being the one having to do the work.

"I hope you're satisfied with his work." Elijah laughed as he walked up to Gray. He leaned over toward Hickok. "I hope you remember it don't pay to make Gray unhappy about a horse's treatment."

"Oh, he's gentle enough with the horse," Gray said. "But he's sure too slow to make a living as a farrier."

Elijah looked at Ally. "When did you take your arm out of the sling?"

Ally looked at her arm and moved it around. "About five days ago. You're sure not very observant."

"I've been working hard the last several days," Elijah said. "I guess I haven't had time to notice."

Josh thought about criticizing Elijah's powers of observation. But, since Ally liked the old fool, he kept his mouth shut. Josh didn't want to upset her, especially since he still hoped for a future with her.

What he wanted was to ask her to walk along the river. Not yet being noon prevented walking. But it didn't stop him from thinking about it. Her blue dress buttoned up the back, and he daydreamed about standing behind her and undoing the buttons, letting the dress fall from her shoulders. That was unlikely to happen. First, he lacked the nerve to try, and second, he doubted she would stand for such behavior. She had been somewhat liberal about letting him kiss her, but he suspected kissing was all she would allow.

Ally herself interrupted his fantasizing when she suggested he spend a little time working with the sorrel while she got lunch ready. Gray, Hickok, and Elijah put the other horses in the newly finished barn, and Josh, now doing his roping, took three attempts but did lasso the horse by himself. The horse no longer objected to a halter, and Josh lunged him around the corral several minutes, getting him to change directions by stepping forward and raising an arm.

Gray and the other two were sitting on the top rail watching. "I think it's time to put a saddle on him," Gray said.

Excitement rippled through Josh while he reached for the blanket. Gray held the lead rope while Josh laid the saddle blanket on the horse's back. The horse jumped away a little when the fabric touched his back.

Gray walked the horse around for a couple of minutes

to calm him down. Satisfied, Gray told Josh to grab the saddle. "Put the right stirrup up and the cinch up over the top of the saddle, then set the saddle on him, don't throw it up there."

The animal stood quiet until Josh let the full weight of the saddle rest on his back.

"Look out!" Gray yelled as the horse left the ground.

The saddle flew forward, and to the right, the blanket straight to the right. The horse changed directions every time he took to the air. Gray held on to the lead rope and managed to at least keep the horse in the corral.

Ally heard all the commotion and Elijah's howling and came back out to watch. They put the saddle back on three more times with the same results. The fifth time he still threw the saddle but calmed down as soon as the saddle was gone. Two more attempts, and the saddle stayed in place.

"You might want to let me reach under for the cinch," Gray told Josh.

Josh gladly took a step back. The horse stood quiet while Gray grabbed the cinch and ran the saddle strap through the ring. He pulled the cinch up against the horse's chest and waited a brief time before snugging the strap up. The animal reached around and tried to bite, but Gray mildly slapped his mouth. The sorrel tossed his head at Gray, but Gray deflected the horse's face with his elbow and pulled the cinch tight.

Gray handed the lead rope to Josh and told him to lead the horse around the corral. "You'll want to do the same thing for a couple of days. Then it'll be time to climb on his back."

"It's an odd thing," Josh said when they sat down for lunch.

"What's odd?" Elijah asked as he ladled Ally's thick beef stew on his plate.

"That I spend so much time with that rank horse, and I'm not dead yet. I believe that's what someone predicted."

"Well, you ain't been on his back yet, either," Elijah said.

"He will be in a day or two," Gray said. "The sorrel's gonna make you a fine horse," he told Josh. "You should be proud of your work with him."

"Are you going to let Josh up first?" Ally caught her lower lip between her teeth.

Josh started to say something, but Elijah cut him off.

"I don't see why who gets on first makes any difference." Elijah snorted. "Ain't nobody likely to stay long." Elijah got to laughing at his own wit. "Gray might last a little longer, but the final result's gonna be the same— somebody's gonna end up in the dirt."

Even Josh grinned a little.

"I just know it ain't gonna be me," Elijah said.

Laughing felt good to Josh. Maybe he did have a place here.

Chapter Seventy-Five

After they finished lunch and Elijah had a brief nap, he and Josh went off to check the cattle. Jimmy Hickok offered to go along, but Josh said they didn't need a third man. Ally discreetly whispered to Gray that she didn't think Josh wanted them alone together. She found the shock on Gray's face slightly amusing.

As soon as Josh and Elijah rode off, Gray said he was going to find out what the sorrel thought about having someone on his back. "We won't tell Josh about this," he said, noticing the perplexed look on Ally's face.

"You really are...a good man." Ally gave Gray a quick hug and followed him out to the corral.

Gray roped the sorrel and spent several minutes brushing him and cleaning out his feet. The horse made one attempt at kicking him when he picked up one of his back feet, but that was the only time he got aggressive.

Gray saddled him with no problem, and surprisingly the horse accepted the bit without a fight. "Well, I guess the time is now." Gray put a foot in the stirrup and stepped on. At first, the horse did not move at all. When Gray squeezed his sides, he took a couple of steps and tore off for a short distance. He bucked, and crow hopped a few times, sunfished a little, not much, and pretty much stopped.

"He didn't put up much of a fight," Ally said from outside the fence.

With urging from Gray, the sorrel started to move again. Gray walked him around the corral for several minutes and then squeezed his sides, moving him into a light lope. He spent a little short of an hour starting, stopping, and moving the horse around the corral. He brought him over to where Ally and Hickok were watching and stepped off. The horse shied a bit when Gray swung his leg over to step down. "I didn't expect much trouble," Gray said. "Sometimes they lose their minds the second or third time you ride them, but I think if Josh stays calm, this guy will be fine." They confirmed their agreement—Josh would think he'd be the first one on the horse.

After dinner, when Josh asked Ally if she wanted to walk along the river, Elijah mumbled something about her pushing Josh in. Elijah got a pole to see if the trout were biting, after asking if it was all right for someone else to use the river.

Josh asked if there were any other poles, saying he and Ally would do a little fishing with him.

"You must promise not to push Josh in," Ally whispered to Elijah, who flushed red since he thought she missed his remark.

When Ally, using grasshoppers for bait, pulled in her fourth nice rainbow to go along with one monster brown trout, Elijah, skunked using worms, decided to give up and head home to bed. Ally told Josh since she caught all the fish, his contribution should be cleaning them.

While Josh cleaned, Ally lay back on the bank and

gazed up at the stars. After he finished, he lay down next to her. "Are you aware after next week—your three months are up?" she asked.

"I hadn't been counting."

She sat up and turned to face him. "A lot has happened since you came," she said. "You said when you came, you wanted to be of some help to me. You have." She sat up and looked out across the river. "I've appreciated the help."

Josh sat up. "You sound like I'm leaving."

"You're no longer obligated to stay."

If Ally intended to marry him, she sure wasn't acting like it. The woman was hard to figure out. She lay back down flat and turned away from him. The silence lasted a full ten minutes before Josh couldn't take being ignored any longer. "Do you want me to leave?"

Ally didn't respond. Josh hated the silence. "I'd appreciate an answer." He sounded a little testy. She sat up but still didn't speak. She stared out across the river. Josh took her by the arm and turned her toward him. "I deserve an answer," he said with some anger now in his voice.

"I don't have an answer! Isn't that obvious?"

Josh also stood up. "I'll be damned if I can understand you."

"Then, don't try." Ally sounded not only unconcerned but completely disinterested.

Now angry, he turned away from her and stared off into the settling darkness. "Fine, I won't," he said.

They were both silent for what was like an eternity. If Josh were a real man, he would leave her standing in the dark, pack his gear, and leave for Fort Laramie tonight. However, as frustrated as she made him, he had feelings for the woman. So, he stayed, like a blamed fool.

At last, Ally turned toward him. "Let's walk up the river."

"No," Josh said, drawing a stunned look from Ally. "I don't want to walk. I want to talk about us. Do you want me to stay or to leave?"

Ally looked at Josh. It was time to be honest. "I don't want to talk about this." That was easy to say. It was the next part, the honest part, that would be hard. Despite her reluctance, she had to talk about it. "Stay if you want; I just don't want to be pressured if you do." Ally had to be careful about what she said. She did not want to be angry, and yet she was so close. A blast of wind, hot and dry, blew across the river and into her face. "Half the time, I do think I want to marry again...someday." She shook her head in frustration.

"And I'm sorry, Josh, but I don't want to marry you." She took a step away. "My marriage was difficult. Haven't you figured that out?" *Why am I getting into this?* Josh standing in front of her looking lost didn't help. "I won't say I didn't love Sam," she said, wondering if any of this was understandable to Josh. "We wanted different things." In truth, Ally was not sure anymore what she wanted. She certainly didn't know what Josh wanted, and she told him that. "I can't do that again," Ally said. "If I ever marry again, we have to want the same things. Too many dreams are already lost. I don't want any more to slip away."

"I want you." Josh took hold of her hands. "I could be happy here if this is what you want. I think together we could make this place a success, successful enough to be able to travel if you want to." He smiled at her. "Or we can go to St. Louis. I was successful in business. I can be again."

Nothing he said changed her mind. Ally had concerns he might be weak, a hopeless quitter.

"The valley where Gray lives would be another possibility. Gray already said his mother wants to stop teaching school. Teaching is something you could do. High Meadows might not be a city, but the place is a town, not an army fort. We're already friends with Gray, his sister, the Laurie girl, Alan Joseph. At least we know them a little; we wouldn't be strangers."

"You're not listening, Josh. I'm not ready to marry, maybe not ever."

Chapter Seventy-Six

The morning was gray, drab—melancholy. Long before Kane's men got up, Kane knew he was going to have a rough start to the day. His throbbing foot had swollen up so much his boot was agonizingly tight. Stumbling around in the dark the night before, he threw his bedroll on hard, rocky ground, which limited his sleep to only about two hours, which came sporadically.

He hobbled his way down to the creek and stuck his foot in, hoping the wet boot might stretch out. It didn't. Mad about his misfortune, Kane limped back into the ratty camp. He fired his pistol to wake up the others. Two men grabbed their weapons, preparing for a fight; the rest sat on the ground, looking resentful about Kane rousing them. "You better git your heads alert," Kane hollered.

"About what?" one of the bolder men grumbled.

"About what we're gonna do today," Kane said in a threatening tone.

"Hell, we ain't doin' nothing right now," the bold-talking man replied.

Kane limped over to the man, drew and cocked his pistol while shoving it in the man's face. "You gonna give me trouble?" The man raised his hands and slowly backed away without saying anything. "You better back off." Kane's lip curled into a snarl. He'd been ready to shoot the man over his sassiness but decided against it. He might need him; Gray would make for a damn tough opponent. Most men didn't have the nerve to stand and fight with the odds against them. Gray did.

"Some of us were wondering," Kane's new foreman said. "If you're so set on hurtin' the Hart woman, why don't you let us use her for a little fun before you cut her all up? We'd enjoy passing her around." Kane found the idea appealing. Why not put that brash female through some added humiliation before killing her? Being naked in the dirt while a dozen stinking men used her would pain her damn pride.

Kane smiled at his new foreman. "Tell somebody to cook up some of the bacon we brought. We'll eat and get moving. I'm lookin' forward to this little celebration," he said.

Chapter Seventy-Seven

Since finishing the breakfast dishes, Ally had been leaning against the corral, watching Gray brush his blue roan stud. She barely said anything, and since he seldom talked much, the morning had been a quiet time. "I believe you're sad, again," Gray finally said.

"No, only a little tired," Ally said. "Josh and I came back from the river pretty late."

"Swimming?"

"No." Ally chuckled. "I only swim with one swimming partner."

Gray laughed and winked at her.

"I told Josh no."

Gray didn't look surprised.

"I know," she said. "I should have told him sooner. I didn't have the heart."

"How did he react?"

The question bothered her, at least a little. Josh's reaction was hard to describe. Just typical Josh. "He didn't get angry. He didn't do anything except pout." She didn't understand why she told Gray. It was undoubtedly inconsequential to him. Perhaps, she told him because deep down, she still wanted his advice. Why was a mystery. He probably didn't know anything about love—horses, cattle, Sioux, and Cheyenne, maybe killing, but probably not love. "Do you think telling him now was the right thing?"

"He needed to know," Gray said.

"I'm serious," Ally said, taking a couple of steps toward the man who had become her trusted friend.

"Ally, what I think of him shouldn't matter."

"Well, it does," Ally said.

Ally could see in his eyes there were a lot of things Gray would have preferred to face: she assumed blizzards, hunger, thirst, men shooting at him, his sister haranguing him about staying home. She knew he'd find them all better than trying to answer her question.

"Ally, your matrimonial choices, or those of any other woman for that matter, are none of my business. I make enough mistakes making my own decisions. I don't need to be making mistakes for others."

Ally's eyes narrowed, the same way Jean and Annie did when he was going to lose an argument to them. Giving up, he told Ally that Josh wouldn't be the one for him.

Ally sighed. "Why do I bother to ask for your advice? You never give any."

"My advice is, make up your mind and live with your decision."

Ally rubbed the horse's neck, and for a moment, laid her forehead in his mane. "The problem is after I said no, I started worrying about it being the right answer. I'm not sure about anything." She turned and looked at Gray. "He says we can stay here, or if I want, go to St. Louis." She put her hand on Gray's wrist. "He also says we could go to High Meadows, where you live." She paused for a deep breath. "Do you think we'd be welcome? It's not St. Louis, but at least there'd be people."

Gray put his hands on the woman's shoulders, surprising her. "Ally, you worry too much," he said. "You think too much about what might go wrong and not enough about what might go right." He laughed a little, although Ally didn't consider anything humorous. Gray briefly touched her face. "Yes, you'd be welcome. And I think you might like High Meadows. Everyone's friendly. We help each other. We have a couple of churches, a store, a café. We've even got a doctor. Although, I don't think he's worth much."

Ally appreciated Gray's efforts to paint quite a picture of life in his valley. "We work hard, but we hold socials, community dances, fireworks on the Fourth of July." He playfully gave Ally's hair a slight tug. "Our valley is a regular, what do they call that place in England...Camelot. Maybe you ought to marry the scoundrel, move up, and enjoy life. If marrying him doesn't work out, you can always shoot his big toe off and send him packin'."

"You said I look sad," she quietly said as she leaned back against the corral as if the rails would somehow protect her from the emotions welling up inside. She was having a difficult time talking. By looking at her, Gray was making the situation more awkward. "I am sad...I guess."

"Why?"

When she didn't answer, Gray quietly asked again.

Ally didn't answer immediately. Probably because she questioned the truth of what she was about to say. "I didn't think I wanted to be alone," she said, looking up at Gray as if looking for comfort. "The idea of loneliness terrifies me." She stepped toward her friend. "I've learned something," she said as she touched his arm. She enjoyed touching him. Being with him felt good. She couldn't imagine the pleasure of making love with him.

"Ally?"

The sound of his voice snapped her back to reality.

"I recognize I can make it alone." Ally took her hand off his arm. "I'm afraid that's what makes me sad."

The other three men rode up. "Cattle are fine," Josh said

as he dismounted.

Seeing neither Josh nor Elijah armed, Gray told them it might not be a bad idea to be wearing a gun, adding Kane wasn't going to leave them alone forever. When Josh and Elijah went off to arm themselves, Hickok told Gray and Ally he could only stay a couple more days. He was already past due in Missouri to pick up freight for New Mexico.

Hickok's leaving distressed Ally. "I wish Kane would do whatever he's going to do," Gray said. "I don't care much for waiting." Elijah and Josh came walking back, both wearing Navy Colts. Elijah was carrying a ten-gauge shotgun. "That'll stop a man if he's close enough."

"If I'm gonna shoot a fella, I intend to stop him," Elijah said.

Chapter Seventy-Eight

"I doubt we're more'n two miles from her place. Make sure your guns are loaded." A couple of the men looked insulted by Kane's remark. One whispered something to the new foreman. "Remember, a hundred dollars and first choice of her horses for killing Gray. But Alice Hart is mine," Kane said.

"How are we supposed to know which one is Gray?" one of the men asked.

"He'll be the one killing a bunch of you," Kane said.

A few minutes later, Ally Hart's house and barn were in plain sight. Seeing the barn rebuilt peeved Kane a considerable amount. He told a couple of men to light the torches they'd made and throw one through a window of the house and the other in the barn.

Elijah was standing by the corral biting off a chunk of

tobacco when Kane's men rushed the ranch. The attack started with a lot of yelling. He didn't hear the shot until a terrible burning in his belly knocked him to the ground. A man on horseback threw a flaming stick into the barn. Elijah wanted his shotgun, but the double barrel Greener leaned on the corral out of reach. Pulling his pistol took every bit of his strength. He cocked it and shot at the man who threw the torch. Elijah made a mortal shot, but the wounded man didn't die until he shot Elijah a second time, this time hitting an artery in his thigh.

Elijah bowed his head, studied the bloody holes in his stomach and leg. Violent coughing sent blood spewing out of his mouth. He shot another of Kane's men, a runt wearing a greasy Mexican sombrero and poncho cut out of an old tarp. Elijah's bullet penetrated his lower back, crippling him. He was face down in the dirt, swearing at Elijah in Spanish.

"I can't understand Mex talk. You may as well shut up." Elijah held up his pistol in both hands and sent a .44 cartridge right into the runt's face. Elijah, no longer able to sit up, slid down against the corral post. The burning in his belly greatly depressed him. He was helpless. There was nothing to do but wait for someone to finish killing him.

At the sound of the shooting, Josh peeked out of the barn. The scene was frantic, not a planned out battle, pure chaos. Before hurrying back into the barn Josh did muster the courage to fire at two of Kane's men who were rushing toward Elijah. Josh foolishly fired all six of his shots, forcing their retreat, but hit no one. Looking for a safe place to reload, in truth to hide, he ducked back into the barn while two bullets went singing past him.

Josh's fighting was done. He cowered in the darkest corner of the barn, his nerve gone, his hands shaking so violently he couldn't reload his cap and ball pistol. The shooting outside was deafening. His pistol dropped to the ground when he put his hands over his ears. Men were dying, groaning above the gunfire. Hunkering down behind a hogshead barrel, Josh could see Elijah slumped down in the bright sunlight, leaning against the corral.

The front of Elijah's shirt dripped blood. Every time he coughed blood and phlegm spewed from his mouth, his arms drooped uselessly at his side. Josh hid, taking in the whole scene in lurid detail. Nothing mattered. Not Elijah still being alive, not his desperate need of help, Elijah's peril didn't matter. Death prowled out in that bright sun. Josh wouldn't, couldn't help. The barn air was beginning to reek with the pungent stink of burning sulfur. It made him think of blood. His eyes burned. He squeezed them shut, trying to shut out the fight. The darkness didn't help.

Gray and Hickok had been at the river when the shooting started. They came running back to the house, shooting as they ran. Unlike Josh, they did not miss. They shot twice each, killing four of Kane's men, making the odds much more even. The horse Kane's new foreman was riding spooked during all the shooting, throwing his rider. Before the man got back to his feet, Gray shot him in the back of the head.

A man carrying one of the torches threw it through a window, where the flame caught Ally's curtains on fire. Kane himself dismounted and hobbled up Ally's steps and across her porch.

He burst through her door, not more than ten feet away from where Ally was trying to put out her curtains. "You whore," he hollered. "I'm going to cut you to pieces." He swung his skinning knife at her slashing her forearm. He hit her in the face with his fist, knocking her down. Kane, awkward and off-balance because of his toeless foot, fell while trying to kick her. Ally jumped over him, trying to escape. Bleeding badly, the bleeding, along with the brutal hit to her face, made her unsteady.

Before she could escape, Kane jumped back on her. He hit her in the back of the head with his fist. The force of the blow sent her face through a window, cutting a deep gash in her eyebrow. When Kane grabbed at the neck of her dress, it ripped, momentarily freeing her. She got hold of a coat tree and managed to hit Kane in the side of the head, but not hard enough to stop him.

Outside, Kane's men were in a state of confusion. Gray and Hickok had killed another man and wounded two more as the men tried to escape behind the house. One of them hid behind the oak tree where Ally buried Sam; the other jumped down behind the riverbank. Hickok came racing over to the side of the house, where Gray shot another of Kane's men.

"Can you shoot 'em from here?"

"Not 'til they stick their damn heads up," Gray said, as one did just that and fired a shot at them. The bullet glanced off the corner of Ally's house and zipped out across the yard next to the well. The man hiding behind the riverbank popped up and fired, knocking Hickok's hat off. Before the man ducked back down, Gray put a shot in the middle of his forehead.

"That fella ruint my hat," Hickok griped. "I'm glad you parted his hair for him."

"You keep this one trapped behind the tree. I'm goin' back to the front." Gray hugged the side of the house as he darted back to the front.

With only Kane and two of his men still unscathed, Kane's attack was turning into a debacle. With eight of their pack dead, a ninth on the ground dying, Kane's remaining men were losing interest in fighting. Fleeing now seemed like a better idea.

Inside the house, instead of killing Ally, Kane was set on hurting her. He threw her against a wall, twice. He slammed his fist into her stomach, causing her to collapse on the floor. She made it up to her hands and knees. "I'm going to cut you open, you whore." Instead, he kicked her in the chest so hard it lifted her in the air and over backward, right next to the open front door. Somehow, she burst out the door, stumbling as she tried to go down the steps, landing not far from the Sioux lance.

Kane came lurching down the steps, his head bleeding profusely from the blow Ally landed with the coat tree. Still swearing and threatening Ally, he relished in her anguish and in her being helpless. Except she wasn't.

While Kane lumbered his way toward her, she pulled the yellow and red feathered lance out of the ground. She managed to rise to her knees. When Kane charged her, skinning knife in hand, she shoved the lance in below his ribs and gave the shaft a second shove, trying to force it clear through him.

Kane didn't look like he was in pain. He looked astonished. He grasped the lance with both hands and tried to pull it out, but he could not budge the thing. He fell to his knees, spitting blood and shrieking for Ally's damnation. Kane shrieked for her doom until he didn't have the strength to shriek.

In the end, he whimpered, "You killed me."

There was no sympathy in Ally's eyes. "I'm not a whore."

About the time Ally got to her feet, the man behind the oak tree decided the riverbank would be better cover than the tree and dashed for the river. Hickok put two bullets in his rib cage. The last two men only wanted to flee. Hickok might have let them. He would never know because Gray Wehr let no foe escape. If men tried to kill him, he did not give them a second chance.

Gray had them trapped behind a boulder out past the well. He made a wild dash at them, circling wide to the left to go around behind them. Gray shot both raiders, the last one with his pistol nearly against the man's chest, when the man ran out of bullets. The muzzle was so close the flash set the man's shirt on fire, not that the brute noticed.

Gray and Hickok both ran to Ally. Blood was gushing out of the slash on her arm. Both of her lips were split open and badly swollen. The gash in her eyebrow had blood flowing down her face staining the front of her dress.

Once the shooting ended, Josh came slinking out of his hiding place in the barn and told them Elijah was down. It was the first time the other three found out Elijah was shot.

Ally, barely able to stand, demanded Gray help her to Elijah. "I'll get something to wrap Ally's arm," Josh said as the others headed off toward Elijah.

Elijah was still alive when they got to him, but barely. "I'm awful shot up, Mrs. Hart." His voice was hardly audible. "My belly hurts a considerable amount, and I can barely see." Elijah moaned from deep within. "Did you kill that damn Dierden Kane?"

"We did," Ally said. "Lie quietly."

"That's good. Now you'll have some peace." Elijah tried to point to the man who shot him, or at least in his direction. "I believe I got the fella who shot me. At least I got that satisfaction." Ally sat down next to him and pulled Elijah close to her. "Sorry I won't be here to help you anymore. I always enjoyed helping you, Mrs. Hart."

For some reason, Ally suddenly regretted not being a crier. Elijah had been perhaps the most genuine friend she had ever had. He deserved crying over.

"Mrs. Hart, would you maybe do me one favor? I'm afraid it's kind of a big one."

"Just ask. Anything, anything."

"The tintype of you sitting over the fireplace, do you think I might be buried with your picture in my hand?"

Ally wanted to tell him he would be fine. In two weeks, he'd be helping her. They both knew differently, and they didn't lie to each other. Ally looked up at Gray. "Would you go get it?"

When Gray got back, Josh was with him, carrying bandages for Ally's arm. "Here it is," she whispered as she placed the tintype in Elijah's hands and squeezed his fingers around it.

Elijah weakly put the picture to his lips and kissed it. "Now, I'll always have you with me." When he said that, Ally cried. He was the one dying, but it was Ally his heart was breaking for.

"Your eye looks like it hurts," he said, reaching toward her face and gently wiping some of the blood.

"Not as much as Kane's belly," Hickok said.

Elijah glanced at Hickok. Elijah laughed as much as possible. "Good," he said, smiling.

"Now, you must do me a favor." Ally leaned down and gently kissed her dear friend. "Call me Ally...please, just one time."

Chapter Seventy-Nine

Seven days passed, one week since they buried Elijah Yancey. Virtually no work had been done since the day of the fight. The fort surgeon stitched up Ally's arm and eyebrow, Hickok left for Independence, Missouri. Josh paid no attention to the once-rank horse. Ally mostly grieved over her friend. Gray groomed his blue roan and talked about going back to High Meadows.

On this particular rainy afternoon, Ally trifled around in the kitchen, her arm again in a sling, while Josh sat at the kitchen table doing absolutely nothing. Ally, weary of putting off what she was going to do, handed Josh a cup of coffee and sat down across the table from him. No reason to hesitate any longer, so Ally didn't. "Josh," she said before pausing until he looked at her. "I think it will be best if you leave."

She didn't expect Josh to answer, and he didn't. He stiffened, clenched, and unclenched his fists. "This harsh land is not the right place for you. I think that should be clear to you. I've never been willing to admit it, but I fit here in this wilderness. Unkind and unforgiving as the life is, this is my home. I want, for the first time, I want to be part of making this land a good place to be. You never will."

"I appreciate your making that decision for me."

"I'm not making decisions for anyone," Ally said. "Not anyone except myself."

Josh waited for her to continue, but she didn't.

"You want everybody to think you're sweet and kind," he said in an angry voice. "You're not."

Josh continually discouraged and exasperated her. For the last week, she honestly tried hard not to be angry with him, not disappointed in him. Nevertheless, Ally was both.

Before she said no to his *sort of* marriage proposal, Josh talked about redeeming himself, accomplishing things, but at the end of the day, he stayed a quitter. The man hid in the barn through the entire fight with Kane. He didn't even try to pull Elijah to a safe place. He just left him slumped by the corral. He admitted not helping Elijah. For Ally, that was unforgivable. She had no idea if Elijah was first shot in the stomach or the leg, but McCormick, the spineless cud, should have helped him, might have saved him.

"How do you think you're going to be able to make it here, all by yourself?"

At first, Ally wasn't going to answer. Answering, in all honesty, was pointless. Her answer wouldn't change anything.

"You have no idea, do you?" Josh was disrespectful. The disrespect quickly turned into anger.

"I'm going to High Meadows, where Gray lives."

"I guess I'm not surprised," Josh said.

The scorn and contempt in his voice offended Ally. She flushed and lashed out. "There is nothing between Gray and me!" She responded, not because her life was any of his business but because she resented his insinuation.

"Oh, of course not," Josh yelled, flinging the coffee cup across the room.

For a moment, Ally thought he might hit her and backed away. Thankfully, he didn't turn violent with her.

Three days later, with virtually no interaction with Ally or Gray, Josh packed his belongings on his red roan horse and climbed up on the once rank sorrel Ally called rightfully his. He started toward St. Louis, or at least somewhere other than the Wyoming territory. He wouldn't openly say. Maybe he didn't have a place in mind.

To Ally, he would always be a coward, something she could not get beyond. Still, she made an honest attempt to express gratitude to the man, going as far as saying she wished him happiness. Ally tried again to explain, perhaps more gently, why marriage would not work for them. Josh, without responding or saying goodbye, simply rode off. After he left, Ally told Gray she genuinely hoped Josh would find peace, redemption, a decent life.

It took a little more than a month, but Ally sold her ranch and her livestock to a young family from Nebraska. She only kept Elijah's horse and the cowy sorrel, the one who had spun out from under Joshua McCormick that seemingly long-ago day he and Ally moved cattle together.

On a pristine fall day in the Bighorn Mountains, Ally Hart got her first look at High Meadows and her new valley home. Its beauty took her breath.

Maybe, just maybe, here in her new home, she would find the peace and love she desired. Only time would tell.

CPSIA information can be obtained
at www.ICGtesting.com
Printed in the USA
FSHW020230180821
83896FS